Mary Stewart, one of the most popular novelists, was born in Sunderland, County Durham and lives in the West Highlands. Her first novel, *Madam, Will You Talk?* was published in 1955 and marked the beginning of a long and acclaimed writing career. All her novels have been bestsellers on both sides of the Atlantic. She was made a Doctor of Literature by Durham University in 2009.

Praise for Mary Stewart and *Madam, Will You Talk?*:

'The tension mounts rapidly until it reaches breaking point, while the terrible thirsty heat of the Provençal summer, the noise of the cicadas, the dust of the country buses, all add to the unfolding of the story. This is not only an excellent tale of mystery. It is a well written novel.'
The Times

'She set the bench mark for pace, suspense and romance – with a great dollop of escapism as the icing'
Elizabeth Buchan

'A comfortable chair and a Mary Stewart: total heaven. I'd rather read her than most other authors.'
Harriet Evans

MARY STEWART

Madam, Will You Talk?

HODDER

First published in Great Britain in 1955 by Hodder & Stoughton
An Hachette UK company

This edition 2011

1

A CIP catalogue record for this title is available
from the British Library.

ISBN 978 1 444 71120 2

Printed and bound in the UK by
CPI Mackays, Chatham ME5 8TD

Hodder & Stoughton policy is to use papers that are natural, renewable
and recyclable products and made from wood grown in sustainable
forests. The logging and manufacturing processes are expected to
conform to the environmental regulations of the country of origin.

Hodder & Stoughton Ltd
338 Euston Road
London NW1 3BH

www.hodder.co.uk

For my Mother and Father

I

Enter four or five players.

The whole affair began so very quietly. When I wrote,
that summer, and asked my friend Louise if she would
come with me on a car trip to Provence, I had no idea
that I might be issuing an invitation to danger. And
when we arrived one afternoon, after a hot but leisurely
journey, at the enchanting little walled city of Avignon,
we felt in that mood of pleasant weariness mingled with
anticipation which marks, I believe, the beginning of
every normal holiday.

No cloud in the sky; no sombre shadow on the
machicolated walls; no piercing glance from an enig-
matic stranger as we drove in at the Porte de la
République and up the sun-dappled Cours Jean-
Jaurès. And certainly no involuntary shiver of apprehension as we drew up at last in front of the Hôtel
Tistet-Védène, where we had booked rooms for the
greater part of our stay.

I even sang to myself as I put the car away, and when
I found they had given me a room with a balcony
overlooking the shaded courtyard, I was pleased.

And when, later on, the cat jumped on to my

balcony, there was still nothing to indicate that this was the beginning of the whole strange, uneasy, tangled business. Or rather, not the beginning, but my own cue, the point where I came in. And though the part I was to play in the tragedy was to break and re-form the pattern of my whole life, yet it was a very minor part, little more than a walk-on in the last act. For most of the play had been played already; there had been love and lust and revenge and fear and murder – all the blood-tragedy bric-à-brac except the Ghost – and now the killer, with blood enough on his hands, was waiting in the wings for the lights to go up again, on the last kill that would bring the final curtain down.

How was I to know, that lovely quiet afternoon, that most of the actors in the tragedy were at that moment assembled in this neat, unpretentious little Provençal hotel? All but one, that is, and he, with murder in his mind, was not so very far away, moving, under that blazing southern sun, in the dark circle of his own personal hell. A circle that narrowed, gradually, upon the Hôtel Tistet-Védène, Avignon.

But I did not know, so I unpacked my things slowly and carefully, while, on my bed, Louise lay and smoked and talked about the mosquitoes.

'And now – a fortnight,' she said dreamily. 'A whole fortnight. And nothing to do but drink, and sit in the sun.'

'No eating? Or are you on a cure?'

'Oh, that. One's almost forgotten how. But they tell me that in France the cattle still grow steaks . . . I wonder how I shall stand up to a beefsteak?'

'You have to do these things gradually.' I opened one of the slatted shutters, closed against the late afternoon sun. 'Probably the waiter will just introduce you at first, like Alice – Louise, biftek; biftek, Louise. Then you both bow, and the steak is ushered out.'

'And of course, in France, no pudding to follow.' Louise sighed. 'Well, we'll have to make do. Aren't you letting the mosquitoes in, opening that shutter?'

'It's too early. And I can't see to hang these things away. Do you mind either smoking that cigarette or putting it out? It smells.'

'Sorry.' She picked it up again from the ash-tray. 'I'm too lazy even to smoke. I warn you, you know, I'm not going sight-seeing. I couldn't care less if Julius Caesar used to fling his auxiliaries round the town, and throw moles across the harbour mouth. If you want to go and gasp at Roman remains you'll have to go alone. I shall sit under a tree, with a book, as near to the hotel as possible.'

I laughed, and began putting out my creams and sunburn lotions on what the Hôtel Tistet-Védène fondly imagined to be a dressing-table.

'Of course I don't expect you to come. You'll do as you like. But I believe the Pont du Gard—'

'My dear, I've seen the Holborn Viaduct. Life can hold no more . . .'

Louise stubbed out her cigarette carefully, and then folded her hands behind her head. She is tall and fair and plump, with long legs, a pleasant voice, and beautiful hands. She is an artist, has no temperament to speak of, and is unutterably and incurably lazy.

When accused of this, she merely says that she is seeing life steadily and seeing it whole, and this takes time. You can neither ruffle nor surprise Louise; you can certainly never quarrel with her. If trouble should ever arise, Louise is simply not there; she fades like the Cheshire Cat, and comes back serenely when it is all over. She is, too, as calmly independent as a cat, without any of its curiosity. And though she looks the kind of large lazy fair girl who is untidy – the sort who stubs out her cigarettes in the face-cream and never brushes the hairs off her coat – she is always beautifully groomed, and her movements are delicate and precise. Again, like a cat. I get on well with cats. As you will find, I have a lot in common with them, and with the Elephant's Child.

'In any case,' said Louise, 'I've had quite enough of ruins and remains, in the Gilbertian sense, to last me for a lifetime. I live among them.'

I knew what she meant. Before my marriage to Johnny Selborne, I, too, had taught at the Alice Drupe Private School for Girls. Beyond the fact that it is in the West Midlands, I shall say nothing more about the Alice Drupe as it is virtually impossible to mention it without risking a heavy libel action. Louise was still Art Mistress there, and owed her continued health and sanity to the habit I have described, of removing herself out of the trouble zone. As far as it was possible to do this at the Alice Drupe, she did it. Even there, she saw life steadily. At any rate she saw it coming.

'Don't speak too soon,' I warned her. 'You may yet

come across Lloyd-Lloyd and Merridew sipping their Pernod in the restaurant downstairs.'

'Not *together*, my dear. They don't speak now. The Great Rupture paralysed the whole school for weeks . . .' She paused and wrinkled her nose. 'What a revolting metaphor . . . And *not* Pernod, Charity; Vichy water.' She lit another cigarette.

'What happened?'

'Oh, Merridew put up a notice without asking Lloyd, or Lloyd put one up without asking Merridew, or something desperately frightful like that,' she said indifferently. 'I wasn't there.'

Naturally not.

'Poor things,' I said, and meant it.

Louise flicked her ash neatly into the bowl, and turned her gold head on the pillow.

'Yes, you can say that. You're out of it now for good, aren't you? You're lucky.'

I didn't answer. I laid Johnny's photograph gently back in the case, where I had just come across it, and picked up a frock instead. I shook it out and laid it over a chair, ready to put on. I don't think my expression changed at all. But Louise happens to know me rather well.

She ground out her cigarette, and her voice changed.

'Oh God, Charity, I'm sorry. I forgot. I am a fool. Forgive me.'

'Forget it,' I said, lightly enough, 'I do.'

'Do you?'

'Of course. It's a long time now. I'd be silly and unnatural not to. And I *am* lucky, as you said.' I grinned at her. 'After all, I'm a wealthy widow . . . look at these.'

'My dear girl! What *gorgeous* undies. . . .'

And the conversation slipped comfortably back to the things that really matter.

When Louise had gone to her own room, I washed, changed into a white frock with a wide blue belt, and did my face and hair very slowly. It was still hot, and the late sun's rays fell obliquely across the balcony, through the half-opened shutter, in a shaft of copper-gold. Motionless, the shadows of thin leaves traced a pattern across it as delicate and precise as a Chinese painting on silk. The image of the tree, brushed in like that by the sun, had a grace that the tree itself gave no hint of, for it was merely one of the nameless spindly affairs, parched and dust-laden, that struggled up towards the sky from their pots in the hotel court below. But its shadow might have been designed by Ma Yüan.

The courtyard was empty; people were still resting, or changing, or, if they were the mad English, walking out in the afternoon sun. A white-painted trellis wall separated the court on one side from the street, and beyond it people, mules, cars, occasionally even buses, moved about their business up and down the narrow thoroughfare. But inside the vine-covered trellis it was very still and peaceful. The gravel between the gay little chairs was carefully raked and watered; shade lay gently across the tables, some of which, laid for dinner, gleamed invitingly with glass and silver. The only living thing in the court was a thin ginger cat, which was curled round the base of my spindly tree, like – who was it? Nidhug? – at the root of Yggdrasil.

I sat down by the half-shuttered window and began to think about where I should go tomorrow.

Avignon Bridge, where one dances, of course; and after Avignon itself, the Pont du Gard – in spite of the fact that I, too, had seen Holborn Viaduct. I picked up the Michelin Guide to Provence, and looked at the sketch of the great aqueduct which is on the cover . . .

Tomorrow, I said to myself, I would take things easy, and wander round the ramparts and the Popes' Palace. Then, the day after . . .

Then fate, in the shape of Nidhug, took a hand.

My cue had come. I had to enter the stage.

The first hint I had of it was the violent shaking of the shadows on the balcony. The Chinese design wavered, broke, and dissolved into the image of a ragged witch's besom, as the tree Yggdrasil vibrated and lurched sharply under a weight it was never meant to bear. Then the ginger cat shot on to my balcony, turned completely round on a space the size of a six-pence, sent down on her assailant the look to end all looks, and sat calmly down to wash. From below a rush and a volley of barking explained everything.

Then came a crash, and the sound of running feet.

The cat yawned, tidied a whisker into place, swarmed in a bored manner up an impossible drain-pipe, and vanished on to the roof. I got up and looked over the balcony railing.

The courtyard, formerly so empty and peaceful,

seemed all of a sudden remarkably full of a boy and a large, nondescript dog. The latter, with his earnest gaze still on the balcony, was leaping futilely up and down, pouring out rage, hatred and excitement, while the boy tried with one hand to catch and quell him, and with the other to lift one of the tables which had been knocked on to its side. It was, luckily, not one of those which had been set for dinner.

The table, which was of iron, was very heavy, and the boy seemed to be having some difficulty in raising it. Eventually he let go the dog, and taking both hands to the job, succeeded in lifting the table almost half-way. Then the dog, who appeared to be a little slow in the uptake, but a sticker for all that, realized that his prey was gone from the balcony and leaped madly in several directions at once. He crashed into the boy. The table thudded down again.

'*Oh Rommel!*' said the boy, surprisingly enough.

Before I could decide what language this was, the boy looked up and saw me. He straightened, pushed his hair back from his forehead, and grinned.

'*J'espère,*' he said carefully, '*que ce n'etait pas votre chat, mademoiselle?*'

This, of course, settled the question of his nationality immediately, but I am nothing if not tactful. I shook my head.

'My French isn't terribly good,' I said. 'Do you speak English, monsieur?'

He looked immensely pleased.

'Well, as a matter of fact, I *am* English,' he admitted. '*Stop* it, Rommel!' He grabbed the dog with decision.

'He hadn't hurt the cat, had he? I just saw it jump for the balcony.'

'It didn't look very worried.'

'Oh, that's all right, then. I can't persuade him to behave decently, as – as befits a foreigner. It seems funny to *be* foreigners, doesn't it?'

I admitted that it did indeed.

'Have you just arrived?'

'At about four o'clock. Yes.'

'Then you haven't seen much of Avignon yet. Isn't it a funny little town? Will you like it, do you think?'

'I certainly like what I've seen so far. Do *you* like it here?'

It was the most trivial of small-talk, of course, but his face changed oddly as he pondered the question. At that distance I could not read his expression, but it was certainly not what one might expect of a boy – I judged him to be about thirteen – who was lucky enough to be enjoying a holiday in the South of France. Indeed, there was not much about him at that moment, if you except the outward signs of crumpled shirt, stained shorts, and mongrel dog, to suggest the average boy at all. His face, which had, even in the slight courtesies of small-talk, betrayed humour and a quick intelligence at work, seemed suddenly to mask itself, to become older. Some impalpable burden almost visibly dropped on to his shoulders. One was conscious, in spite of the sensitive youth his mouth, and the childish thin wrists and hands, of something here that could meet and challenge a quite adult destiny on its own ground, strength for strength. The burden, whatever it was, was quite obviously recognized and accepted. There had been some hardening process at work, and recently. Not a pleasant process, I thought, looking at the withdrawn profile bent over the absurd dog, and feeling suddenly angry.

But he came out of his sombre thoughts as quickly as he had gone in – so quickly, in fact, that I began to think I had been an over-imaginative fool.

'Yes, of course I like it. Rommel doesn't, it's too hot. Do you like the heat?' We were back at the small-talk. 'They said two English ladies were coming today; that would be you – Mrs. Selborne and Miss Crabbe?'

'Cray. I'm Mrs. Selborne,' I said.

'Yes, that's it.' His grin was suddenly pure small-boy. 'I'm bad at remembering names, and I have to do it by – by association. It sometimes goes awfully wrong. But I remembered yours because of Gilbert White.'

Now most people could see the connection between cray and crab, but not many thirteen-years-olds, I thought, would be so carelessly familiar with Gilbert White's letters from his little Hampshire village, which go under the title of *The Natural History of Selborne*. I had been right about the intelligence. I only knew the book myself because one is apt to be familiar with most of the contexts in which one's name appears. And because Johnny—

'My name's David,' said the boy. 'David Shelley.'

I laughed.

'Well, that's easy enough to remember, anyway. How do you do, David? I shall only have to think of the Romantic poets, if I forget. But don't hold it against me if I address you as David Byron, or—'

I stopped abruptly. The boy's face, smiling politely up at me, changed again. This time there could be no mistake about it. He went suddenly rigid, and a wave of scarlet poured over his face from neck to temples, and receded as quickly, leaving him white and sick-looking. He opened his mouth as if to speak, fumbling a little with the dog's collar. Then he seemed to make some kind of effort, sent me a courteous, meaningless little smile, and bent over the dog again, fumbling in his pocket for string to fasten him.

I had made a mistake, it seemed. But I had not been mistaken when I had sensed that there was something very wrong somewhere. I am not a person who interferes readily in other people's affairs, but suddenly, unaccountably, and violently, I wanted to interfere in this one.

I need not have worried; I was going to.

But not for the moment. Before I could speak again we were interrupted by a woman who came in through the vine-trellis, from the street. She was, I guessed, thirty-five. She was also blonde, tall, and quite the most beautiful woman I had ever seen. The simple cream dress she wore must have been one of Dior's favourite dreams, and the bill for it her husband's nightmare. Being a woman myself, I naturally saw the enormous sapphire on her left hand almost before I saw her.

She did not see me at all, which again was perfectly natural. She paused a moment when she saw David and the dog, then came forward with a kind of eye-compelling grace which would have turned heads in Piccadilly, Manchester, on a wet Monday morning. What it did in Provence, where men make a hobby of looking at women, I hesitated to think. I believe I had visions of the cafés along the Rue de la République emptying as she passed, as the houses of Hamelin emptied a different cargo after the Pied Piper.

She paused by the upturned table and spoke. Her voice was pleasant, her English perfect, but her accent was that of a Frenchwoman.

'David.'

No reply.

'*Mon fils . . .*'

Her son? He did not glance up.

She said, evenly: 'Don't you know what the time is? And what on earth happened to the table?'

'Rommel upset it.' The averted head, the sulky-sounding mumble which David accorded her, were at once rude and surprising. She took no notice of his manner, but touched him lightly on the shoulder.

'Well, put it right, there's a good boy. And hurry up and change. It's nearly dinner-time. Where have you been today?'

'By the river.'

'How you can—' She laughed and shrugged, all at once very French, then reached in her bag for a cigarette. 'Well, put the table up, child.'

David pulled the reluctant Rommel towards a tree, and began to tie him to its stem. He said flatly:

'I can't lift it.'

A new voice interrupted, smoothly:

'Permit me, madame.'

The man who had come quietly out of the hotel was dark and singularly good-looking. His clothes, his air, no less than his voice, were unmistakably French, and he had that look of intense virility and yet sophistication – the sort of powerful, careless charm which can be quite devastating. It was all the more surprising, therefore, that the woman, after a glance of conventional thanks, ignored him completely, and lit her cigarette without glancing in his direction. I would have gone to the stake for my conviction that she, where men were concerned, was the noticing type.

The newcomer smiled at David, lifted the heavy table without apparent effort, set it straight, then dusted his hands on a handkerchief.

'Thank you, sir,' said David. He began untying Rommel again from the tree.

'*De rien*,' said the Frenchman. 'Madame.' He gave a little bow in her direction, which she acknowledged with a faint polite smile, then he made his way to a table in the far corner of the courtyard, and sat down.

'If you hurry,' said David's mother, 'you can have the bathroom first.'

Without a word the boy went into the hotel, trailing a somewhat subdued dog after him on the end of the string. His mother stared after him for a moment, with an expression half puzzled, half exasperated. Then she gave a smiling little shrug of the shoulders, and went into the hotel after the boy.

The Frenchman had not noticed me either; his

handsome head was bent over a match as he lit a cigarette. I went quietly back through my window, and stood for a moment in the cool shade of the room thinking over the little scene which, somehow, had hidden in it the elements of oddity. The exquisite film-starry creature, and the dilapidated dog . . . Christian Dior and Gilbert White . . . and she was French and the boy's accent was definitely Stratford-atte-Bow . . . and he was rude to her and charmingly polite to strangers.

Well, it was no affair of mine.

I picked my bag up and went downstairs for a drink.

2

Ther saugh I first the derke ymaginyng
Of felonye . . .

(Chaucer)

When I got down into the little courtyard, it was beginning to fill up. Louise was not down yet, so I found a table in the shade, and ordered a Cinzano.

I looked about me, resigned to the fact that almost everybody in the hotel would probably be English too. But the collection so far seemed varied enough. I began to play the game of guessing at people's professions – and, in this case, nationalities. One is nearly always wrong, of course, and it is a game too often played by those self-satisfied people who are apt to announce that they are students of human nature . . . but I played it, nevertheless.

The two men at the next table to me were Germans. One was thin and clever-looking, and the other was the fat-necked German of the cartoons. And since I heard him say '*Ach, so?*' to his companion, it didn't need any great insight to hazard the rest. There was a young couple, honeymooning at a guess, and, at another guess, American. Then there was the handsome

Frenchman, drinking his Pernod by himself in the corner, and another man sitting alone near the trellis, reading a book and sipping a bright green drink with caution and distrust. I puzzled for a long time over him – he might have been anything – until I saw the title of the book. *Four Quartets*, by T. S. Eliot. Which seemed to settle it. There were two other parties who might have been anything at all.

At this point Louise joined me.

'I have been kept from my drink,' she complained, bitterly for her, 'by the *patronne*, who is convinced that I cannot wait to know the history, business, and antecedents, of everyone in the hotel. And who, incidentally, was panting to find out mine and yours.'

Her vermouth was brought, and she tilted it to the light with a contented sigh.

'*L'heure de l'apéritif.* What a civilized institution. Ah, that must be M. Paul Véry.' She was looking at the Frenchman in the corner. 'Madame said he was handsome enough to suicide oneself for, and that hardly applies to anyone else here. He's from Paris. Something to do with antiques.'

'This is thrilling.'

'The other lonely male is English, and a schoolmaster. His name is John Marsden and he is almost certainly a Boy Scout and a teetotaller as well.'

'Why on earth?' I asked, startled.

'Because,' said Louise drily, 'any lonely male I ever get within reach of these days seems to be both, and to eschew women into the bargain. Is that the right word, eschew?'

'I believe so.'

'At any rate, one would not suicide oneself for *that* one. I wonder why he looks so solemn? Do you suppose he's reading *Whither England*, or something?'

'It's T. S. Eliot,' I said. '*Four Quartets.*'

'Oh *well*,' said Louise, who does not consider poetry necessary. Mr. Marsden was dismissed.

'I suppose that couple are American?' I said.

'Oh yes. Their name is Cornell, or they come from Cornell, or something. My French had a breakdown at that point. And Mama and Papa under the palm tree are hot from Newcastle, Scotland.'

'Scotland?' I said blankly.

'So Madame informed me. Scotland, zat is ze Norz of England, *n'est-ce pas*? I like the daughter, don't you? The Young Idea.'

I looked cautiously round. The couple under the palm tree might have sat anywhere for the portrait of Suburban England Abroad. Dressed as only the British can dress for a sub-tropical climate – that is, just as they would for a fortnight on the North-East coast of England – they sat sipping their drinks with wary enjoyment, and eyeing their seventeen-year-old daughter with the sort of expression that barnyard fowls might have if they suddenly hatched a flamingo. For she was startling to say the least of it. She would have been pretty in a fair English fashion, but she had seen fit to disguise herself by combing her hair in a flat thick mat down over one side of her face. From behind the curtain appeared one eye, blue-shadowed to an amazing appearance of dissipation. Scarlet nails, spike-heeled sandals, a flowered dirndl and a cotton jersey filled to frankly unbelievable proportions by a frankly impossible figure . . . Hollywood had come to Avignon by way of the Scotswood Road. And it became apparent that this not inconsiderable battery of charm was turned full on for someone's benefit.

'The man in the corner . . .' murmured Louise.

I glanced towards M. Paul Véry, who, however, appeared quite indifferent to the effort being made on his behalf. He had a slight frown between his brows, and he was tracing a pattern with the base of his glass on the table-top as if it were the only thing that mattered in the world.

'She's wasting her time, I'm afraid,' I remarked, and, as if he had heard me (which was impossible) the Frenchman looked up and met my eyes. He held them deliberately for a long moment in a cool, appraising stare, then, just as deliberately, he raised his glass and drank, still with his eyes on me. I looked away to gaze hard at the back of the fat German's neck, and hoped my colour had not risen.

'She is indeed wasting her time,' said Louise softly. She raised an amused eyebrow at me. 'Here's metal more attractive.'

'Don't be idiotic,' I said with some asperity. 'And control your imagination, for goodness' sake. Don't forget this is Provence, and if a woman's fool enough to be caught staring at a man, she's asking for it. That's what's called an *œillade*, which is French for leer.'

'All right,' said Louis tranquilly. 'Well, that's all that Madame told me. I think the other lot are Swiss –

nobody else except Americans could afford a gorgeous vulgar car like that – and are just *en passant*. The only other resident is a Mrs. Bristol, who's either a widow or divorced. *Et voilà tous.* Shall we have another drink?'

Then the blonde appeared, threading her way between the tables, to sit down near the trellis, two tables away from Mr. Marsden. She crossed one exquisite nyloned leg over the other, took out a cigarette, and smiled at the waiter. There was a sort of confusion, which resolved itself into three separate movements – the fat German beat the waiter and Mr. Marsden by a short head – to light her cigarette. But Mr. Marsden won on points, because the German's lighter refused to work, and Marsden had a match. She flung a smile to Fat-Neck, an order for a drink to the waiter, and a look across the flame of the match to Marsden that made the flame look awfully dim. At any rate he read *Burnt Norton* upside down for quite some time afterwards. I had been right about the Pied Piper.

'Eschew,' said Louise, 'was definitely *not* the right word. I suppose that is Mrs. Bristol.'

It was on the tip of my tongue to correct her when the waiter, travelling like a Derby winner, brought the drink.

'Madame Bristole's drink.' He bowed it on to the table, and himself away.

She settled back in her chair, and looked about her. Seen at close quarters, she was as lovely as ever, which is saying a lot. It was a carefully tended, exotic loveliness, like that of a strange flower. That is a hackneyed metaphor, I know, but it describes her better than any

other . . . her skin was so smooth, and her heavy
perfume seemed part of her. Her eyes, I saw, were a
curiously bright blue, and large. Her hands were restless, and at the corners of mouth and eyes I could see
the faint lines of worry. These deepened suddenly as I
watched her, and then I realized that David had come
out from the hotel. He followed the waiter, who was
bringing another drink for Louise, and, as he passed
our table, saw me. He gave me a sudden little half-
apologetic grin, which the waiter masked, I think, from
the woman. Then the queer sullen look came down
over his face again, and he sat down opposite her. She
looked approvingly at his clean shorts and white shirt,
and said something, to which he did not reply. She
looked at his bent head for a moment, then resumed
her casual scrutiny of the tables.

The place was filling up rapidly now, and the waiters
were handing round the menus.

'Have you met that boy before?' asked Louise, 'or
was that just another leer?'

I said that I had spoken to him for a moment in the
courtyard. For some reason which I could not analyse,
I did not want to talk about it and I was glad when she
dropped the subject without further question.

'We'd better order,' she said.

We studied the menu with some enthusiasm . . .

But when Louise asked me if I wanted *côte d'agneau*
or *escalope de veau*, I replied 'Shelley' in an absent sort
of way, and between the *petites pommes de terre sautées*
and the *tarte maison* I was still trying to fit the lovely
(and French) Mrs. Bristol in with Gilbert White and

that appalling dog and the expression on a child's face of something being borne that was too heavy for him to bear.

And I didn't mean the iron table, either.

After dinner Louise announced that she was going to get her book, and sit over her coffee and cognac until bedtime. So I left her to it, and went out to explore Avignon alone.

Avignon is a walled city, as I have said, a compact and lovely little town skirted to the north and west by the Rhône and circled completely by medieval ramparts, none the less lovely, to my inexpert eye, for having been heavily restored in the nineteenth century. The city is dominated from the north by the Rocher des Doms, a steep mass of white rock crowned by the cathedral of Notre Dame, and green with singing pines. Beside the cathedral, taking the light above the town, is the golden stone palace of the Popes. The town itself is slashed in two by one main street, the Rue de la République, which leads from the main gate straight up to the city square and thence to the Place du Palais, at the foot of the Rocher des Doms itself.

But these things I had yet to find. It was dusk when I set out, and the street was vividly lit. All the cafés were full, and I picked my way between the tables on the pavement, while there grew in me that slow sense of exhilaration which one inevitably gets in a Southern town after dark. The shop windows glittered and flashed with every conceivable luxury that the mind of the tourist could imagine; the neon lights slid along satin and drowned themselves in velvet and danced over perfume and jewels, and, since I have learned in my twenty-eight years to protect the heart a little against too much pity, I kept my eyes on them, and tried not to think about the beggars who slunk whining along the city gutters. I went on, carefully not thinking about those beggars, until I reached the end of the street, where the Rue de la République widens out and becomes the main square of the city, and where all Avignon collects at night, together with, one would swear, every child and every dog in France.

The square is surrounded with cafés, which overflow the narrow pavements with a froth of gay little tables and wicker chairs, and even cast up a jetsam of more little tables across the roads and into the centre of the square itself. Here, as I said, Avignon collects at night, and for the price of a cup of coffee, which secures you a chair, you may sit for an hour and watch France parade for you.

I paid for my coffee, and sat in the milk-warm air, marvelling, as one has to in Provence, at the charming manners of the children, and the incredible variety of shapes possible among the dogs, at the beauty of the half-naked, coffee-brown young men in from the fields, and the modest grace of the young girls. One in particular I noticed, an exquisite dark creature who went slowly past with downcast eyes. Her dress was cut low over her breasts, and gathered tightly to a tiny waist, but her face might have been that of a nun, and she walked demurely between her parents, stout, respectable-looking folk who made the girl as difficult of access, no doubt, as Danaë. And she was followed, I could see, by dark-eyed glances that said exactly what had been said to Bele Yolanz and fair Amelot, five hundred years before, when the troubadours sang in Provence.

'Excuse me,' said a woman's voice behind me. 'But didn't I see you at the hotel?'

I turned. It was Mamma from Newcastle, Scotland, and she was smiling at me rather hesitantly from a nearby table.

'I'm Mrs. Palmer,' she said. 'I hope you don't mind me speaking, but I saw you at dinner, and—'

'Of course I don't. My name's Charity Selborne.' I got up and picked up my coffee-cup. 'May I join you?'

'Oh, do.' She moved her chair to make way for me. 'Father and Carrie – they go off walking about the place, exploring they call it – only sometimes they seem to take so long, and—'

'And it seems longer when you don't know anyone to talk to,' I finished for her.

She beamed as if I had said something brilliant. 'That's exactly how I feel! Fancy! And of course it's not like home, and what with people talking French it's different, isn't it?'

I admitted that it was.

'Of course if I go in for a cup of tea at home,' said Mrs. Palmer, 'in Carrick's, you know, or it might be Fenwick's, there's always someone I know comes in too, and you can have a nice chat before you get the bus. That's why it seems kind of funny not knowing anybody here, and of course it isn't tea anyway, not *real* tea, as you might say, but I just can't seem to fancy this stuff they give you with lemon in, can you?'

I said on the whole, no, and how very brave of her to come all this way for a holiday.

'Well,' said Mrs. Palmer, 'it wasn't really me that suggested it, it was Carrie. I'd never have thought of a grand holiday like this, you know. But I just thought to myself, why not? You always read about the South of France and what's the good of just going every year to Scarborough and reading about the South of France? Well, I just thought, we can afford it, and why not? So here we are.'

I smiled at her, and said why not indeed, and good for her, and what a splendid idea of Carrie's.

'Of course she likes to be called Carole,' said Mrs. Palmer hastily. 'I think it's these films, you know. She will try to dress like them, say what I will.'

I said Carole was a pretty girl, which was true.

'Now that Mrs. Bristol, poor thing,' said Mrs. Palmer. 'She *does* look the part, the way Carrie never will. Of course she *was* on the stage or something, before It Happened.'

I sat up straight.

'Before what happened, Mrs. Palmer?'

'Oh, didn't you know? I recognized her straight away. Her photo was in all the Sunday papers, you know. Before she married that dreadful man, I meant.'

'What dreadful man? *What* happened?'

'The murderer,' said Mrs. Palmer, lowering her voice to a whisper. 'He was tried for murder, the Brutal

Murder of his Best Friend, it said in the papers.' The quoted headlines echoed queerly. 'He thought his friend was carrying on with *her* – with his wife – so he murdered him. It was all in the papers.'

I stared at her stupid, kindly, half-excited eyes, and felt a bit sick.

'David's father, you mean?' I asked numbly. 'David's father a *murderer*?'

She nodded.

'That's right. Strangled with a blind cord. Horrible. An Act of Jealous Madness, it said.'

I said, inadequately, looking away from her:

'Poor little boy . . . how long ago was all this?'

'The trial was in April. Of course, she's not the boy's mother, you know, she was his second wife. But of *course* she took the boy away: she couldn't leave David to *him*. Not after what happened.'

'What do you mean? D'you mean he's still alive?'

'Oh yes.'

'In prison?'

She shook her head, leaning a little closer.

'No. That's the awful part of it, Mrs. Selborne. He's At Large.'

'But—'

'He was let off. Insufficient evidence, they called it, and they acquitted him.'

'But perhaps he's not guilty. I mean, the courts of law—'

'Guilty,' said Mrs. Palmer, tapping my arm. 'Guilty as hell.' She broke off and went rather pink. 'That's what Mr. Palmer says, you understand, Mrs. Selborne.

And it's my belief he was mad, poor soul, or he'd never have gone for the boy like he did, murder or no murder.'

'Gone . . . for the boy?' I repeated, a bit shakily.

'Yes. Terrible, isn't it?' I could see the easy moisture start into her pale kindly eyes, and I warmed towards her. There was nothing of the ghoul about Mrs. Palmer; she was not enjoying the story, any more than I was. 'They found David unconscious in the bathroom near the bedroom where the body was found. He'd been knocked on the head.'

'Did he say his father had done it?'

'He didn't see who hit him. But it must've been the murderer. Caught in the Act, as you might say. Oh, it was an awful business; I'm surprised you don't remember it, really. The papers went on about it for long enough.'

'No, I don't remember it.' My voice sounded flat, almost mechanical. Poor David. Poor little boy. 'I don't remember hearing the name before at all. It's – it's terrible.'

Mrs. Palmer gave an exclamation, grabbed her handbag, and rose.

'Oh, there's Father and Carrie, off down the other side of the square, they can't have seen me . . . I must run. It's been lovely having a little chat, Mrs. Selborne, really lovely.' She beamed at me. 'And don't take on about poor Mrs. Bristol and the little boy. She's divorced from that Man, you know. He can't do a thing. And children do get over things, they say.'

Over some things, yes.

'I'm glad you told me,' I said, 'I might have said something . . . I had no idea.'

'Well, if you didn't see the photos—' said Mrs. Palmer. 'Of course, Bristol isn't their real name, so you wouldn't have heard it. The real name was Byron. Richard Byron, that was it. And now I must run. Good night, Mrs. Selborne.'

She went across the square, away from me, and I sat there for a long time before I even realized she had gone.

3

Sur le pont d'Avignon
L'on y danse, l'on y danse
Sur le pont d'Avignon
L'on y danse, tout en rond.
(French nursery rhyme)

By ten the next morning it was already as hot as on the hottest day in England, but with no sense of oppression, for the air was clear and light. Louise, true to her word, retired with a book and a sketching pad to the little green public gardens near the hotel.

'You go and play tourist,' she said. 'I'm going to sit under a tree and drink grape juice. Iced.'

It sounded a tempting programme, but tomorrow would be no cooler than today, and in any case the heat does not worry me unduly, so I set off for a gentle tour of exploration. This time I went out of the city gate, and turned along under the massive outer walls, towards the quarter where the Rhône races under the Rocher des Doms and then round the western fortifications of the city. It was a dusty walk, and not a very pleasant one, after all, I discovered. The verges of the narrow road were deep in dust and grit, the only vegetation, apart from the trees along the river, being thistles as dry as crumbling paper. Even along the flat edge of the Rhône itself, under the trees, there was no grass, only beaten dirt and stones, where beggars slept at night on the bare ground. A pair of enormous birds dipped and circled above the river.

But presently, round a curve in the city wall, the old bridge of the song came into view, its four remaining arches soaring out across the green water to break off, as it were, in midleap, suspended half-way across the Rhône. Down into the deep jade water glimmered the drowned-gold reflection of the chapel of St. Nicholas, which guards the second arch. Here, held by a spit of sand, the water is still, rich with the glowing colours of stone and shadow and dipping boughs, but beyond the sand-bank the slender bridge thrusts out across a tearing torrent. Standing there, you remember suddenly that this is one of the great rivers of Europe. Without sound or foam, smooth and incredibly rapid, it sucks its enormous way south to the Mediterranean, here green as serpentine, there eddying to aquamarine, but everywhere hard in colour as a stone.

And then I saw David, playing with Rommel beside the pool under the chapel. Both boy and dog were wet, David, since he was in bathing trunks, more gracefully so than Rommel, who looked definitely better when his somewhat eccentric shape was disguised by his wool. I was on the bridge, actually, before I saw them below me. They seemed absorbed, David in building a dam, Rommel in systematically destroying it, but almost at once the boy looked up and saw me sitting in the embrasure of the chapel window.

He grinned and waved.

'Are you going to dance up there?' he called.

'Probably not,' I called back. 'It's too narrow.'

'What's in the chapel?'

'Nothing much. Haven't you been up?' I must have sounded surprised.

'No money,' said David, succinctly.

'Tell the concierge I'll pay for you on my way down.'

'I didn't mean that, you know.'

'No, I know. But I did. Only for heaven's sake hang on to Rommel. There's no parapet, and he'd be at Marseilles by tea-time if he fell into this.'

Boy and dog vanished into the concierge's lodge, and presently emerged on to the bridge, slightly out of breath, and disputing over Rommel's right to hurl himself sportingly straight into the Rhône.

But presently Rommel, secured by the inevitable piece of string, was reckoned as being under control, and the three of us cautiously went to the very end of the broken arch – cautiously, because the bridge is only a few feet wide and there is always a strong breeze blowing from the North – and sat down with Rommel between us. We sang '*Sur le pont d'Avignon*' in the style of Jean Sablon, and David told me the story of St. Bénézet who confounded the clerics of Avignon, and built the bridge where the angel had told him, and we watched the two big birds, which were kites, David said, and which soared and circled beautifully up in the high blue air.

Then we went down to the road, and I paid the concierge, and David thanked me again, and we set off back to the hotel for lunch.

It seemed impossible, on this lovely gay morning, that David's father might be a murderer, and that David himself had been struck down, for no reason, in the dark, by a hand that must surely have belonged to a madman.

'Where do you spend most of your days?' I asked.

'Oh, by the river, mostly. You can swim under the bridge at the edge, inside the sand-bank where there's no current.'

'You haven't seen – well, the countryside? The Pont du Gard, and the arena at Nîmes, and so on? Perhaps you don't bother with that sort of thing?'

'Oh *yes*. I'd love to see the arena – do you know they have bull-fights every Sunday and one of the matadors is a woman?'

'Well I should hate to see a bull-fight,' I said decidedly. 'But I intend to go and see the arena tomorrow anyway, and if you'd like to come, there's plenty of room in the car. Do you think your mother would let you?'

'My step-mother,' said David distinctly.

He shot me a little sidelong look and flushed slightly. 'That's why we have different names, you see.'

'I see. Would she let you come? That is, if you would like to come?'

He hesitated oddly for a moment, and once again I saw the mask fall across his face, and as before, for no reason that I could guess. It was as if he considered some grave objection, rejected it eventually, and finally shrugged it away.

'I should like it very much, thank you,' he said formally. 'And I don't think my step-mother will object at all. It isn't her kind of thing, you know,' naïvely enough, 'but she doesn't much mind what I do.'

When we reached the hotel, people were gathering for *apéritifs* in the cool courtyard. I came down from my room to find Mrs. Bristol already installed at a table beside an orange tree. She smiled at me, and made a gesture of invitation, so I went over and sat down at her table.

'I hear you have been with David,' she said to me, 'so very kind of you to trouble.'

'Not at all. We met by accident – I enjoyed the morning immensely.' I murmured commonplaces, and she thanked me charmingly for what she called my kindness.

She bought me a drink and we talked nothings about the heat, and the town, and the shops for some time. She was very charming and talkative, but I noticed that the worried lines round her mouth seemed rather more pronounced today, and that whenever David's name cropped up in the conversation, there seemed to darken in her eyes the same shadow – of wariness, was it? – that had crossed David's face when I spoke of the trip to the arena at Nîmes.

'I had thought of taking the car to the Pont du Gard tomorrow,' I said at length, 'and then on to Nîmes, to look round a bit. If you have no objection, I should like to take David with me? I don't know whether my friend will want to go, and I should very much like to have David's company.'

She was lighting a cigarette when I spoke, and she paused with the flame of the lighter an inch from the cigarette-end, in the queerest, most exact repetition of David's own deliberation. I saw her assimilate the question, look at it carefully, hesitate, and then decide. For the life of me I couldn't understand why a proposal for a day's sight-seeing tour (which was surely what one came to Roman France for anyway?) should raise such problems as mine apparently did.

'It's so very kind of you,' said Mrs. Bristol, and the lighter finally made contact with the cigarette. 'I'm sure David will enjoy it.' She made a charming grimace. 'These antiquities – they are not for me; I am for Paris, the cities, the people – places where one amuses oneself . . . you understand?'

'Oh yes – but I rather like it both ways,' I laughed. 'And I'm afraid I adore sight-seeing. I'm a born tourist, but I don't like to go in a crowd. But what on earth do you find to do in Avignon if you don't like – er, antiquities?'

She hesitated again, and sent me a quick look from under her darkened lashes.

'We do not stay long – we pass through to Monte Carlo. We rest a few days in Avignon on the way.'

'Well, thank you for the drink, Mrs. Bristol,' I said, getting to my feet. I had caught sight of Louise, who had taken a corner table, and was looking at the lunch menu. We murmured more civilities, and I turned to go, but the strap of my bag caught on the back of the chair, and as I swung round again quickly to disentangle it, I saw Mrs. Bristol staring at me, with her lovely eyes narrowed against the smoke of her cigarette, and in them a look of half-pleased, half-apprehensive speculation that puzzled me considerably.

That evening, as Louise was no more inclined than formerly to go for a walk, I left her sketching in a café in the city square, and went alone up the little dark street that leads to the Popes' palace and the gardens among the pines, high up on the Rocher des Doms.

Unlike the main square, the Place du Palais was almost empty, the buildings on three sides dark and blank, while on the right the great façade of the Palace soared up out of the living rock, shadowy yet luminous in the starlight. I lingered for a while gazing up at it, then went slowly up the sloping zigzag walk through the pines towards the high gardens, which lie at the very edge of the city, and are girdled in by the city wall itself. Very few people appeared to be up there that evening, and only occasionally, it seemed, I heard the murmur of voices and the soft scrunch of the gravel under someone's foot. The air was still, and the cicadas were quiet at last, but the pines kept up a faint continuous murmuring overhead, almost as if, in sleep, they yet gave back the sound of the wind that sweeps down the river all winter, and, in summer, lingers in them still.

Climbing slowly up through the winding alleys of evergreens, I came at length to the topmost edge of the gardens, above the Rhône, and leaned over the low battlemented wall to rest. Below me the wall dropped away vertically, merging into the solid cliff which bounded the river. The Rhône, beneath, slipped silently under the darkness on its wide and glimmering way.

It was very quiet.

Then suddenly, from somewhere behind me, came a man's voice, speaking low, in French.

'So this is where you are!'

Startled, I turned my head, but behind me was a thick bank of evergreen, and I could see nothing. I was alone in my little high corner of the wall. He must be on the lower walk, screened by the bushes. A woman's voice answered him.

She said: 'You're late. I've been here a long time. Have you a cigarette?'

I heard the scrape of a match, then he said in a voice which sounded sullen: 'You weren't here when I passed ten minutes ago.'

'I got tired of waiting, and went for a walk.' Her voice was indifferent, and I heard the gravel scrape, as if he made an angry movement.

I had no intention of letting myself be marooned in my corner while a love scene went on within hearing, and I determined at this point that, as I would have to pass them to get back to the main path, I had better emerge before anything passed that might make my appearance embarrassing. But as I turned to move, the woman spoke again, and I realized, suddenly, two things: one, that the voice was that of Mrs. Bristol, and secondly, that she was very much afraid. I suppose

I had not recognized the voice immediately because I had previously only heard her speak in English, but as her voice rose, edged with fear, I recognized it.

She said: 'It's happened. I knew it would happen. I knew . . .'

His voice cut in sharply, almost roughly: 'What's happened?'

'He's here. He's come. I had to see you, I—'

He interrupted again.

'For God's sake, pull yourself together. How do you know he's here?'

She spoke breathlessly, still with the tremor in her voice.

'I got a phone call tonight. His car's been seen. They traced it as far as Montélimar. He must be coming this way. He must have found out where we are—'

'Loraine—'

'What are we going to do?' It was a desperate whisper. I leaned against the wall in my little corner; not for anything could I have come out now. I could only trust they would not seek its greater privacy for themselves.

I heard the man (I think it was he) draw in a long breath. Then he spoke quietly and with emphasis.

'There is nothing that we can do, yet. We don't know for certain where he is, he may be anywhere in Provence. When was he seen in Montélimar?'

'Yesterday.'

He exploded with wrath. 'God in heaven, the clumsy fools! And they only telephoned tonight?'

'They weren't sure. It was a big grey car with a GB plate, and they think it was his. It was the first glimpse they'd had since Chartres.'

'They should have been sure. What the hell are they paid for?' he said angrily.

'Can't we find out where he is? I – I don't think I can stand much more of this – this suspense.'

'No, we must do nothing. We'll find out soon enough, I've no doubt.' His voice was grim. 'And for God's sake, Loraine, take hold of yourself. You shouldn't have got me up here tonight, you don't know who's about, and this is such a tiny place. Anybody from the hotel—'

Her voice was sharp with new alarm: 'You don't think he's got someone planted in the hotel? Do you mean . . .?'

'I don't mean anything,' he returned shortly. 'All I'm saying is, that we mustn't be seen together. You know that as well as I do. Anyone might see us, they might mention it to David, and he has little enough confidence in you anyway, as far as I can see.'

'I do try, I really do.'

'I know you do,' he said more gently. 'And I know David's not easy. But it's not David I'm thinking about, so much as *him*. If *he* ever got to know we were connected I'd be a hell of a lot of use to you, wouldn't I? He'd find a way to get me out of the road first, and then—'

'Don't, please!'

His voice softened: 'Look, my dear, stop worrying. It'll be all right, I promise. I got you out of the mess before, didn't I? I got you away from England, didn't I? and the boy too?'

She murmured something I couldn't catch, and he went on: 'And it'll be all right again, I swear it. I know it's hell just sitting around wondering what's going to happen, but I'm in charge and you trust me, don't you? Don't you?'

'Yes. Yes, of course.'

'Here, have another cigarette.' I heard him light it for her, and there was a pause.

'Those damned English police,' she said bitterly. 'If they'd known their job this would never have had to happen. He ought to be dead and done with.' The way she repeated it made me shiver, 'Dead and done with,' she said.

'Well, he's not,' said the man briskly, sounding as if he were dragging back the conversation, with an effort, on to a less dramatic and more practical level. 'He's here, in France. And there's nothing to be scared of. He can't do a thing to you, after all. All you've got to do is keep your nerve and hang on to David. We ought to go back, I think. You go first – come down to the corner with me till we see if there's anyone about.' He must have turned to go, for his voice grew suddenly fainter.

She stopped him for a moment. Her tone was calmer, and the note of fear was gone, but I could hear the tautness of her nerves through it, for all that.

'I meant to ask you – that girl, Selborne I think her name is – she offered to take David out in her car to-morrow. I suppose it's all right?'

There was another pause. I think he took her arm, because I heard them begin to move off together, but I heard his reply, faintly, before they went out of earshot.

'Quite all right, I imagine. In fact, it might be a good idea . . .'

The palms of my hands, I found, had been pressed so hard against the stone of the parapet that they were sore. I stood perfectly still for some time after they had gone, slowly rubbing my hands together, and thinking.

It was not a particularly pleasant thought, that somewhere near at hand, possibly even in Avignon at this moment, was a man who was probably a murderer; a man vindictive enough, if I had understood aright what I had heard, to pursue the wife who had divorced him after the trial, and dangerous enough to frighten her as Loraine Bristol was being frightened. She was not, I thought, a woman who would frighten easily.

Why was he apparently following her? Did he want her back, was he hoping for reconciliation . . . no, that wouldn't do, she wouldn't be so afraid if that were all. Then was he angry at her action in divorcing him at such a time, was it revenge he was after? No, that was absurd; people just didn't behave that way at all, not rational people . . . that must be it, I thought, and went cold . . . he was *not* rational. Mrs. Palmer had said that he was mad, and no sane man, surely, would have struck down his own son . . .

David.

It wasn't Loraine he was pursuing at all, it was David.

I pressed my now tingling hands to my cheeks, and thought of David and the dog Rommel, building dams under the Pont St. Bénézet, and as I thought, some of the loneliness of the child's situation dawned on me, and made me feel chilled. I knew a lot about loneliness. And I knew that, come murderers, come hell, come high water, I should have to do something about it.

I slowly descended the zigzag walk to the level of the Palace square, on the alert in case I should run into Mrs. Bristol, who might be waiting about somewhere to give her companion a start.

Her companion? I had not recognized the lowered voice, the rapid French. But that it was someone at the hotel I felt sure.

Then, in the narrow dark little street that skirts the foot of the rock where the palace is built, I saw someone standing, a man. He did not see me, but stood gazing in the direction of the main square, and, as I paused in the darkness under the palace steps, I saw him slip out of the shadows, and saunter down the street and into the light.

I recognized him all right.

It was Marsden.

4

Old moniments . . .
(Spenser)

Towards mid-morning the next day I eased the Riley down the narrow main street of Avignon, and out on to the perimeter road. Louise sat beside me, and in the back were David and Rommel, wrangling as usual over the necessity of chasing every cat we passed. We skirted Avignon, following my route of the previous day, but before we reached the old bridge of St. Bénézet, I turned the car over the narrow suspension bridge which crosses the Rhône. We crept across its swaying, resounding metal surface, then swung through Villeneuve-lès-Avignon and headed south for Nîmes.

The heart of Roman France . . . I thought of the legions, tramping behind their eagles through the pitiless heat and dust, across this barren and hostile country. The road was a white and powdery ribbon that twisted between slopes of rock and scrub. Whin I recognized, and juniper, but most of the shrubs were unfamiliar – dark green harsh foliage that sucked a precarious life from the cracks among the screes and faces of white rock. Here and there houses crouched under the heat, clinging to the edge of the road as if to a life-line; occasionally a grove of olives hung on the slopes like a silver-green cloud, or a barrier of cypress reared its bravery in the path of the mistral, but for the most part the hot and desert slopes rose, waterless and unclothed by any softer green than that of gorse and scrub.

'Mustn't they have felt hot in their helmets?' said David, breaking into my thoughts as if he had known exactly what I was thinking. 'Though I suppose Italy's just as hot.'

'And they fought all summer,' I said. 'In winter they retired—'

'To winter quarters – I remember that,' said David, grinning. 'In my Latin Grammar, if they weren't going to the city to buy bread, they were always retiring to winter quarters.'

'I believe they went to the coast. There's a nice little place east of Marseilles where Caesar made a sort of spa for his veterans.'

'Aren't the Michelin guides wonderful?' murmured Louise. 'And incidentally, Charity – I hate to interfere, but you *have* seen that bus, haven't you?'

'I could hardly avoid it,' I said drily. 'It's in the middle of the road.'

'Oh, I just thought – what's the French for "break-down"?'

'*Dépannage*. Or in this case, just plain *accident*. Haven't you got used to the French way of driving yet? You should have.'

We were rapidly overtaking a bus which was indeed thundering along in the very centre of the narrow road. But I knew my stuff by now, after the hundreds of heartbreaking miles before I had discovered that the 'courtesy of the road' means very different things in France and England. I swung to the left, bore down on the bus with every appearance of intending to ram it, and put the heel of my hand down hard on the horn. The bus, responding with an ear-splitting klaxon, immediately swerved to the left, too, straight into our path. I didn't even brake, but put my hand on the horn and kept it there. The bus, with an almost visible shrug, moved over about a foot to the right, and we tore by.

Louise let out a long breath. 'I'll never get used to that!'

'If he'd seen the GB plates we'd never have done it. The British are despicably easy to bully on the roads.'

'Did you see who was on the bus?' said David.

'No, I was busy. Who was it?'

'That man from the hotel. I think his name's Marsden. He sits at the table by the big palm.'

'Oh. Yes, I've noticed him.'

I eased my foot off the accelerator, and glanced at the bus in the driving-mirror. It might conceivably turn off at Pont du Gard for Tarascon, but I had the idea that the Avignon-Tarascon buses went another way. In which case, this must be the bus for Nîmes, and Marsden was on it. And after what I had heard last night up at the Rocher des Doms, I was not quite sure what I thought about the possibility of Marsden's following us to Nîmes.

I slowed down a little more. With a triumphant screech of its klaxon, the bus overtook the Riley, and demanded the road.

I glanced in the mirror as it loomed up behind the car. Yes, unmistakable, even in mirror-image: NIMES.

I put my foot down again, and we drew away. I was trying to think, but I had too little to go on. It was like groping for a window through curtains of spiders' webs, only to find that it was dark outside the window, and that when the webs were all torn down, the window would be still invisible.

I thrust the problem aside, and passed a small Citroën with concentrated care.

At Pont du Gard we drew in under the shade of the trees, opposite the hotel. Louise began to gather her things together.

'David,' I said. 'Will you do something for me?'

'Of course. What?'

'Ask up at the hotel what time the bus gets here. How long it stays. What time it gets to Nîmes. Will your French stand up to that, do you think?'

David gave me a look, and scrambled out of the car with Rommel.

'Of course,' he said again; then, with a sudden burst of honesty – 'It's not so much *asking*, because you can practise on the way up, but it's understanding what they tell you – 'specially when it's numbers. But I'll try.' He gave me his swift engaging grin, and ran off through the gravel terrace of the hotel.

'Are you sure you don't want to come on to Nîmes, Louise?'

'Quite, thanks. I'll go down by the river and paint the bridge – oh, all right, aqueduct – I'll have lunch here first. What time are you coming back?'

'I'm not sure. When d'you want to be picked up?'

Louise looked through the trees towards the river, where could be seen a glowing glimpse of golden stone.

'I don't know, honestly. I'll tell you what, Charity – we won't tie ourselves down. You go on to Nîmes and look at your remains in your own time. If I'm sitting at one of those tables when you come back, pick me up. If not, I'll have gone back on the bus, so don't bother. You won't want to come back much before dinner-time, anyway, and I'll have finished painting long before that.'

David came panting across the road to the door of the car.

'*Midi-vingt!*' he announced with triumph. 'The bus gets here *midi-vingt*. It waits half an hour, and it gets to Nîmes at half-past one. Is that what you wanted to know?'

'That's fine,' I said, glancing at my watch. 'It's barely twelve now, and the bus doesn't get here till twenty past. We'll have time to look at the bridge – sorry, Louise, aqueduct – after all.'

I took the ignition key out and dropped it into my bag.

'What *do* you mean?' asked Louise. She was looking at me curiously. 'I thought that's one of the things you came for? What's the bus got to do with it?'

I felt the colour creep into my face. I had been thinking aloud, without realizing how queer it must have sounded.

'Nothing,' I said, rather lamely. 'I was thinking about lunch. We'll have lunch in Nîmes, so we won't stay here too long.'

I need not have been afraid that Louise would pursue the subject. She was already rummaging for her pencils, and hardly listened to my reply. But as I turned from the car, I saw David looking at me. A long, unreadable look . . . and again I sensed that all those impalpable defences were up. Then Rommel gave an impatient tug to his string, and we all went down towards the bank of the river, under tall trees harsh with the shrilling of the cicadas.

5

O bloody Richard!
(Shakespeare)

Whenever I look back now on the strange and ter-rifying events of that holiday in Southern France, I am conscious of two things which seem to dominate the picture. One is the continuous dry and nerve-rasping noise of the cicadas, invisible in the parched trees, the other is the Roman aqueduct over the Gardon as I first saw it that brilliant day. I suppose the ten or twelve minutes that David and Rommel and I spent gazing at those golden arches spanning the deep green Gardon were like the last brief lull before the thunder.

We stood near the edge of the narrow river, on the water-smooth white rock, and watched Louise settle herself in the shade of some willows, where the aqueduct soared above us, its steep angle cutting the sky. On the under-sides of the arches moved the slow, water-illu-mined shadows, till the sun-steeped stone glowed like living gold. Except for the lazy sliding silver of reflected light under the striding spans, nothing stirred. Not a leaf quivered; there was no cloud to betray the wind. You would have sworn that the gleaming river never moved . . .

The sound of an engine on the road above recalled me abruptly. We said good-bye to Louise, who hardly heard us, and climbed the dusty track again to the car.

Not until we had swung out on to the road to Nîmes did either of us speak.

Then David gave a queer little sigh, and said:

'I'm glad I did come, after all.' Then he flung a quick glance at me, and flushed. 'I mean – I didn't mean—'

'It doesn't matter. I'm glad you're glad you came.'

He glanced at me again, and I could sense, rather than see, a long and curious scrutiny.

'Mrs. Selborne—'

'Yes?'

He hesitated. I could feel his body beside me, tense as a runner's. I kept my eyes on the road and waited. Then he gave another odd, sharp little sigh, and bent his cheek to Rommel's shoulder.

'Oh, nothing. How far is it to Nîmes?'

And for the rest of the way we talked about the Romans. I was not to be allowed to help, after all. And I knew better than to force confidence from a boy of his age – a boy, moreover, who had so much the air of knowing exactly what he was up against, and what he was going to do about it. But stealing a look down at the childish curve of the thin cheek laid against the dog's fur, I wasn't so sure that he could deal with whatever queer situation he was in. And again, I knew that I wanted most desperately to help. It was irrational, and I can't explain it, even today. It was just the way David made me feel. I told myself savagely that I was a fool, I said unpleasant things under my breath about a frustrated mother-complex, and I kept my eyes on the road, my voice casual, and I talked about the Romans.

And so we drove into Nîmes, parked the car off the square outside the church, and had lunch in a restaurant in a side street, out of sight of the place where the buses stop.

'The Arena first!' said David. 'I want to see where they keep the bulls!'

'Bloodthirsty little beast, aren't you? But there's no bullfight today, you know. Sunday nights only. The better the day, the better the deed.'

'Look, there's a poster – a Corrida, and this Sunday, too!' He looked at me wistfully. I laughed.

'*No*, David. I won't. And you wouldn't like it either, really. You're English – you'd be on the side of the bull. And think of the horses.'

'I suppose so. Golly, look! Is that it?'

We climbed the sloping street towards the enormous curve of the Arena, and made our way round half its circumference until we found the way in through its massive and terrible arches. I bought tickets, and we went into the barred shadows of the lower corridor. There were a few other tourists there, staring, chattering, fiddling with cameras. We followed a little group of English people up the main steps, out into the sunlight of the Arena until we emerged in what must have been the ringside seats, looking down into the great oval where the beasts and the Christians used to meet in blood and terror under the pitiless sun. I went forward to the edge and looked down at the sheer sides of the Arena, just too high for a man to leap, even if he were in terror of his life. David came to my side. He, at any rate, was not haunted by the things that had been done here. His face was excited and a little flushed and his eyes shining.

'Golly, Mrs. Selborne, what a place! I saw a door down there labelled TORIL. D'you suppose that's the bull? Do they use Spanish names here? Where does the bull come out to fight?'

I pointed to the big double doors at the end of the oval, where, in white letters, the word TORIL stood again.

'*Golly!*' said David again. He leaned over the parapet and gazed down with concentration. 'Do you suppose we could see bloodstains?'

I moved back into the shadow of the stairway. The heat reflected from the stones was almost unbearable. I heard, behind and below me, the monotonous voice of the concierge doling out tickets to a new batch of tourists. Two or three people came up the steps beside me, and another group, I noticed, went through a doorway near the foot of the steps, that apparently led out into the arena itself.

I leaned back against the cool stone in the shadows and watched David idly as he sauntered along the ringside tier, periodically stopping to lean over – looking for bloodstains, I supposed. Well, at least that disposed of an idea that the boy was a neurotic – a healthy desire for bloodstains was, I knew, part of the normal boy's equipment.

I closed my eyes. The concierge's voice rose and fell. There was a murmur of talk in French, in German, in American. Somewhere near me a camera clicked. Some more tourists came up the steps beside me, talking vigorously in German. For once we seemed to be the only English people there. But no sooner had the idle thought crossed my mind than I was proved wrong, for down below, on the arena floor itself, I heard some people talking English. And suddenly, a man's voice, sharp, distinct, edged with bad temper:

'This is *not* the wrong blasted ticket. It was issued at the Maison Carrée.'

Then someone passing on the steps jostled me, and my bag slipped from my lax fingers. I opened startled eyes, and made a grab for it. The culprit – it was a pleasant-looking woman of about forty – stooped for the bag and handed it to me with a soft-voiced apology in a charming American drawl.

'My own fault, I was half asleep.'

'It's this turrible heat,' she said. 'You do better in the shade. Come along, Junior.' As they turned to go, I became aware of David at my elbow. He spoke breathlessly:

'Mrs. Selborne!'

'What – why, what on earth's the matter, David?'

He had hold of my sleeve. His face was flour-white, and in the shadow his eyes looked enormous.

'Don't you feel well?'

'No – I – that is—' The hand on my arm was shaking. He began to pull me down the steps. 'May we go now? I don't want to stay here – do you mind?'

'Of course not. We'll go straight away. I was only waiting for you.'

He hardly waited for me to finish; he went down the steps as if his feet were winged, and out through the gate into the hot street, with Rommel close at his heels.

I followed, to find him heading back the way we had come.

'Why, David, don't you want to see the other things? This is the way back to the car.'

He paused a moment as we rounded the street corner, and put out a tentative hand again.

'I – I don't feel too good, Mrs. Selborne. I suppose it's the heat. D'you mind if I don't see the other things with you? I–I can wait for you somewhere.'

I took him by the arm.

'I don't mind at all. Of course not. I'm sorry you're not feeling well, though. Shall we go back to the car?'

We retraced our steps to the square, then he stopped and faced me again. He looked better now; he was still very pale, but he had stopped shaking, and even smiled at me.

'I'll be fine now, Mrs. Selborne. I'll sit in the church till you come back. It's lovely and cool in there. Please don't worry about me.'

'What about a drink? An iced mint? Here's a café.'

But he shook his head.

'I'll just go and sit in the church.'

'What about the dog?'

'Oh—' he glanced uncertainly at the church door. 'Oh. I expect it'll be all right. I'll sit near the back, and it's not the time for service. He could stay in the porch anyway . . .'

In the end he had his way. I watched him into the cool shadow of the west doorway, then I turned away to look for the temple and the gardens. At least nobody appeared to have forbidden Rommel's entry, and the church was the best place David could choose in this heat. I realized that, if he thought his indisposition had spoiled my day, he would be very embarrassed, so I decided to continue my sight-seeing tour of Nîmes, but to complete it as quickly as I could.

I saw the lovely pillared Maison Carrée, then I made my way along the stinking street beside the canal to the beautiful formal gardens which are the pride of Nîmes. The heat was terrific, and by the time I reached the gardens – so beautifully laid out around their stagnant and pestilential pools – even my enthusiasm for Roman remains had begun to waver.

I stood for a moment gazing up at the ranks of pine trees on the steep slope which leads up to the Roman Tower. It was very steep; the cicadas were fiddling in the branches like mad; the heat came out of the ground in waves.

'No,' I said firmly.

I turned my back on the tower, and made like a homing bee for the little ruined Temple of Diana – which has a café just beside it, where one can drink long iced drinks under the lime trees.

After two very long, very cold drinks, I felt con-siderably better. I still could not face the Tour Magne, but out of self-respect, as a tourist, I must use up the part of my tourist's ticket dedicated to the Temple of Diana. I left my chair and went through the crumbled arches into the tiny square of the temple.

It was like being miles from anywhere. Behind me, back through the crumbled archway, was the hot white world with its people and its voices; here, within, was a little square of quiet and green coolness. Trees dipped over the high broken walls, shadows lay like arras in the pillared corners, fronds of ferns lent softness to every niche and crevice. And silence. Such silence. Silence with a positive quality, that is more than just an absence of sound. Silence like music.

I sat down on a fallen piece of carved stone, leaned back against a pillar, and closed my eyes. I tried not to think of Johnny . . . it didn't do any good to think of Johnny . . . I must just think of nothing except how quiet it was, and how much I liked being alone . . .

'Aren't you well?'

I opened my eyes with a start.

A man had come into the temple, so quietly that I had not heard him approach. He was standing over me now, frowning at me.

'What's the matter? The heat?' He spoke with a sort of reluctant consideration, as if he felt constrained to offer help, but hoped to God I wasn't going to need it.

I knew there were tears on my eyelashes, and felt a fool.

'I'm all right, thanks,' I said crisply. 'I was only resting, and enjoying being alone.'

He raised his eyebrows at that, and the corner of his mouth twitched sourly.

'I'm sorry.'

I got up, feeling still more of a fool.

'I'm sorry too. I didn't mean that – I didn't mean to be rude. I – it was actually the literal truth. I wouldn't have said it, but you caught me a little off balance.'

He did not answer, but stood looking at me; I felt myself flushing like a schoolgirl and, for some idiotic reason, the tears began to sting again behind my eyes.

'I'm not usually rude to perfect strangers,' I said. 'Especially when they have been kind enough to – to ask after my health. Please forgive me.'

He didn't smile, but said, kindly enough:

'It was my fault for catching you – off balance. Hadn't you better have a cigarette to put you back on again before you go out?'

He handed me his case, and added, as I hesitated: 'If you don't accept cigarettes from perfect strangers either, we had better remedy that. My name's Coleridge. Richard Coleridge.'

I took a cigarette. 'And mine's Charity Selborne. Though it ought to be Wordsworth, I feel.'

He lit a match for me, and his look over it was sardonic.

'Don't tell me you feel a bond between us already?'

'No . . . though as a matter of fact I did wonder for a moment if we'd met before. There's something famil-iar—'

He interrupted, his voice rough again: 'We haven't. I don't know any Selborne outside of Gilbert White.'

I lifted my head, startled.

'Gilbert White?'

'Yes. You know the book—'

'Of course. It was just that somebody else the other day connected me with it too, and not so very many people read it now. And I was surprised at David, because he's only a boy.'

I suppose I should have been more careful; I suppose I should have heard the way his voice altered then. But I was still embarrassed, wanting to get away, chattering aimlessly about nothing.

He said, very quietly: 'David?'

'Yes. David Shelley. That's who I was thinking of when I said I should have been called Wordsworth. All the Romantic poets seem to be in—'

'Where did you meet this David Shelley?'

I heard it then. I stopped with my cigarette half-way to my lips and looked at him. His hand was quite steady as he flicked the ash from his cigarette, and his face showed no expression. But there was a look behind his eyes that made my heart jolt once, sickeningly.

He said again, softly, almost indifferently: '*Where did you meet this David Shelley?*'

And looked at me with David's eyes.

Shelley–Coleridge–Byron. I knew now. I was alone in that quiet little temple with Richard Byron, who had been acquitted of murder on the grounds of insufficient evidence, and who was looking at me now as if he would like to choke me.

He threw away his cigarette and took a step towards me.

6

Escape me?
(Browning)

'Excuse me, monsieur.'

Richard Byron stopped and swung round. The concierge stood just inside the doorway of the temple, looking at him with a sort of mournful reproach.

'Your ticket, monsieur. You nevaire show it.' His limp moustache drooped with rebuke. His eyes were pale watery brown, and slightly bloodshot. I thought I had never seen anybody I liked better. I ground out my cigarette with shaking fingers, and started – oh, so casually! – for the door. But the concierge must have thought that Richard Byron and I were together, for he stood his ground.

As I fished hurriedly in my bag for my ticket, Byron handed over his paper slip with an abrupt gesture of impatience. The concierge took it, eyed it with the same spaniel-like reproach, and shook his head.

'It is torn, monsieur. It is defaced. It is perhaps not the right ticket. . . .'

Richard Byron spoke harshly: 'I cannot help its being torn. It was torn when I got it.'

'Where did monsieur get it?'

'At the Maison Carrée.'

Something else jolted in my mind. The voice in the Arena, protesting about the same ticket in almost the same words; and David, who had been leaning over the parapet gazing into the Arena, coming flying down the steps to me, and dragging me away. David, white and shaking, going to hide in the church.

David had seen his father all right, and was even now hiding in the church like a rabbit in its burrow. At the thought of David, I was suddenly not afraid of Richard Byron any more. I held out my ticket again to the concierge, who took it, looked mournfully at it, and clipped it. Then I was out in the sunlight again walking past the café tables, back towards the canal. I was trying desperately to think of some way to get back to David and the car without Byron's seeing me. But the lovely gardens stretched ahead of me, open as a chess-board, and then there were the long, straight streets . . . I began to hurry; if only the concierge would keep him . . . but he must have squared the old man somehow, for I had hardly gone fifty yards towards the canal when I heard his step behind me, and he said:

'Just a minute. Please.'

I turned to face him.

'Look,' I said, pleasantly, casually, 'it's been very pleasant meeting you, and thank you for the cigarette. But I must go now. Good-bye.'

I turned to go, but he was at my elbow again.

'I just wanted to ask you—'

I tried to freeze him – to act as if I thought this was

just the usual pick-up, and to get away before he could ask any more questions.

'Please allow me to go,' I said icily. 'I prefer to go alone, as I said to you before.'

'I want to talk to you.'

'I'm afraid I—'

'You said you knew a boy called David Shelley.' He was scowling down at me, and his voice had an edge that I by no means liked. Against this direct attack I felt helpless, and in spite of myself, panic started to creep over me again. I wanted time to think – to think what to do, what to say. 'Where did you see him?'

'Why do you want to know?' I must have sounded feeble, but I could only stall weakly for time.

'I know him,' he said shortly. 'If he's hereabouts, I'd like to look him up. He's – he's the son of an old friend. He'd want to see me.'

Like hell he would, I thought, hiding away like a panic-stricken rabbit in the church, poor little kid.

I said: 'I'm sorry, I don't really know him.'

I could see people approaching up the long flight of steps from the gardens below, and I felt better. He could hardly detain me, make a scene, when there were people there. When they reached us I would break away from him, move off with them, lose myself among the other tourists . . .

I looked candidly into Richard Byron's angry grey eyes: 'I only met him casually on a sight-seeing trip – the way I met you. I couldn't tell you where he's staying.'

'When was this?'

'Two days ago.'

'Where?' The question was quiet, but somehow I could sense behind it some intolerable strain. I was reminded sharply again of David.

'In Tarascon,' I said, at random, some memory of the morning's encounter with the bus no doubt still in my mind. The people were nearly up the steps now, were pausing on a landing to look back at the view. . . .

'Whereabouts in Tarascon? Did he say if he was staying there?'

'No. I told you I didn't know. I only met him for a short time when we were looking at—' Panic flooded me for a moment. What *was* Tarascon? What did one look at in Tarascon? I plunged on a certainty – 'At the Cathedral.'

I heard him take in his breath in a long hiss and looking up I saw his eyes narrowing on me in a look that there was no mistaking. It was not imagination this time to see violent intentions there. If ever a man looked murder at anyone, Richard Byron looked it at me on that bright afternoon between the flaming beds of flowers in the gardens of Nîmes.

Then the little group of tourists was round us, and I turned to go with them. Anywhere, so long as I was among people, safe in a crowd, safe from the danger of betraying David to this hard-eyed man who stood in the sunlight looking like murder.

'Why, hallo,' said a soft American voice. 'Didn't I see you before – down at the bull-ring? Kind of a quaint l'il place, isn't it? Where's yuh li'l boy?'

It was the woman who had picked up my bag. She

smiled charmingly at me, but my mouth felt stiff. I just looked at her.

'Mom,' came a plaintive voice, 'Hi, Mom! Can yuh fix this film for me?'

She smiled at me again, and hurried towards Junior, who was wrestling with his Kodak at a café table. I started to follow, but a hand closed round my wrist, and gripped it hard.

'Just a minute,' said Richard Byron again.

He pulled me round to face him. I turned as if I were a wax doll – I had no more resistance. His grip was hurting my wrist, and he pulled me close to him. The group of tourists, self-absorbed and chattering, moved by, paying no attention. He drew me behind a group of statuary.

'Let me go!'

'So you were in the Arena today with a boy?'

'Let go my wrist or I'll call the police!'

He laughed, an ugly little laugh. 'Call away.'

I bit my lip, and stood dumb. The police – the questions – my papers, my car – and I still had to get quietly out of Nîmes with David. Richard Byron laughed again as he looked down at me.

'Yes, you'd be likely to call the police, wouldn't you?' His grip tightened, and I must have made a sound, because his mouth twisted with satisfaction before he slackened his hold. 'Now, where's this boy you were with?'

I couldn't think. I said, stupidly: 'She's mistaken. He wasn't with me. I was just talking to him. It wasn't David.'

He sneered at me.

'Still lying? So you were just talking to him, were you? The way you talked to David Shelley in the Cathedral at Tarascon?'

I nodded.

'Would it surprise you to be told,' said David's father, 'that Tarascon is a small and dirty village whose main claim to fame is a castle on the Rhône? And that, though I suppose there must be one, I have never even seen a church there?'

I said nothing. I might have known. Johnny always said I was a rotten liar.

'And now, damn you,' said Richard Byron, 'take me to David.'

And he pulled my arm through his own, and led me towards the steps.

He did not speak as we went down the long shallow flight of stone steps to the lower gardens, and I was grateful for the chance to think. Why he was acting like this I could not imagine, and I did not intend to waste time thinking about it yet. I must think of nothing but how to shake him off, and get out of Nîmes and back to Avignon without his following me or seeing David.

One thing was certain, I thought, remembering the boy's panic-stricken flight from the Arena on hearing his father's voice, David was mortally afraid of meeting his father. So all that mattered for the moment was that David should get away. If only he had told me then, we could have left Nîmes straight away. And after meeting

Richard Byron, I knew that, sooner than let him get his hands on David, I'd murder him myself.

I stole a glance at his profile, with its expression of brooding bitterness, and the unpleasant set to the mouth. Then I remembered, with a queer cold little twist of the stomach, what Mrs. Palmer had said.

'He must have been mad . . . they ought to have locked him up . . . *he must be mad*!'

Panic swept over me again, and at the same time a queer sense of unreality that I believe does come to people when they are in fantastic or terrifying situations. This could not be happening to me, Charity Selborne; I was not walking along the canal-side in Nîmes, Provence, with my arm gripped in that of a man who might be a murderer. A man who had hurt me and cursed me, and looked as if he would like to kill me. These things didn't happen . . . my mind spiralled stupidly; I wonder if Johnny thought it couldn't be happening to him, when he came down over France with his wings in flames . . .?

'Well?' said Richard Byron.

He had paused at the corner leading to the Arena, and looked down at me.

I said nothing, and his brows came down sharply into a scowl.

'Well?' he repeated with the sneer in his voice. 'You beautiful little bitch, what about it?'

Then suddenly, gloriously, I was angry. Someone once described it as a 'chemically useful reaction'; I believe it is. At any rate, my mind cleared at that moment and I forgot to be afraid of him, madman or no. And I knew what to do.

I looked up the street that leads to the Arena, and saw, parked at the extreme end of it, a big grey car, and I remembered Loraine's panicky whisper . . . 'A big grey car with a GB plate . . .' I looked the other way towards the square; there was a bus standing there, and I could see its destination: MONTPELLIER.

Then I put a hand to my eyes, and my lip quivered.

'All right,' I said. 'I was lying to you, but you frightened me, and I wanted to get away. I *was* with David Shelley in the Arena.'

His arm moved sharply under mine.

'That's better. Where is he now?'

'I don't know.'

'Now look here, my girl—'

I shook my head impatiently: 'Can't you see I'm telling the truth now? He didn't want to go up to the Tour Magne with me. He went off on his own.'

'Where are you meeting him again?'

I hesitated, and I could feel him tensing.

'In the square,' I said reluctantly. Oh, David, I prayed, if it doesn't work, forgive me!

'When?'

'In time for the bus. You're making me late.'

He whirled round, his eyes on the square. There was no sign of David.

'The Montpellier bus,' I said sulkily.

His eyes showed his satisfaction.

'That's the Montpellier bus standing there now,' he said. 'When does it go?'

I peered towards it, screwing up my eyes. 'Is it? Yes, it is.' I saw the drivers standing about in the sun, as if they had all the time in the world, and once again I took a chance. 'It goes in about ten minutes.' Then I looked up at him, and my eyes really did swim with tears. 'And now, please may I go? I – I'm sorry if I annoyed you, but you scared me so.'

He hesitated, and I tried not to hold my breath. Then he dropped my arm abruptly, and said: 'Very well. I'm sorry I scared you, but I thought – well, you shouldn't have told me those lies. I'm a little anxious about David, you see, and I thought you were stalling me off. I'll see him at the bus.'

He started quickly up the street towards the parked car. I walked as casually as I could to the corner, then, once out of sight, I broke and ran for the church as if hounds were out and I was the hare.

Luckily there was no one about in the porch to see me tear into the building as if I were bent on sacrilege. If David weren't there – I couldn't think beyond that possibility. But he was, curled up in a big pew in a side aisle with Rommel asleep at his feet. He straightened up with a jerk when he saw me.

'David,' I said breathlessly. 'Don't ask questions. He's looking for you. Come to the car – quick!'

He threw me one scared and wondering look, and came. As we reached the porch I hesitated for a moment and scanned the square, but could not see the big grey car. We turned right and tore across the open space, and as we ran I saw out of the tail of my eye the bus for Montpellier slide out of the rank and turn on to the Montpellier road.

Then we had found our side street and the car, and

were threading a maze of narrow streets away from the square.

'Our luck's in . . .' I breathed. 'The Montpellier bus . . . it left early . . . he'll follow it until he finds out, and by that time—'

Two minutes later the Riley slipped out of Nîmes and took the Avignon road.

7

Never—
(Browning)

We were some way out of Nîmes before either of us spoke. Then I said carefully: 'You saw your father at the Arena, didn't you, David?'

'Yes.' His voice was low and expressionless, and I didn't look at him; my eyes hardly ever left the driving mirror, where I was watching for a big grey car with a GB plate. 'I heard him speak first, then I looked over and saw him. I didn't think he'd seen me.'

'He hadn't. I gave you away by mistake. I met him up at the Temple of Diana. Up in the gardens.'

'What happened?'

'Oh, he tried to make me tell him where you were. I told a few lies and got caught out in them – I never did have much luck that way. Then I managed to make him think we were getting the Montpellier bus.'

'I suppose he'll follow it?'

'Yes, I'm hoping so,' I said cheerfully. 'And it's in quite the opposite direction from Avignon.'

'Yes, I know.'

Something in his tone made me glance quickly at

him. He was sitting, hugging Rommel between his knees, and staring in front of him with an expression I found it hard to read. He was still very white, and there was a look of strain over his cheek-bones, as if the skin were stretched too tight. His eyes looked enormous, and as he turned to answer my look I could see in them misery and a kind of exaltation, through the tears that were slipping soundlessly down his cheeks. My heart twisted uncomfortably, and I forgot to be casual any more. I put out my left hand and touched him on the knee.

'Never mind, David. Is it very bad?'

He did not answer for a bit, and when he did his voice was coming under control again.

'How did you find out about my father?'

'I'm afraid there was some gossip at the hotel. Someone who'd followed the – the case recognized your stepmother. Did you know he might be in Nîmes?'

'No. I thought he might be following us down here, but I didn't know . . . I thought it couldn't do any harm to have one day out. You – you didn't tell him we were staying in Avignon?' The terror was back in his voice as he half turned to me.

'Of course not. It's very important that he shouldn't find you, isn't it?'

He nodded hard over Rommel's head.

'Terribly important. I can't tell you how important. It – it's a matter of life and death.' And somehow the hackneyed over-dramatic words, spoken in that child's voice with a quiver in it, were not in the least ludicrous, and were uncommonly convincing.

'David.'

'Yes.'

'Would it help you to talk about it?'

'I don't know. What did they tell you at the hotel?'

'Not very much. Just what was in the papers at the time. You see, if you'd told me about your father when you saw him first in Nîmes, this needn't have happened. From what I had heard at the hotel, I gathered that it might be – undesirable – for your father to find you again, and then when I met him in Nîmes and realized that it was his voice that had frightened you in the Arena, I knew that whatever happened you didn't want him to catch you. That's all.'

The driving mirror was still blank of anything but a narrow white road snaking away from the wheels.

'That's all there is,' said David at length. 'Except for one thing. Mrs. Selborne, there's one thing that's terribly important too.'

'What's that, David?'

He spoke with a rush: 'Don't tell anyone – *anyone*, what's happened today!'

'But, David – how can I help it? Your step-mother ought surely—'

I saw his hands move convulsively in the dog's fur, and Rommel whined a protest. 'No! Oh, please, Mrs. Selborne, *please* do as I say. It would only worry her terribly, and it couldn't do any good. It won't happen again, because I won't go out, and anyway, we leave in a few days for the coast. So please keep it a secret! I wouldn't ask if it didn't matter.'

I was silent for a moment, and the Riley sang up a

steep rise in the road. A little way ahead I could see the deep trees and the golden arches of Pont du Gard.

'All right,' I said. 'I don't know why, but I'll do as you say. Though I still think I ought to tell your stepmother. But I won't.'

'Cross your heart?' I don't suppose the childish oath had ever been administered with such an agony of urgency. I smiled at David.

'Cross my heart.'

There was a little sigh beside me. 'You're awfully nice, aren't you?' said David naïvely.

'Thank you.'

'How – how did he look?'

I slowed down and pulled in behind a big brake van with a Vaucluse plate. Still nothing in the mirror. But in front of my eyes rose Richard Byron's face, dark and angry, with scowling brows and hard mouth, and I could feel the bruises on my wrist where he had hurt me.

'He looked well enough,' I said carefully, 'but of course he was pretty angry, and so he wasn't too pleasant. I don't blame you for being scared, you know; I was scared silly. I wondered—' I broke off abruptly.

'You wondered if he was mad?' said the small voice beside me. 'Well, I think he is – I think he must be. Quite mad.'

And we drove into Pont du Gard and drew up in front of the hotel.

★   ★   ★

A hasty look through the tables on the terrace satisfied us that Louise must have already gone home, so we set off once more for Avignon.. On the second half of the journey we hardly spoke; I watched the driving mirror and drove as fast as I dared, while David sat crouched together beside me holding the dog. We swung through Villeneuve-lès-Avignon shortly before six o'clock, and crawled over the suspension bridge. It was queer, after only two days, how much coming back into Avignon felt like coming home; I suppose that after the events of the day the hotel was a refuge, a bolt-hole, where one could hide and lock a door.

I took the car straight in through the Porte del'Oulle this time, feeling that another ten minutes of exposed driving on the perimeter road was more than I could stand. We threaded the narrow streets as fast as a homing cat, and the Riley ran into the garage and stopped with a little sigh, just as the clock in the Place de l'Horloge struck the hour.

L'heure de l'apéritif. And Louise would be sitting in the quiet courtyard drinking her vermouth, just as she had done yesterday and the day before.

I smiled at David, and got out of the car.

'I think a bath before dinner, don't you? And we had a very pleasant, very ordinary day in Nîmes. You were very impressed with the Arena, I remember.'

He managed a smile. 'Thank you for taking me,' he said.

I watched him through the court into the hotel, then I turned sharply, and went back into the street. I almost ran back to the gate which commanded the suspension bridge, and there, in a crowded little café, sitting well inside, against the wall, I had my drink – a cognac, this time. For half an hour I sat there, watching the narrow bridge that joined the city with Villeneuve-lès-Avignon.

But no big grey car with a GB plate crossed the bridge. So after a while I got up and went back to the hotel.

I found Louise, not in the courtyard, but in her room, thumbing through her sketch-book. The inevitable vermouth stood on her dressing-table.

'I just came to make sure you were back. I thought you must be when we didn't see you at Pont du Gard.'

'I came back after the light began to change,' she said. 'Did you have a good day, or were you broiled alive?'

I pushed the hair back off my forehead, and sat down on the edge of the bed.

'It was fearfully hot,' I admitted. 'I didn't finish the course, I'm afraid. I just could *not* climb the last long mile to the Roman tower. But the other things were well worth a visit. How did the sketches go?'

Louise knitted her smooth brow at her sketch book.

'Oh, so-so. The shapes are wonderful, but oh Lord, the light. It can't be got. If you leave out the reflections the arches look like American cheese, and if you put them in they look like fat legs in fish-net nylons. The colours just aren't there in the box.'

She sipped her drink, and her eyes considered me. 'Are you sure you haven't overdone it a bit, Charity?

You look done up. Don't forget you're not quite as tough as you think you are.'

'I'm all right.'

'Well, be careful, that's all. This isn't the climate to take risks with—'

'I'm all right,' I said again. 'Or at least I shall be when I've had that dinner I'm beginning to dream up.'

I went to my room to change. I hadn't time for a bath, but I took a quick cool sponge down, and put on my pale green dress. I looked in the mirror as I brushed my hair, and saw with a faint surprise that under their faint tan my cheeks were quite without colour. I leaned closer to the mirror. Something about the eyes and the corners of the mouth reminded me vividly of David's face as he had turned to me in the car, some trace seemed to be there of strain – and fear. I frowned at my reflection, and then fished in a drawer for some rouge, annoyed that my encounter with David's father, which I had been trying to put out of my mind until I could think it over without disturbance, should have apparently had such a profound effect on me. After all, what did it amount to? A bruised wrist and some abuse? The natural fear of a sane person confronted with the unreasonable? For certainly no sane man – even discounting David's terrible little confession to me on the homeward drive – would have behaved in that way to a strange woman, even if she were apparently obstructing him in his desire to see his son.

I smoothed the rouge faintly over my cheek-bones, back towards the hair-line, then dusted over with powder. That was better. My coral lipstick next, and the face that looked back at me was an altogether braver affair. Thank God for cosmetics, I thought, as I put them into my bag; one not only looks better, one *feels* better, with one's flag at the top of the mast again. I would not think about Richard Byron again this evening. He had not come to Avignon, of that I was sure. David had only to lie low for a few days more, then he was to go to the coast, and surely France was big enough for a small boy to get lost in? There was nothing more that I could do, and up to date, even if I was left with food for a nightmare, I hadn't done so very badly.

I picked up my bag, and as I did so, I caught sight of the blue marks on my wrist. I turned the arm over, and examined the dark prints where Richard Byron's fingers had bitten into the flesh. Then I remembered my wide silver bracelet, and, hastily searching for it, clasped it round my wrist, over those tell-tale bruises. To my fury, I found that I was shaking again.

'Oh *damn* everything!' I said aloud, with unwonted viciousness, and went to get Louise.

The dinner that I had dreamed up proved to be every bit as good as the dream. We began with iced melon, which was followed by the famous *brandade truffée*, a delicious concoction of fish cooked with truffles. We could quite contentedly have stopped there, but the next course – some small bird like a quail, simmered in wine and served on a bed of green grapes – would have tempted an anchorite to break his penance. Then *crêpes Suzette*, and, finally, coffee and armagnac.

We sat over this for a very long time, and then we went up to the Place de l'Horloge and had more coffee and sat again. Louise talked a bit about light, and reflections, and a picture by Brangwyn of the Pont du Gard that she had seen in a Bond Street exhibition, but I was not listening very hard. I was not even thinking, at any rate not usefully. I just sat and drank black coffee and felt very, very tired.

We went back to the hotel at about half-past ten, to find the courtyard empty save for the thin cat at the foot of the tree Yggdrasil. I said good night to Louise and went to my room. The tired feeling still persisted, and it was with slow mechanical movements that I took off the green frock, creamed my face, brushed my hair, and went through all the motions of getting ready for bed. I was even too tired to think, and with the edge of my mind I remember feeling glad about this.

Finally I wrapped my housecoat round me, and went along the corridor to the bathroom, which was at the far end from my room.

I was in the bathroom, and was in the act of closing the door softly behind me, when I heard a quick tread in the corridor, a man's tread. A door opened, and I heard an urgent whisper:

'*Loraine!*'

I froze. It was the voice of the man I had overheard with Loraine Bristol on the Rocher des Doms.

'*Loraine!*'

'*You! What is it? What has happened?*'

'*Loraine, he's here! I saw him. Today. In Nîmes.*'

There was a sound like a deep-drawn breath of

terror. Then the door shut behind him, and I heard the click of a lock.

I shut the bathroom door and leaned against it for a moment, my brain revving up like a tired engine.

Marsden. On the bus to Nîmes. I had forgotten all about Marsden.

I must ask David where Marsden came into the picture. I crept out of the bathroom without a sound, and paused outside Loraine Bristol's door. There was the barest murmur inside, of voices. I tip-toed on, round the angle of the corridor, to David's door, and lifted my hand to scratch at the panel, wondering as I did so if Rommel slept in the room with him, and if he would bark.

Then I stopped, with my hand half-way to the panel, and froze again.

From inside the room came the sound of a child's desolate sobbing.

I stood there for a long moment, then my hand dropped to my side and I went back to my own room.

8

– While I am I, and you are you,
So long as the world contains us both . . .
While the one eludes, must the other pursue:
                        (Browning)

All things considered, I did not sleep too badly. I was wakened at about nine o'clock the next morning by Louise, who stopped to knock on my door on her way down to breakfast.

I got up slowly, and dressed. The shadows under my eyes were still there, and so were the marks on my wrist, but I put on my coffee-cream linen dress and my silver bracelet, and felt pretty well able to face what might come. I went down to the courtyard for breakfast.

David was there, looking as if he had not slept too well, but he gave me a gay little smile of greeting, and Rommel, under the table, wagged his silly tail. Loraine Bristol looked up from lighting one cigarette from the half-smoked butt of another. She, too, looked as if she had not slept, and the lines from nostril to mouth were sharply etched on her lovely face, giving her suddenly an older, harder look. I felt sorry for her.

She said: 'Good morning, Mrs. Selborne. It was so good of you to take David yesterday. He has been telling me how much he enjoyed the day.'

I said, lightly: 'That's all right, it was a pleasure. Nîmes is a lovely place, except for the smells. I hope David will be able to come with me for another trip some day.'

I saw David's swift upward glance, then Mrs. Bristol said: 'It's so nice of you. Perhaps. But we plan to leave Avignon soon, and we will go then to Nice.'

'I hope you enjoy it,' I said, and we smiled at one another like two mechanical dolls, and then I went to our own table and sat down.

Over the coffee and *croissants* I looked round me. Mamma and Papa from Newcastle were there, and Mamma waved cheerfully when she caught my eye. Carole, apparently, was not up yet, or perhaps it took her a long time to complete her fearsome toilette. The young American couple, each-in-other-absorbed, sat with heads close together in their corner. The Frenchman, Paul Véry, was nowhere to be seen. But Marsden sat at his table beside the vine-covered trellis, imperturbably eating his *croissants* and reading *Little Gidding*.

'At breakfast!' said Louise in an awed voice. 'A man who can read poetry at breakfast would be capable of anything.'

You're probably right at that, I thought, remembering the decisive voice in the dark . . . *I got you out of the mess before, didn't I? . . . I'm in charge, and you trust me, don't you?*

'More sight-seeing today?' came Louise's voice. I

shook myself free of my thoughts, and poured another cup of coffee.

'I'll do what you do,' I said.

'Sit in the shade and drink iced grape-juice?'

'Just that.'

'Tired?'

'A bit. You were right. The heat did take it out of me yesterday. I'll stay at home today and think up something good for tomorrow.'

Presently people began to move, the tourists discussing the day's programme. The Germans went off, arguing over a guide book, and soon afterwards the American couple strolled out into the Rue de la République, arm-in-arm. David got up then, and went into the hotel with Rommel, and in a few moments Marsden went in too. Loraine Bristol lit another cigarette and stared in front of her. I made some excuse and got out of my chair. Perhaps now I could get to David's room and ask him about Marsden – why Loraine Bristol, if she did know Marsden, and if he had helped her and David in the first place, had not told David of the connection. Perhaps David would feel safer if he knew that there was a man on guard between him and Richard Byron.

It was possible, of course, I thought as I climbed the stairs, that David did know, but he had betrayed no such knowledge yesterday when we had seen Marsden on the bus, nor had any sign of recognition passed between Marsden and himself, beyond the casual recognition of fellow-guests in a hotel.

Marsden was in the upper corridor, so, without going near David's door, I went into my own room,

and collected the things I should want for the morning,
my sun-glasses, a book, my Michelin guide. Then,
after a few minutes, I went out again into the corridor,
only to find that my plan of having a private word with
David would have to wait, for he and Rommel and
Marsden were together, making for the stairs.

'. . . So I thought I'd go up there this morning,'
David was saying, 'instead of to the river.'

'I'm walking up that way myself,' said Marsden.
'Mind if I come with you?'

'Not at all, sir . . .' The voices faded. I went back
into my room, thinking that it certainly did not sound
as though David knew of any intimate connection
between Marsden and his own affairs. Then I heard
them come out into the courtyard, below the balcony,
and I moved towards the window.

'. . . The tower at the north corner,' said Marsden.
'Though how he ever got a mule up it I don't know.
Have you ever been in?'

'No,' said David. I saw him stop beside his step-
mother's table. 'I'm going up to the Rocher des Doms,'
he told her. 'Mr. Marsden's coming too. You get a
marvellous view of the ferry-boat from there; it has to
cross with a rope, in case it gets swept away.'

Yes, I thought, watching them go together up the Rue
de la République, and you also get a marvellous view of
the suspension bridge that leads in from Nîmes and
Montpellier. And I wondered just how much of his day
David would spend up on the battlements, watching for
a big grey car with a GB plate.

*   *   *

The day dragged by. Louise and I spent the morning in the gardens, according to plan, drinking iced grape-juice and idly watching the circular sprays watering the vivid lawn. Then she got out her sketch book and began to make rapid clever little drawings – of the children, thin and brown, of the old women who sat squarely on the narrow seats, knitting and watching them, of the ragged-trousered half-naked men who raked the gravel, of the frocked priests moving to and from the church across the way. I took out my book and tried to read, but between my eyes and the page swam perpetually two angry grey eyes under their black brows, and a mouth twisting with sudden murderous fury. I blinked it away and began to read with steady concentration, only to find after several minutes that I had read the same page over and over again, and had not taken in a single word of it, and that my brain was mechanically repeating, like a damaged record . . . *you little bitch, you little bitch, you little bitch.* I pushed back my hair as if by the action I could brush my mind clean of memories, but I gave up the attempt to read after a while, and sat, fidgeting with my sun-glasses, and wishing I could draw – do anything to take my mind off the wheel that it was treading, over and over again.

'Louise.'

'Mm?'

'Let's go and have lunch.'

'Already?'

'It's time. We may as well go back to the hotel, don't you think?'

But though we sat for a long time in the court, over a leisurely lunch and cigarettes, David did not appear and nor did Marsden. Paul Véry was in his corner, and smiled at me over his *apéritif*, but apart from him and ourselves, all the other residents, including Loraine Bristol, seemed to be lunching elsewhere. At length I got up.

'I think I'll go and rest,' I said, and went up to my room.

To my own surprise I slept deeply and dreamlessly for a long time, and woke in the late afternoon, feeling refreshed and in my right mind. As I washed and slipped into the pale green dress I felt singularly light-hearted, as if some heavy cloud had lifted off the landscape, and had left nothing but a shining prospect of sun upon the wet spring grass. I had had an unpleasant experience, which had upset me considerably; very well, now it was over, and the memory of Richard Byron's crazy furious behaviour could be thrust back with all the other nasty things into the woodshed. I sang as I clipped the silver bracelet on over the bruises, and I smiled at my reflection as I brushed my hair.

And as for David – the lifting cloud cast a momentary shadow there; but the fresh wind of common sense blew it away into rags. David's problem was a tragic one, certainly, but a comparatively simple one, after all. There were two adults to look after him, and, if the conversation on the Rocher des Doms meant anything, Loraine Bristol would eventually marry her helper.

The only problem was to keep David out of his father's way, and surely that wouldn't be so very difficult to manage? And, whatever I felt about it, I could do nothing for David. It was Mrs. Bristol's problem, and I was a stranger. And I would see the last of them in a few days' time anyway. There was only one sane thing to do, and that was to forget the whole business.

I went lightly along to Louise's room, and found her doing her hair.

'Louise, I've had an idea. I'm feeling as restless as a gipsy, and I'm sick of doing nothing. I'm going to take the car and drive up to Les Baux for a night – or even a couple of nights. D'you want to come?'

'Les Baux? Where's that and what is it?'

'It's a ruined village, a hill village south of Avignon. I believe it's a queer wild sort of place – just ruins and a deserted village and an inn and a wonderful eerie view. It's just what I feel like, anyway, miles from anywhere.'

Louise put away her brush and comb and began to do her face.

'Do you want me to come – I mean, do you *not* want to go alone?'

'I don't mind whether I go alone or not. That's not why I was asking. If you'd like the drive, come by all means. If not, I'll be perfectly happy.'

She looked at me in the mirror. 'Sure?'

'Perfectly. I take it you *don't* want to come?'

'Not particularly. I'd rather laze about here and draw. But if you—'

'Then forget it. It was a sudden idea, and it suits the way I'm feeling, but you needn't let it affect you. I'll go and ring up and see if they've a room at the inn, and I'll drive up there for dinner.'

Louise sat down to put on her sandals. 'You know,' she said, with an upward look at me, 'I was wondering last night – well, is anything up?'

'Not a thing,' I lied cheerfully. 'I was tired, but after that sleep this afternoon I feel wonderful. But I feel a bit stifled in Avignon, and I want to be off up to Les Baux tonight. You're sure you don't want to come?'

Louise shook her head.

'No. You go off and commune with nature and the ghosts in the ruined houses. It sounds terrible. I'll see you when I see you, I suppose.'

So I went downstairs and telephoned the inn at Les Baux, where I was lucky in being able to secure a room for one night at least, with the probability of the next, if I should wish it. Feeling something like a released prisoner, I hurried back to my room, pushed a night-dress and a few toilet necessities into my big handbag, went down again and saw Madame, then said good-bye to Louise and went out to get the car.

It was all done so quickly, and I was out of Avignon and heading for Orgon, before I really had time to think what I was doing. But when I did think about it, pushing the car along at a comfortable speed in the evening light, it still seemed a good thing to do. I wanted, above all things, to be out of Avignon, out of that *galère*, even for a short time. And I wanted to be alone. I was glad Louise had elected not to come, though, knowing Louise, I had never really for a moment suspected that she might want to. Somehow, the picture I had formed of Les Baux, the empty little mountain village, where night was so quiet and dawn so beautiful, just represented the sort of thing I very much needed.

About David Byron I steadfastly refused to think, and about Richard, his father, I did not think at all, except for a little twist of wry amusement when I looked at the map and saw that soon I would be turning on to the Tarascon road.

The evening was drawing down, and the light deepened. Away behind me I caught a last glimpse of the towers of Avignon, like torches above the trees. Around me the landscape grew wilder and more beautiful, muted from the white and dusty glare of day to the rose and purple of evening. The sun set, not in one concentrated star of fire, but in a deep diffusion of amber light, till the sharp black spires of the cypresses seemed to be quivering against the glow, and flowing upwards like flames formed of shadows.

It did not seem long before the Riley climbed the last hill, and I berthed it outside the inn not long before seven o'clock.

9

Oi deus, oi deus, de l'alba! tan tost ve.
(Ah God, ah God, but the dawn comes soon)
(Medieval French lyric)

The deserted town of Les Baux, in medieval times a strong and terrible fortress, stands high over the southern plains. The streets of eyeless houses – little more than broken shells – the crumbling lines of the once mighty bastions, the occasional jewel of a carved Renaissance window, clothed with ferns, have an uncanny beauty of their own, while something of the fierce and terrible history of the 'wolves of Les Baux', the lords of Orange and Kings of Arles, still seems to inhere in these broken fortifications. The prospect is wild enough, and strange enough, to satisfy anyone who, like myself that evening, felt so pressingly the need for quiet and my own company. With faint amusement I perceived slowly creeping over me the mood of melancholy in which the not-quite-romantics of the eighteenth century in England found such gentle pleasure.

I sat near the window of the little inn's dining-room, watching the evening light on the distant slopes, and enjoying my lonely dinner. I ate slowly, and the light was dying from the land when at length I took my coffee and chartreuse outside on to the little terrace, and prepared to let the past have its way with me.

I got out my book, and read the *chansons de toile* again, the songs of lovely Isabel, Yolande the beautiful, Aiglentine the fair, who had sat at their embroidery, singing, so very long ago, in this same land. Then I shut the book, and sat dreaming, with my eyes on the broken lines and ghost-filled terraces of the town, trying to pave the streets and cut back the vegetation and fill the empty ways with horses and men and the glint of armour and the scarlet of banners.

I sat there till darkness had drawn over the scene, and then I went down to the car and drove it away from the inn door, round the open sweep to face the road again. I left it parked there, two wheels on the verge. Then I went up to my room.

Where was it that I had read that to watch the dawn over the ruined town was one of the sights of the world? Looking out of my window into the darkness, tracing the imperceptibly darker shapes of rock and hill, I thought that whatever the book had said it was probably right. I would go out early and wait for the sun to rise, and see if the ghosts of the Kings of Arles really did ride at cock-crow. So I did not undress, but merely took off frock and shoes, and lay down on one of the beds. I was asleep almost at once.

I must have slept for three or four hours, because when I woke and turned my head to look at the window, I could see, not light, but a faint lifting of the darkness. I put a light on and looked at my watch, only to find that I had forgotten to wind it the night before. I put the light off again, got up, and went to the window to lean out. My room faced south-east, and away to my left I could see what looked like the beginnings of a rift in the night, a soft pencilling of light on the underside of a cloud. The air was chill and clear and silent.

I closed the shutters, put on the light again, and got into my frock and shoes. I rinsed my face and hands in cold water to wake myself up properly, then put on my coat, and went quietly out of my room and down the stairs.

I must have made some slight noise, but nobody seemed to hear, or at any rate to bother about it. I supposed the people at the hotel were used to dawn-watchers in Les Baux. The door of the inn was not locked, so apparently there was nothing tangible, at any rate, to fear from the ghostly princes of Orange. Wishing I had a torch, I let myself out with caution and moved carefully towards the deserted buildings. My feet made no sound upon the grass.

How long I sat out there, in a coign of carved stone and rough rock, I do not know. Long enough, I suppose, for my vigil did at length bring in the dawn. I saw the first light, fore-running the sun, gather in a cup of the eastern cloud, gather and grow and brim, till at last it spilled like milk over the golden lip, to smear the dark face of heaven from end to end. From east to north, and back to south again, the clouds slackened, the stars, trembling on the verge of extinction, guttered in the dawn wind, and the gates of day were ready to open at the trumpet . . .

oi deus, oi deus, de l'alba! tan tost ve . . .

Suddenly I was cold. The pleasant melancholy had faded, and in its place began to grow, unbidden, the little germ of loneliness which could, I knew, mature in these dark and wild surroundings all too soon into the flower of desolation. I began to wish violently for a cigarette.

I got up, stretched, stood for a moment looking at the growing light. Waiting, perhaps, unconsciously, for the trumpet to blow its shrill aubade across the stars.

Something moved behind me.

Moved and spoke.

As I whirled, my heart stampeding, my hands to my throat—

'So I've found you again,' said Richard Byron.

He was standing barely three yards away from me. In the darkness I could see him only as a looming shape on the slope above me, but I would have known that voice anywhere, hard, incisive, with an edge to it, and an unpleasant undertone of mockery. He stood where he was, above me in the dark, and I knew that I was as securely trapped in my corner of rock as if I had been in a locked room. To the left of me, and at my back, the rock wall and the remains of a towering buttress; to my right, the sheer drop to the southern plain; and before me, Richard Byron.

I stood still, and waited.

He lit a cigarette, and in the hissing flare of the match I saw again the face of my nightmare, the dark hair falling over the frowning brow, the hard eyes narrowed against the flame.

The match lit a brief arc over the cliff. The cigarette glowed red as he drew on it.

'How did you get here?' I asked, and was annoyed because my voice was not my own at all.

He said: 'You stopped for petrol at St-Rémy. You went across the road and had a drink in a boulevard café while they put oil in and cleaned up for you.'

'Yes, I did. Were – were you in St-Rémy?'

'I was. I was, like you, having a drink while they did something to my car. I went to your garage and waited for you, but when I heard you ask the man for the road up to Les Baux I knew you were safe, so I thought I'd wait. It isn't so public here as it was in St-Rémy, and you and I have something that we want to discuss, haven't we?'

'Have we?'

His voice was unemotional: 'You god-damned little bitch, you know we have. Where's David?'

So there we were again, except that the issue, for me, was slightly clearer. I knew that I was not going to tell him where David was, but I also knew what before I had only suspected, that he was crazy, and would stop at nothing to get what he wanted.

'Where's David?'

'Asleep in bed, I hope,' I said.

He made an impatient movement, and my throat tightened.

'You know what I mean. Where is he?'

'I'm not going to tell you,' I said levelly. If it maddened him, I couldn't help it, but I judge it better to be downright than to prevaricate.

He was silent for a moment, and I saw the cigarette glow again, twice, in rapid succession.

The next question, when it came, took me completely by surprise.

He said abruptly: 'Is it money you want? If so, how much?'

'I've as much money as I want,' I said, when I could speak. 'What were you going to offer – thirty pieces of silver?'

I could feel him staring at me through the darkness. He dragged on his cigarette again.

'But I wouldn't refuse a cigarette,' I said.

I heard him fumble for it, and again a match rasped and flared. This time his eyes were watchful on me across the flame. He lit the cigarette and, coming a step nearer, handed it to me.

'What's the matter?' I said contemptuously. 'Are you afraid I'll push you over if you come any nearer?'

'Listen, my dear,' said Richard Byron evenly. 'This won't get either of us anywhere. I want to know where David is. You do know, and you refuse to tell me. Very well, then I shall have to make you tell me.'

The cigarette wasn't much help after all; I threw it over the cliff. My brief moment of initiative was over, and he was attacking again.

I said, more bravely than I felt: 'And how do you propose to do that? Torture? Be your age, Mr. Byron.'

He said savagely: 'My God, I'd like to try. If I lay hands on you again I'll not answer for myself. I'd like to wring your lovely neck.'

'I see. Gestapo stuff.' But my voice shook.

'And why not? I've seen it done, and to women. It works, as often as not.'

'Don't be a fool,' I said sharply. The nightmare terror was seeping into me again, cold, cold. I could see him a little better now, towering over me, silhouetted against the faintly glowing cast, like some shadow of fear. 'If you so much as moved a finger towards me, I'd scream the place down.'

'Don't worry. I'm not going to hurt you. Not yet. But I think we'll get things plain and clear, you and I.'

He flung away his cigarette, and at the sharp movement my inside twisted over with a little thrill of fear, and I began to feel sick. Cold and sick. I put a shaking hand backwards on to the firm stone, and the hand slipped a bit. It was clammy.

Richard Byron spoke without emphasis, but his voice beat at me with the wince of hammer on steel.

'I gather that you know who I am. I told you I was a friend of David's. That was not true, as presumably you know. I am David's father, and I have an idea that that gives me a right to know where David is.'

I said nothing. I was leaning back against the stone, fighting off the same feeling of unreality and nightmare that I had experienced in the streets of Nîmes. And fighting off, too, waves of sickening blackness that kept washing over me out of the cold night.

'I did a murder once,' said Richard Byron pleasantly, 'and got away with it. They say it's easier the second time. And I assure you, you stupid little fool, that I'd do another today as easily as I'd stub out a cigarette, to get hold of my son.'

The gates of the eastern sky were opening behind him; the aubade must have blown, and I had never heard it. . . . Pure and piercing, the first fingers of the dawn stabbed the sky. Then they were blotted out again by another wave of darkness which washed up from the damp ground at my feet. I was falling . . . I clawed at the stones . . . they were slipping sideways from me . . . the whole world was slipping sideways, away from the sun.

From a great way off, a voice spoke in the blackness.

'Nothing could be easier than murder, you know. . . .'

I put out my hands in a futile little gesture, and his shadow towered over me, then stooped like a hawk. . . .

And I fainted.

I was buried, and they had put a heavy stone on top of me. But I was not dead, and I was struggling to lift it, only they had tied my hands as well, and I could not move . . . I could not even open my eyes. Then, of itself, the stone lifted off me, and I could move my head and my hands a little, in the silence and the darkness. I must have been crying, or had I died of drowning? . . . my face was wet and cold.

I struggled back to the edge of consciousness, and opened my eyes, to find that the darkness, at any rate, was real, and so were the tears on my face. Tears? I slowly put up a hand, and found that not only my cheeks, but my forehead and hair were damp – someone had put cold water on me. That was it. I had fainted, for some reason, and someone had put cold water on my face to bring me round.

Hazily I turned my head. I was lying on a bed beside a window whose slatted shutters were barring out the faint grey light of early morning. I looked into the room. In the darkness I could see the shape of a chest of drawers . . . another bed . . . Someone was lying on the other bed, smoking. I saw the cigarette glow and fade, glow and fade.

I murmured: 'Johnny?'

The voice that answered me dispelled the dream, and brought reality back with a rush. It said: 'So you're round again. Who's Johnny? Is he in this too?'

I didn't answer for a bit. Then I said: 'You can't get away with this, you know.'

'With what?'

'What are you doing in here? Why won't you leave me alone?'

He said lazily: 'This is as comfortable a way of keeping an eye on you as any. And I've told you why I won't leave you alone. You're my link with David, and I'll keep my hand on you till I get what I want.'

I said: 'But this is my room. Don't you imagine the folk at the inn will want to know who you are? You can't get away with this sort of thing, even in France. What if I start to scream?'

The cigarette glowed placidly, and I could hear the smile in his voice, as he said: 'Scream away.'

I bit my lip. Of course I couldn't scream; I could see in my mind's eye the result if I did – the fuss, the explanations, the recriminations, perhaps the police – then names . . . and addresses. No, I couldn't scream.

He laughed in the darkness. 'I'm your husband, anyway. I got here late last night, and didn't want to disturb them. After all, I don't imagine you specified a single room, did you? And all the rooms here are double, which was lucky.'

'What are you going to do?' I said again.

'Stick to you like a leech, my dear, like a lover.' He settled himself comfortably on his bed. I stared into the dark, somehow too exhausted to be afraid; I felt empty and tired. I remembered to be glad that I had not told Madame where I had come from, and that I had registered merely '*en passant*'. He would get no information either from the inn or from the register.

'Won't they think it a bit odd that we each arrive in our own cars?'

'I didn't bring mine up,' he said. 'I left it a couple of hundred yards down, round the bend out of sight. I wasn't going to let you see it, if by any chance you happened to be about when I arrived. Don't worry about that.'

I did not bother to explain how little I was worrying. I turned away towards the window, and turned the pillow over, so that the dry side was against my cheek.

This would have to wait till morning. I could do nothing, and common sense told me that if Richard Byron wanted information out of me, at least he would not murder me in my sleep. Neither, I thought, would he risk trying anything approaching violence, now that people were within call, and now that, if I were frightened enough, I would risk police investigation. I was still in coat and shoes, of course, so I slipped the latter off and wrapped the former warmly round me, and curled up with my back to the other bed.

Richard Byron said: 'Who's Johnny?'

I said shortly: 'I don't want to talk to you. I'm going to sleep.'

I heard a faint scrunching sound as he ground out his cigarette in a tray between the beds. He said nothing. The springs of the other bed creaked heavily, and I tensed myself unconsciously. But he was only settling himself down and relaxing.

After a while, to my own vague surprise, I drifted off to sleep.

10

And Charity chased hence by Rancour's hand
                              (Shakespeare)

I awoke to an empty room, dredged with sunlight through the shutters, and the comforting sounds of breakfast on the terrace below the windows. For a long drowsy moment I wondered why I should be lying so uncomfortably curled up on the top of the quilt, wrapped in my coat. Then I remembered, and sleep fled incontinently as I turned over to look at the other bed. It had not been a nightmare, that strange interview among the dark ruins, my fainting, the implacability of the man who was going to stick to me like a lover – I could see the impression where he had lain on the other bed, the dent left by his head in the pillow, and a little pile of cigarette-butts in the ash-tray between the beds.

I sat up and swung my legs over the side of the bed. I felt a little stiff from sleeping curled up, and as if I had not slept long enough, but otherwise the night's adventures did not seem to have affected me physically to any great extent. But mentally I was in a turmoil. Where was Richard Byron now? What did he propose to do today? And how, how, *how* was I going to get away from him?

I crossed to the door, locked it, then took off my coat and frock and washed, afterwards patting cold water into my cheeks till the skin tingled and I felt fresh and invigorated. I brushed my hair hard, then shook out the green dress, thanking heaven and the research chemists for uncrushable materials, and put it on again. The familiar routine of doing my face and hair did a good deal to restore my confidence. Somehow I would get away from him, get back to Avignon, make some excuse to Louise, and we would drive off some-where else for our holiday, at any rate until Loraine and the boy had left for the coast. Or at worst, if I could not shake my enemy off, I could lead him astray, away from Avignon . . . though I felt a little cold quiver of the familiar fear to think what he might do if I thwarted him again.

At any rate I would get ready for whatever oppor-tunity might come. I put my book, my dark glasses, my toothbrush, all the small things I had brought for the night, into my bulky handbag, glanced round the room to see that nothing was forgotten, then put my coat round my shoulders and unlocked the door and went out into the corridor.

Richard Byron was waiting for me at the foot of the inn's single flight of stairs. He was leaning against the newel-post, smoking the inevitable cigarette, and as I came hesitantly down the stairs he looked up and gave me a sardonic good morning.

'I hope you slept well?' he said, straightening up.

'If we are husband and wife,' I said, 'you ought to know. And I should like a cigarette, please.'

He gave me one, and we went out on to the terrace. One or two people were still breakfasting, but I had slept late, and most of the guests had already gone into the ruined town, or had left in their cars.

He followed me to a table near the edge of the terrace, and held a chair for me.

I sat down in the shade without looking at him or speaking, and watched the smoke from my cigarette curling up in delicate blue fronds towards the hanging vines that clothed the terrace wall. We sat for some minutes in silence, but it was not the comforting silence of companionship; I could feel his eyes on my face, and was intensely conscious of his presence on the other side of the little table, and between us the air positively sizzled with unasked questions and ungiven answers.

So I watched the tip of my cigarette, and then the waiter came with the coffee and *croissants*.

The coffee was smoking hot and delicious, and smelt wonderful in that sunny still air. I put one of the flat oblongs of sugar into my cup, and stirred it slowly, enjoying the smell and the swirl of the creamy brown liquid in the wide-mouthed yellow cup.

'Have a roll,' suggested Richard Byron, and handed me the flat basket where the new hot *croissants* reposed on their snow-white paper napkin. There was something in the ordinary familiar little gesture over the breakfast table that made me suddenly still more sharply conscious of the queer and uncomfortable situation that I was in now, deeply in. I took a roll, still without looking at him, but memory stirred queerly . . . Johnny passing me the toast-rack, the marmalade . . . I bit my lip. Johnny had never seemed so far away, so utterly gone. I said it to myself, deliberately: so dead.

I was alone. Any help I got now would only come from myself, and I was well aware that I am not the stuff of which heroines are made. I was merely frightened and bewildered, and deeply resentful of the situation in which I found myself.

Which is why I sat eating my rolls without really tasting them, and staring at the golden distance of the southern plain beyond the rocks, without really making any plans at all. With every mouthful of hot and fragrant coffee, I felt better, but my brain was numb, and I dared not look at Richard Byron, in case he should see how afraid of him I was. Though, I told myself, if he doesn't know by now that you panic every time he comes near you, my girl, he must be mad.

Mad. The coffee suddenly tasted vile, and I put down my cup unsteadily on the saucer. That was the root of the matter, of course – even a heroine might legitimately be afraid of a mad-man, and a mad-man who had cheerfully, not very long before, admitted to a murder. I had to get away. I didn't know how, but I had to get away.

Then my eyes fell on my car, which was standing where I had left it, facing down the hill, about fifty yards from the terrace steps. And I remembered something Richard Byron had said last night . . . something about leaving his car a short way down the road, parked off the track. If I could somehow get to my car without him, get a start, I might get away. The Riley was fast and utterly reliable; I had not seen, in Nîmes, what make of car he drove, but I knew the Riley could be depended upon to give the average touring car a run for its money. And I had filled up last night with petrol and oil. Everything I had brought with me was in my handbag . . . I had only to go.

And if Richard Byron had posed as my husband, then Richard Byron could do the explaining, and pay the bill.

My heart was beginning to thump again, and I dared not look at him. I fumbled in my bag, ostensibly for a handkerchief, but in reality to make sure of my car keys. I took out my book of Provençal poetry, and laid it on the table, while I rummaged beneath my nightdress in the bag. My fingers closed over the keys, and I slipped them into a top compartment where I would be able to reach them easily, then I took out my handkerchief and a cigarette, put the book back, and closed the bag.

Richard Byron struck a match and held it for me across the table. I tried not to look at him, but something drew me to raise my eyes across the flame, and I saw that he was watching me with a curious expression on his face.

'What did you come up here for anyway?' he asked.

I tried to speak lightly: 'What does anyone come up here for? To see the lair of the wolves of Orange.'

'I can't help wondering,' he said slowly, 'just where you come into all this. And who is Johnny?'

My fingers tightened on my bag. 'Do you mind?' I said. 'I don't particularly want to talk to you. And I don't feel too good this morning.'

I saw his hand make an abrupt movement of impatience, and he bit back something he had been going to say. We were alone on the terrace now, and the waiter had vanished. A couple of sightseers came out of the inn, paused for a moment in the shade of the terrace roof, then stepped out into the blinding morning sun. The girl was wearing white, and swung a scarlet bag in one hand. The man, in khaki shorts and a loose linen jacket, carried an enormous camera. They were laughing. They strolled past us, below the terrace, and away towards the ruins, and disappeared round a high wall of rock, and as they went, the normal safe and happy world seemed to go with them and suddenly I was, again, alone with Richard Byron, caught in the dark circle of his little personal hell.

For a short while we sat there, in the hot silence, while the sunlight moved a fraction, and laid its slanting glare across the toe of my sandal. Somewhere, a cicada started to rasp, dry and rhythmic.

I dropped my half-smoked cigarette and ground it out gently on the floor. I leaned my forehead on my hand.

'Is there any more coffee?' I said, as if with difficulty.

I felt him glance sharply at me.

'No. It's finished. What's the matter?'

I shook my head a little. 'It's nothing. It's only—' My voice trailed away, and I said nothing.

There was another short silence, while I could feel

him staring at me. I sensed the puzzlement and suspicion that there must be in his glance, but this time I had an advantage I had not had in Nîmes – there must have been no possible doubt about the genuineness of my faint last night, and I must be looking quite definitely the worse for it this morning. I lifted my head and looked at him, and I know my eyes were strained and shadowed, and my lips, under the brave coral paint, were dry.

'I'm all right, thanks,' I said, 'but would you ask the waiter for some water – or a cognac; yes, a cognac?'

I don't know quite what I was planning to do. I had some general idea of establishing the fact that I was too rocky to make any violent attempt at escape; I think, too, that with hazy memories of thrillers I had read, I toyed with the idea of throwing the cognac into his eyes and making a run for it before he could recover.

But suddenly the opportunity was there, and for once, like every other heroine, I took it, and took it fast.

Richard Byron called the waiter, called again. I drooped in my chair, indifferent. But the waiter, whether because he did not hear, or because he was busy and we were so late – I suspect he helped in other ways in that little inn besides waiting at table – at any rate, the waiter did not come. After calling, and going up to the inn door to peer into the empty lobby, Richard Byron, with a long backward look at me, went into the inn.

It was all the start I needed.

As I ran the fifty yards between the terrace and the car, I snatched out the keys. It took three seconds to open the door and slip into the driving seat, leaving the car door silently swinging. That blessed engine came to life at a touch, and the Riley slid forward on the slope as I lifted the brakes.

As she gathered way I saw, out of the tail of my eye, Richard Byron, with the *patronne*, emerging from the inn door. He started forward, and I slammed the car door and went into gear. As the car rounded the first bend, gathering speed, I saw the *patronne*, gesticulating wildly, catch Byron's sleeve, so that he had to turn and speak to her . . .

Well, let him do the talking, I thought grimly, then I began to laugh. Let him explain why his wife bolts without a word, let him get out of the silly mess of his own making – *and* pay the hotel bill into the bargain.

The Riley sighed down the curling hill, round another sweeping bend, and there, by the verge, parked in a bay of rock, stood a big grey car. A Bentley.

A Bentley, I thought savagely, braking hard. It would be. Something that could give me a fairly alarming chase, unless I did something drastic to it first. I slipped out of the car, with thoughts of tyre-slashing, taking sparking-plugs, and other acts of thuggery storming through my mind. But there was a garage at the hotel, and who knew what spares might be available? As I stumbled across the stones to the grey car I thought wildly. Not the rotor-arm, for the same reason – and I had nothing to slash tyres with anyway . . . The bonnet was unlocked, and I lifted it, with half an eye on the road behind me.

It came automatically after all; it was the way Johnny

had taught me to immobilize the car during the war, when we had to leave it parked for hours at the R.A.F. Station dances, and when the young officers, after about one in the morning, thought nothing of 'winning' someone else's car for a joy-ride with a girl in the blackout. Not a usual method at all, but one very difficult to detect, and which could give an awful lot of trouble . . . And so simple. I whipped off the distributor-cap, gave one of the screws a turn and a half with the end of my nail-file, to break the electric contact, put back the cap, closed the bonnet, and raced back to the Riley, all in less time than it takes to tell.

My hands were shaking and slippery on the wheel but when the car leaped forward again down the slope, I began to feel steadier. Down a bank, with a rush like a lift, along an uneven stretch of flat, round another high walled bend . . . and we were out of sight and well away . . . and it might take him some time to find out why the Bentley spluttered and would not start, with everything, apparently, intact.

Presently we dropped gently round the last bend, and swung on to the good surface of the Tarascon road. I turned to the right in St. Rémy, twisted through back streets till I thought I might have confused my trail a little, then, still keeping generally eastwards, hummed along the narrow country roads with elation in my heart.

11

Exit, pursued by a Bear
(Shakespeare)

Anywhere but Avignon. I might have given him the slip altogether, I hoped at any rate that I had delayed him considerably, but I could not risk leading him straight back to Avignon, and to David. Or, for that matter, back on to my own trail, which from Avignon, wherever I went, would be an open book. I sent the car at what speed I dared over the rough narrow roads, between their blinding high hedges of thorn and cypress, while I thought of where to go and what to do.

I would get clear away, if I could, then I would telephone Louise, tell her as much as I knew, and ask her to pack up and come to meet me. She could hire a car; I would pay for it, and it would save her having to wrestle on the crowded trains with two people's luggage. But where would she meet me? I puzzled over it as the Riley crept cautiously over a narrow and manifestly unsafe river-bridge. Then I made up my mind, taking the simplest solution as being also the best. Marseilles. I had always heard, and indeed it was reasonable enough, that a big city was the easiest place to hide in, and here was I within fairly easy reach of one of the biggest cities in France. Another thing, Louise and I had originally intended to visit Marseilles for a day or so, so the obvious thing to do was to ask her to leave Avignon to meet me in Marseilles.

Even as I made the decision, the Riley ran into a small country town – a large village, by English standards – and a glance at a road sign showed me that it was Cavaillon. I turned off the road into a straight little alleyway and berthed the car. Then after I had lowered the hood and made it fast, I got back into my seat and took out the map.

For Marseilles, I saw, I should not have crossed the river, but have turned sharp south at Orgon on to the main Marseilles road. That much of my way, at any rate, I must retrace. I sat biting my lip, gazing down the narrow alley, which gave at the far end on to the main street of the town, and wondering what to do next. If I went back the way I had come, by the side-roads, and Richard Byron had picked up the trail, I would run straight into his jaws. If, on the other hand, he had not followed my actual tracks, he would be on the main road, and if I took that way I should deliver myself neatly into his hands. He had only the two alternatives, I knew, and, now, so had I.

I sat gripping the wheel, in an agony of indecision. Two alternatives . . . and I was wasting time. I looked at the map again, desperately tracing out with my finger the possible routes to Marseilles. There were three things, it appeared, after all, that were possible. I could take a chance, and go back by one of the two ways across the river Durance, on to the main road for Marseilles, or I could go east through Apt, on route 100, by an involved and roundabout way; or I could go back to Avignon.

The last did not count so I dismissed it straight away. And I was through with taking chances; I was through with trusting my luck. I was not going back across the Durance, to meet Richard Byron. I would go east, and take the long road to the coast. With a heavy heart I folded the map, and started up the Riley. We crept along the alley, which was barely car-width. It was roughly cobbled, and gleamed with stinking puddles where thin cats prowled and rummaged in the gutters. The plaster on the houses was peeling, the shutters hung crookedly on rusty hinges. We crawled along towards the main road.

Then stopped dead as I jammed on all the brakes and sat shaking.

In the slash of vivid sunlight which was the main road at the alley's end, a big grey car flashed past, heading east for Route 100.

It was the Bentley.

My first thought was, absurdly enough, a sort of admiration for the speed he had made, even with my spanners in the works. My second was a sharp elation for myself. At any rate, the road to Orgon was now clear, and I could double on my tracks. I pushed the Riley forward to the brink of the alley, then braked again, and getting out of the car, ran forward to peer up the main street of Cavaillon.

The sun was blinding. The street was narrow, and crowded with the usual French country market crowd. There were women with baskets and string bags clustering round the street-stalls piled high with melons and beans and oranges and sleek purple aubergines. There were mule carts and lorries and big gleaming cars. There were dogs and children and half-naked brown men in berets and faded blue trousers.

But the Bentley had disappeared. I fancied I could see its dust still hanging in the hot quivering air at the east end of the street.

I ran to the Riley, and in a flash we were out of the alley and scudding west for the river bridge and Orgon, where one turns south-east for Marseilles.

Now that the Riley had her hood down, I was grateful for the breeze which, with our speed, fanned my cheeks and lifted my hair. But for the wind of our movement, the day was utterly still; under the pitiless sun of late morning the leaves of the planes that lined the road hung heavy, in thick lifeless clusters of yellow-green. The lovely stems of the trees with their dapple-work of silver and russet-peeled bark, shone in their long colonnades like cunningly worked pillars. The blinding road was barred by their shadows.

Regular as the pulse of a racing metronome, the shadow-bars flicked along the bonnet and back over my shoulder. We sailed out of Cavaillon on the verge of the speed-limit, tore through a dusty section of untidy ribbon-building, then suddenly the road writhed out from the plane-trees, and there, in the full glare of the sun, was the Durance and the long river-bridge.

And a queue of vehicles waiting to be allowed to pass over it.

With a sinking heart I took my place in the queue. The bridge, it appeared, was only a temporary one, three hundred yards of wooden boarding, narrow and unsteady, between the newly erected iron spans. At each end was a sentry-box, from which a man in uniform controlled the passage of traffic. At the moment, the stream from the opposite end of the bridge was being given the way, and cars, lorries, and carts crawled slowly and painfully across the narrow boards, while the white baton of the *agent de police* stretched implacably in front of us.

The heat poured down. I could feel it striking up in waves from the upholstery of the car, and gently prickling out in sweat on my body. I could not relax; I sat rigid, with my eyes switching like a doll's eyes from that forbidding white baton to my driving mirror, and back again.

And still the baton held us back, and the opposite stream of traffic crept forward, and all round me, before, behind, and edging forward to the left, impatient French drivers hooted and raced their engines and stamped on their klaxons, and got ready for a mad rush for first place on the narrow bridge . . .

Behind me, in the tiny mirror, a gigantic lorry quivered and roared, almost on my rear bumper; behind him again I could see a mule cart with a round canvas top. To my left a yellow Cadillac had edged up and was ready to slip in ahead, between the Riley and the brake van in front of me.

My nerves began to stretch. The roaring exhausts, the heat, the klaxons, the undisciplined traffic of the French highways . . . would the white baton never drop? The impatient racing of motors round us suddenly became feverish, and again the imperceptible movement forward began; I saw that the other end of the bridge was now barred, and only three or four vehicles were still coming across; presumably as soon as the way was empty we would be allowed to go.

I gripped the wheel tighter, with an eye on the white baton, and another on the yellow Cadillac.

The last lorry lumbered off the reverberating boards. The white baton dropped, and a hand waved us on. The brake van leaped at the gap, and the yellow Cadillac, with a triumphant blare, cut across the Riley's bows and roared in behind it.

I was third in line on to the bridge, when I looked in the mirror again.

And saw the grey Bentley nosing out from behind the covered mule-cart.

At the far side of the bridge stood the other queue now, with wind-screens flashing like morse in the sun. We crawled towards it. Behind me the green lorry edged on to the boards, shaking the whole contraption in a hair-raising manner. And the Bentley—

Richard Byron had reckoned without the Frenchman's utter lack of anything that might be called conscience or courtesy on the road. For as the Bentley drew out to pass the mule-cart, the driver glanced round and saw him, and immediately, with what looked like an imprecation, lashed at his mule, and hauled at its head, so that the cart swung drunkenly across the Bentley's bonnet. The Bentley checked abruptly, and the driver, lashing his mule again, crammed into the vacant place behind the lorry.

I reckoned afterwards that it gave me a good five miles' start. When I slipped off the bridge on to the western bank, the mule-cart was still plodding, only a third of the way over, with the grey car, held fuming, at less than a walking pace behind it.

I put my foot down and kept it there. The Riley tore up the straight good road like a storm. We passed the brake van as if it were standing, and then I put a thumb hard down on my horn and left the yellow Cadillac blinding through my dust at fifty miles an hour.

The needle flicked up . . . sixty . . . seventy . . . seventy-three . . . and ahead in the glare I could see trees across the way . . . A turn sharp to the left. I lifted my foot off the accelerator . . .

Mercifully there was nothing coming. We took the turning on the wrong side, and the back of the car skidded round it in the dust. There was a protesting scream from the tyres, and then the car straightened out and roared along the crown of the road. I felt no fear any more, I could not afford to think of anything but my driving . . . the world had narrowed down to the blinding straight ribbon of the *route nationale*, and the shadow-flecks across it that blurred now into one long flicker of shadows, like an old film.

I don't even remember Orgon. I suppose I must have slowed down for it, and gone through it with some care, but we were through it before I knew, and out on the road again, with my blessed good engine pulling like the horses of the sun.

We flashed by a little farmstead, set among its bronzed ryefields, swung out for a cruising car, and passed a cart as if it did not exist. A long white hill loomed up, between slopes of baking scrub, and then we were up the hill with the smooth rush of a lift, and dropping down the other side as if the hill had never been.

A little hamlet, pink-painted among dark cypress, hurtled towards us, closed in on us, was gone. Two oncoming cars went by, with a smack like the rattle of a drum.

And the long road writhed and turned and rose and fell beneath the roaring tyres to whip back and away in the driving mirror like a flying snake. And in all the world there was nothing but the racing engine and the rushing air and the road that streamed and streamed towards us.

12

And southward aye we fled
(Coleridge)

Then, suddenly, we were not alone any more. Out of the tail of my eye, to the right, I saw the plume of white smoke that meant a railway engine. The line was running parallel to the road, about fifty paces away, and an express came steaming out of a wooded defile, placidly heading south, like a pompous and attendant sprite.

My mind leaped ahead; I tried vainly to envisage the map. Would there be a railway bridge, or would it be one of those level crossings so common in southern France? So common, and so slow. Dear God, I thought to myself, *so slow*. I had waited before now a full twenty minutes for the bar of a crossing-gate to lift on an apparently quite empty line. And I might have grabbed a good start, but I had had some taste of the speed Richard Byron could make. I couldn't lose him on this road, and my only chance was to get into Marseilles with sufficient start to lose him there. Five minutes would do in those swarming streets, I thought grimly, and, with a hunted glance at the train, I put my foot down again.

To this day I do not know whether the driver of that train really did try and race my car or not. It seems impossible that he should have done so, and yet it really seemed to me, pelting along beside the rattle of the express, that the train gave a lurch and a sharp wail, and thereafter really entered into the spirit of the thing. The engine and I had it neck and neck for perhaps four hundred yards, while the driver and his mate leaned out of the cab and waved, and I sat over the wheel and looked neither to right nor left. Then we began to gain. The engine, panting, fell behind, and its pursuing rattle was deadened and then lost round a wooded bluff. For another span of minutes that seemed like hours, I held the car to its speed, then suddenly we slashed up a swift hill between two banks of olive trees, and away ahead, two miles off down a straight stretch of road, I saw, like a brightly painted toy in the distance, the sentry-box and the red and white bars of the level crossing.

It was still open.

But someone, a tiny figure dim in the quivering heat of the distance, was moving out to lower the bars.

I heard myself give a little sound like a groan, as the Riley hurtled down that road like a rocket-bomb.

The sentry-box came towards us with the sickening speed of a hangar towards a homing aircraft. The man lifted his arm to the crank that would release the bars. I put the heel of my hand down hard on the horn, and kept on.

I saw the startled jerk of his head, the white blur as his face turned towards us, his instinctive leap further out of the way.

Then with a roar and a rush and a sickening jerk and sway of springs, we were through.

I heard the bar crash into its socket behind us.

We had come down that two-mile stretch in one-and-a-half minutes dead.

We ran into Salon at a decorous pace, and threaded the main street with innocent care. In my mind's eye I saw the grey Bentley, fuming, stuck behind that maddening red and white bar until long after the train had passed.

I warned myself, through my relief, that I couldn't count on it. Richard Byron was quite capable of bribing the official to lift the bar as soon as the express was through, and the official was no doubt quite capable of obliging him.

So I did not pause in Salon, but held straight on.

But I had begun to feel tired.

So far, I thought, as I held the car at a comfortable fifty between the flickering avenues of plane-trees, so far the breaks had been about even. And the last good break had been mine. I began, I think for the first time, seriously to believe that I might be able to get clean away, lose myself where Richard Byron could not catch up with me, go right away with Louise until the storm-centre moved, and resume our disrupted holiday elsewhere.

Later on, perhaps, when I had time to think about it, I should begin to be angry at the way my time, my liberty – yes, and my person (I smiled wryly at the out-dated phrase) had been tampered with. I had got embroiled in the affair through no fault of my own, but through an impulse I still could not fully understand, the impulse that had led me in the first place to seek David's company, and in the second, to attempt to protect him. But I had certainly not deserved the kind of thing that had recoiled upon me. I ought to be angry, but just at present I was too preoccupied with my immediate problem to indulge in righteous indignation. The fact that Richard Byron was a murderer, and possibly of unsound mind, rendered null and void any prospect of talking reasonably with him. I had to escape, and then, perhaps, I could think.

The road was climbing steadily, towards the band of hills that lies between the Etang de Berre and Marseilles. It was unbearably hot, and I was hungry, but I put the thought aside, and pressed on through that deserted landscape, in a slow steady climb towards the crest of the rocky hills.

Towards the top the air grew fresher, and clumps of pines, looking cool and northern and beautiful, grew here and there beside the road. Then, some way ahead of me, I saw a little *bistro*, just a small yellow-washed house with three Continental pines to the back of it, a red petrol pump, and some small tables outside under a striped awning. Suddenly I felt unbearably thirsty. I tried to persuade myself that my lead from Richard Byron was such that I could afford ten minutes – no, five – with a long cold drink under that gay awning; that I had at any rate time to stop and buy some rolls and a bottle of red wine. But it was no use; I was definitely through with taking chances; it was Marseilles first stop. So I went relentlessly up the last hundred yards of that hill without looking at the *bistro* any more.

Then the decision was taken rudely out of my hands, because I was barely twenty yards short of it when I felt the Riley swerve across the road. I told myself that I must be more tired than I knew, and I straightened her up and crept on towards the crest of the long rise. Then I felt her pull and veer again, and once again I got her into line. It was only as I actually topped the rise that the dismal truth filtered through into my preoccupied and tired mind.

The breaks were even again, and this one was against me. I had picked up a puncture.

But not so badly against me, after all. The Riley, true as ever, had chosen to have her puncture within a hundred yards of an outpost of civilization, so, grateful for this unlooked-for fortune, I backed her slowly in on to the little flat stretch of gravel in front of the *bistro*.

A big stoutish man in shirt-sleeves and a white apron was rubbing glasses behind the bar in the shady interior. I leaned over the door of the car.

'Monsieur . . .'

He put down the glass he was polishing, and came out into the sun with a grin.

'Please, monsieur, I have a puncture as you see. Is there by any chance a garage? I see you sell petrol. Is there anyone here who could change my wheel while I have something to eat?'

He looked a little doubtful.

But he was French, and I gambled on that. I laid a
hand on his arm, looked desperately up at him, and
said, with a quiver in my voice that was not entirely
assumed: 'Monsieur, it's very urgent. I – I'm running
away from someone, and he isn't far behind me. I
daren't let him see me, and if I'm stuck here with a
puncture he—'

The most complete comprehension flashed across
his face.

'Your husband?'

'Yes, my husband. He's following me, and – and, oh,
monsieur, *do* help me!'

He was wonderful. In two minutes we had the Riley
parked round at the back of the house, in two more he
had routed out a lanky and capable youth from (I
think) his afternoon siesta, and started him jacking up
the car. Within seven at most I was inside the house, in
a cool little room at the back, and he was asking me
what I would have to eat.

'And madame need have no fear,' he said largely,
with gestures, 'for tonight she will sleep with her lover
in safety.'

I didn't argue, but I asked for an iced mint drink, a
long, long one, and whatever food he could manage in
the time it would take to change the tyre.

'An omelette? A herb omelette? It will only take five
minutes. We will find something for madame.
Madame is tired? She should have something reviving
with her omelette, yes?'

In a very little more than five minutes it was there, a
fluffy fragrant omelette, flanked with fresh rolls, butter,

honey and coffee. I swallowed down my cold drink and started on it. I don't think I have ever tasted anything so wonderful as that perfect little meal that I ate hastily in the little back room of that *bistro*, while Jean-Jacques, outside the window, was yanking off my wheel.

I was actually getting up to go, gulping the last of my coffee, when I heard the whine of another car coming up the hill outside, and the check and deepened note as she changed gear. Then the swish of gravel under her tyres as she turned off the road and stopped in front of the *bistro*.

I stood frozen, with the cup half-way to my mouth.

His voice came quite clearly through the nearly shut door. After the conventional greetings—

'No, nothing to drink, thank you,' he said, but I heard the rustle of notes. 'I haven't time. I stopped to ask you if you had seen an English car pass here within the last half-hour, a dark green car with the hood down. Did you happen to notice?'

There was another rustle.

'A dark green car . . .' repeated the *patron* slowly. I heard the clink of a glass, and could imagine him picking it up and deliberately starting to polish it again while he considered.

'A dark green car, English . . .' he paused, and I don't know which must have waited in the most tension, I or Richard Byron, one on either side of the door. 'With a young demoiselle driving?' asked the *patron*.

'Yes.' I could almost see the flicker in Richard Byron's eyes as he leaned forward.

The *patron* said, indifferently: 'A young woman

driving a dark green open car went by here some time ago. She was going fast. Would that be the one monsieur means?'

'That's the one. How long ago?'

In a voice that sounded like a shrug: 'About twenty minutes, twenty-five, half an hour – who knows, monsieur? I paid no attention, but I remember the car you speak of because of the speed . . . and the pretty girl.'

Something passed with a rustle, I heard a mumble of thanks from the *patron* and then, almost immediately, the roar of the Bentley's engine and the sound of rapidly engaged gears. The engine sang across the crest of the hill, and dwindled and died, so that soon the only sound was the rustle of the pines in the little hill-top breeze, and the clink of a glass from the bar.

The *patron* came back grinning.

'He was not far behind you, that one,' he said. 'But if you give him time now he will lose himself ahead of you. Madame cannot go back now the way she came?'

I thought for a moment, then shook my head. I would not lead the chase back into the Avignon area, come what might.

I would wait here, smoke a couple of cigarettes, then drive into Marseilles by the side road, and go to ground and call Louise. And I would tell Louise everything, when I saw her again; I was tired of playing this alone. I didn't feel that David would hold me to my promise of not speaking, after what had happened.

I said: 'Is there another way into Marseilles besides by the main road?'

'Yes, there are many. After one has passed Les Assassins—'

'*Les assassins?*' I asked, startled.

'It is a place at the top of these hills, where one begins to go down into Marseilles. The road goes between walls of rock, a little gorge.'

'But why is it called Les Assassins?'

'Because much rock has fallen there, and the old road used to wind in among the cliffs and boulders, and it was the place where brigands waited, in ambush, for the coaches and the carts of merchants.'

'And after that?'

'Then there is the long run down into Marseilles, and before one reaches the suburbs there are roads which branch and which, if one has a map, will take one into the city by a different way. There is no need to go down the main road into the town.' He smiled suddenly. 'He is to meet you there, *hein?*'

'He – who? Oh, yes, of course,' I said. I had momentarily forgotten that I had a date with a lover in Marseilles that night. 'You have been more than kind,' I told the *patron*, and he shrugged expansively.

'It is nothing, nothing at all. If one cannot help a *belle demoiselle* in distress – what would you? One might as well be dead.'

He went out, beaming good-will, and I sat for a while, quietly smoking, while time passed softly. I felt, gradually, a sense of peace descending on me, a feeling that this was a safe little harbourage that I should be sorry to leave. I sat, relaxed, and I believe I even dozed a little, for over an hour longer. And then, when I saw by my watch that it was nearly three o'clock, I rose reluctantly, and prepared to go.

I found the *patron*, and paid for what I had had, renewing my thanks, and including a thousand-franc note, over and above what I owed him, and a substantial tip for Jean-Jacques.

I found that the latter had occupied his time not only in changing my wheel, but, when told there was no need to hurry, in finding and mending the puncture in the discarded wheel. This, mended now and serviceable, was strapped in place as spare. I thanked him gratefully, and, pursued by good wishes, and frank promises of joy to come from the *patron*, I drove the Riley back round the house and out again on to the road.

Soon the little *bistro* was lost to sight behind us, round a bend in the track, and we were off on our travels again, with the sun for company, and the tall pines whispering above the humming engine. I did not hurry. For one thing, there was now no need, and I would not unnecessarily abuse the car on the rather stony road, and risk picking up another puncture – which I would have to deal with myself. For another, the strain of the previous night, and of the hectic and nerve-racked morning, were beginning most definitely to tell on me. My head was aching a little, and a sort of lassitude, an almost don't-care-ishness, bred of fatigue and lack of sleep, was making itself felt. I knew that, even if the occasion should arise, I would be quite unequal now to the sort of demands that had been made on me that morning. If suddenly called upon for headlong speed, I would probably drive the car off the road at anything over fifty miles an hour.

So I nursed the engine up the long inclines, and took the car gently over the rough surface, with half of my mind on my driving, and the other half trying to recall the street plan of Marseilles and the way I had planned to take.

The white rocks gave way, as we climbed higher, to red. The country, deserted before, was here desolate, stripped even of its olives and its vines. The red rocks, slashed with hard cobalt shadows, rose sheer from the road on either hand, and the only green was the dark cresting of the pines, swaying richly against the dazzling blue. As we approached what appeared to be the summit of the hill, I could see how the cliffs had split and crumbled, till on either side of the road were bare boulders and pylons of rock. Among the strewn red fragments to the left I saw where the old track had wound tortuously across the hill-crest behind the pines and fallen rocks. But the new road went through the sheer red cliff like a white slash.

Les Assassins.

And, in the blue distance, the Mediterranean.

As the Riley gained the summit, I changed up, and she slipped into the long descent with a sigh. Before me the road sank in an interminable and gentle hill towards the enormous untidy sprawl of Marseilles, set on the edge of the loveliest shore in the world.

We started slowly down the last stretch. To the left of the road, several yards ahead, I saw where the old track emerged again on to the road, behind a knot of pines. We slid past it and down.

I suppose I should have seen it coming, but I confess I had not. There was no reason I could see why Richard Byron should not believe the *patron* of the *bistro*, and race on towards Marseilles in the hope of catching me. But of course, he had not believed him.

The grey Bentley glided out of that knot of pines, and closed in behind my car without a sound.

13

Re-enter Murderer
(Stage direction)

There was nothing to be done, of course.

Even if I had not been so tired, I still could not have hoped to drive away from him with no start, and no advantage. I was beaten, and I knew it. I would go quietly.

Without thinking very much of anything at all, except that my head ached and I would be glad to stop driving and get out of the sun, I went on down the long stretch towards Marseilles as if there were no grey car behind me, and no angry man in it who had, by this time, quite a big account to settle with me.

In a very short time we were in the suburbs of Marseilles. The main road runs for perhaps two miles or more through streets of tattered houses and little grubby shops, where the plaster and the paint hangs in peeling festoons, and where beautiful ragged children and hideous mongrel dogs play together among the refuse of the gutters. Soon the tram-lines begin, and the traffic of the city begins to close in. Lorries, mules, carts of all shapes and sizes, cars of assorted vintages and nationalities – all the world on wheels seems to drive through the narrow streets of Marseilles, hooting, shouting, pushing for places, in a rich and strange confusion.

I steered mechanically through it all, changing gear, stopping, swerving, going through all the rapid actions necessary to getting a vehicle more or less undamaged through that incredible *tohubohu*. Behind me, like a shadow, the big grey Bentley swerved and checked and swept forward again on my track, never more than ten yards behind me, never less than four.

I didn't even bother to watch it, except as I would watch anything so close on my tail, in order to give it the necessary signals.

I was finished. I wasn't trying any more. My temples throbbed and I felt as if a heavy weight were pressing down on my shoulders. My mind, even had I tried to make it, would have refused to contemplate what was going to happen after this.

Which is why, when the miracle happened, I did not even notice it.

The first I knew of it was when it gradually filtered through to my stupid senses that there was no grey car reflected in the driving mirror. There was only a mule-cart, and nothing behind that that I could see.

I stared stupidly for three seconds, then I stole a look back over my shoulder. I had come about a hundred yards from where it had happened. A lorry, emerging from a blind side street, had swung across the path of the Bentley, and grazed a passing tram. The Bentley, caught between the two, had had to stop, but whether it was touched or not I could not, of course, tell. But it was stuck fast enough, that much was apparent. Already the beginnings of a crowd had gathered, and excitement was mounting . . . And there were the police . . .

It might take him minutes, or even hours, to get himself out of that.

Like a fainting man who makes a last desperate conscious effort before he goes under, I turned the Riley down a side street, and trod on the accelerator . . . left, right, right, left again – no, that was a cul-de-sac – right, in and out like a twisting hare . . . then before me was a garage, where behind a row of pumps yawned the dark cave of an enormous shed, half filled with lorries, cars, buses, in varying stages of repair. I turned in, ran the car as deep into the shadow as I could, and berthed it finally behind a solid rank of wagons.

Still mechanically, I switched off the engine, collected my bag, maps, glasses and coat, and got out of the car.

I cannot remember what instructions I gave to the proprietor, who had hurried up, but I paid him something in advance, and only just retained enough wit to ask for his card with the address of the garage. I tucked this inside my bag, and went slowly out into the sunshine of the back street.

I turned right, away from the city centre, towards where I imagined the sea to lie, and walked for some way through shabby streets that nevertheless seemed moderately respectable. And soon the name of a little hotel caught my eye, a name I had seen in the Michelin guide. It would, in that case, be clean and comfortable, so I went into its cool tiled lobby, signed my name, and climbed a steep spiral of marble steps to a stone landing on the third floor, where Madame showed me a small and spotless room.

The door clicked shut behind her. I sat down slowly on the bed, and for a full five minutes I don't suppose I even moved an eyelash. The shutters were closed against the sun, and so were the windows, so that the hum and clash of traffic from Europe's noisiest city surged up, muted and drowsy, into the high little room. There was a wash-basin, a foot-bath, a narrow comfortable bed with a snow-white cover, a carafe of water on the table beside the bed . . .

I drank deeply. I stood up, and after I had locked the door, I slowly undressed, shaking out my clothes one by one, and laying them neatly on the bed. I had a leisurely cool wash, bathing and drying my whole body, standing on the warm floor with the slatted sunlight barring me from head to foot. Then I slipped on my fresh nylon nightdress, and brushed my hair thoroughly.

I moved my clothes to the back of a chair, had another long drink, and lay down on the bed.

The day began to recede, grow confused, grow dim, as the sound of the traffic blurred with distance . . . Richard Byron might be miles away, he might be in jail, he might be just outside the door . . . it didn't matter at all.

I slept.

It was just before six when I awoke, and at first, swimming up from the warm depths of sleep, I could not tell where I was, lying on a strange bed with the deepening rays of the sun slanting through the shutters. The light had mellowed from gold to amber, and the sound of the traffic below, too, seemed to have mellowed its note to a subdued rushing like the rushing of an underground sea.

I lay still for a while, enjoying the relaxed warmth of my body and the softness of the bed. Then I got up and began leisurely to dress again in the green frock. It looked fresh enough, considering the wear and tear of the last night and day, I thought, as I buckled the wide belt round it, and slipped into my shoes.

I was hungry, and the first problem I intended to face was that of finding a meal. I toyed with the idea of buying food and wine, and locking myself safely in my room to eat, but decided I might as well eat at a café if I was going out to buy food. And Marseilles was a big and crowded city, not like Nîmes, or Avignon. I would go out, avoiding the main streets, and dine in some small restaurant where I was not likely to be seen. Then I would come back to the hotel and ring up Louise.

I remembered what I had read of Marseilles – that the city was sliced in two by the straight line of the Canebière, the busiest street in Europe, where, sooner or later, all the world passed by. It was said that if you sat in the Canebière long enough, you would see passing by you every soul that you knew. If I were

Richard Byron, I thought, that's where I'd go. I'd select a table in a boulevard café on the Canebière, and sit and watch for the girl in the pale green dress.

So the girl in the pale green dress would go elsewhere.

I took my key downstairs, spoke politely to Madame and the marmalade cat in the foyer, and went down the three stone steps into the street. It was still warm, but the sunlight was deep copper-gold, and the shadows lay long on the pavements.

The exhausted feeling had passed, leaving only, as an aftermath of that deep sleep, a profound sensation of unreality, as if I were moving, effortlessly and bodiless, through a dream. People passed me, traffic rattled by, but these movements seemed to have no connection with the world in which I found myself; men were 'like trees walking', without character or feature or sound, irrelevant creations in the background of my nightmare. The only living person was myself, Charity Selborne, to whom none of these things could possibly be happening . . .

I walked fairly rapidly to the end of the street and glanced to right and left. To the right a vista of still meaner streets and warehouses met my eyes, so I turned left through a narrow way towards the sea. After a while I realized that I was making for the harbour – I could see masts and the gleam of a gull's wing and a flash of early neon lights at the end of the street.

I hesitated. One had heard such tales of Marseilles, the wicked city . . . and was it not near the harbour that the wickedness congregated? A street led off to my left, and I paused in my walk, and glanced up it.

Then made for the harbour without another second's hesitation. For he was there, my enemy, hesitating like myself at the far corner of that street, which, I found later, gave straight on to the Canebière: – I had been right, as far as it went. I did not think he had seen me, but the hunt was up again, and I made for the Old Port of Marseilles without another thought of the wickedness there abounding. I believe I would almost have welcomed the offer of a free trip to Buenos Aires at that moment.

Where the street led into the harbour I hesitated again. It was so open. The Old Port was a vast open space, criss-crossed by tram-lines and railway tracks, bounded on three sides by houses and restaurants all flashing their gaudy neon signs in the face of the sunset, and open on the fourth side to the sea. The harbour waters were crowded with boats of all shapes and colours, and in the amber light the forest of masts swayed and bobbed amid the glancing web of their ropes.

I only hesitated for a second, then made across the open square towards the nearest crowd of people, hoping to lose myself among them, and get somehow to the other side of the square. There were about twenty or thirty people standing there, talking and laughing, between the railway tracks and the edge of the quay. I reached them and joined the crowd, ignored a pressing invitation from a couple of sailors obviously ashore for the evening, and took refuge behind what appeared to be a family party, papa, mamma, and two little boys in sailor suits with red pompoms on their bonnets. I threw a cautious glance at the mouth of the street I had just left. He was not there.

Then I discovered why the crowd had collected there on the quay.

An old boatman, with scarlet cheeks, a quantity of white whiskers, and a liquid and lascivious eye, suddenly appeared up a short gangplank which led from the quay beside us to the stern of a motor-boat moored below.

'This way!' he yelled. 'This way for the Château d'If!'

Simultaneously, another old man, with whiskers slightly less white, and an eye proportionately more lascivious, shot up in rivalry in the next boat.

'This way,' he screamed. '*This* way for the Château d'If!'

The crowd, showing neither fear nor favour, turned as one and began to file down the twin gangplanks. It looked as if, my cover gone, I was going to be left high and dry on the edge of the Old Port.

I flung a look at the street corner, just in time to see Richard Byron emerge, glance once back over his shoulder, then turn to scan the square, but he was not looking at the quay; he was looking the other way towards the din of the Canebière.

I scuttered down the nearest gangplank and sat down under the awning, as far forward as I could get. The boat lay well below the level of the quayside, and I knew he could not see me from where he stood.

But it looked as if, bating Buenos Aires, I were going on a trip to the Château d'If.

The boatman, with a good deal of quite unnecessary noise, cast off, and soon we were churning through the milky waters of the bay towards the harbour mouth.

I cannot pretend that I enjoyed any part of that trip to the Château d'If. I was caught again in the noose of the old fear, and now it was worse, threaded through as it was with the drab strands of hopelessness. It seemed that I literally could not get away from him, almost as if there were something so linking this dark and dangerous man with myself, that wherever I went, he was there. In the whole of Marseilles, to meet him the first moment I ventured out: in the whole of Provence, to meet him in the ruins of Les Baux. To whatever shifts I resorted, he found me: whatever falsehoods my brain devised, he knew the truth behind . . . this, at any rate, is how I was thinking, and how much was due to hunger and how much to inescapable fate I was in no fit state to judge . . .

I sat on the low parapet of the turret of the Château d'If, watching the white stone slowly flush to a tender rose. I watched the softly breaking water of the tideless sea wash and wash across the whispering white pebbles, aquamarine rippled through with liquid gold.

I saw it all in a kind of dream; and the whisper of the sea came like a dream's echo.

The boat went, and I sat where I was. Another came, and discharged its noisy cargo of sightseers, who streamed chattering into the castle, and crowded through the prison-cells and across the wide flat roof where I was sitting. I got up suddenly, and went down to the boat which was waiting. My watch told me I had been on the island already over an hour: he would have gone, I said to myself, without conviction. With rather more conviction, and a good deal more common sense, I told myself that this state of numbed fatalism was the result of hunger and fatigue, and the sooner I got back and got a meal the better I should be.

The journey back seemed much shorter than the outward trip. It was almost dark by now, and along the shore the lights were strung out like a necklace. There were no waves, but bars of darkness slid softly towards the land to lap against the dim rock.

We shut off our engine and drifted towards the quay followed by our arrowing wake. The port was gemmed with neon lights, white, scarlet, green and amethyst, and under the more subdued orange glow of the street lamps the evening crowds were gathering. The city of the night-time was waking up. I sat in the silently moving boat, relaxed now, still in the trance-like drifting state of acute reaction from strain. I scarcely bothered to scan the quay in the twilight, to see if this last absurd bid for escape had worked. I knew it could not. I knew that there was something far stronger than anything I had known before, that would lead Richard Byron straight to the gang-plank to wait for me.

We were tying up at the quay-side. The boatman yelled to a boy on shore, and between them they threw out the gangway. The other people in the boat got up, calling to one another and laughing, and trod awkwardly up the plank. I followed.

I hardly even looked at Richard Byron as he took my arm and helped me on to the quay.

14

Fate, I come, as dark, as sad
As thy malice could desire;
Bringing with me all the fire
That Love in his torches had.
                    (Marvell)

I walked across the quay beside him, his hand under my elbow. People passed us, walked at our shoulders, even jostled us, but we might as well have been alone. I saw the crowd vaguely, darkly through a glass, and the sounds of them were remote, in an anaesthetized distance. The only sound I heard in all the clamour was the tread of our feet on the cobbles, and the breathing of Richard Byron beside me.

He said, not ungently: 'We still have to have our little talk, you know.'

Something deep inside me seemed to snap. The anger I had been too scared, too tired to feel, suddenly jetted up. I stopped abruptly, and swung to face him. People streamed past us, but they were not there at all; there was only myself and my enemy, in a little circle of anger.

I looked him straight in the eyes. I said furiously: 'We

can have as many little talks as you want, since you seem prepared to make such a damned nuisance of yourself to get them. But I can tell you one thing now, and it's the most important thing of all, and it's this. *I am not going to tell you anything about David.* I know perfectly well where he is, and you can bully me and threaten me as much as you like, but you'll find out nothing. Nothing.'

'But I—'

I swept on as if he hadn't spoken: 'You told me outright that you were a murderer. Do you think I am going to be a party to handing a child over to you, a child who, for all I know to the contrary, you *did* bash over the head in the dark the night you murdered your friend? Think again, Mr. Richard Byron. David is a darling, even if he *is* your son, and I – I'd murder you myself if you laid a finger on him!'

The hot tears were welling up in my eyes, tears of anger, anxiety and strain. I felt them spill over and begin to run down my cheeks. I could not see his face through them, and he did not speak for a long moment.

'My God,' said Richard Byron at length in a curious voice. But I hardly heard him.

'Apart from which,' I finished, 'you – you've ruined my holiday, and I've been looking forward to it for ages.'

After which remarkably silly speech I suddenly broke; I began to cry helplessly, with my hands to my face, and the tears dripping out between my fingers. I turned blindly away from Richard Byron, stumbled over a rail-track, and would have fallen, but that his hand caught me again by the elbow and steadied me.

Then he said, in the same curious voice: 'You'll feel better when you've had something to eat. Come along.'

The neon-lighted cafés were a blur. I felt him piloting me along the sidewalks, and I fought for self-control, groping in my bag for a handkerchief. Then suddenly we were in out of the street, in a little, beautifully appointed restaurant where the tables were set back in alcoves, lit softly by wall-lights. I caught a confused glimpse of napery and glass and silver, and a great spray of yellow flowers, then I was comfortably settled on a deep wall-seat upholstered with wine velvet, and Richard Byron was putting a glass into my hand. My own was shaking, and his hand closed on it, holding it steady until I regained sufficient control to raise it to my lips.

I realized, as from a great distance, that his voice was very gentle. He said: 'Drink it up. It'll make you feel better.'

I gulped some of it down. It was spirit of some kind, and it seemed to burst and evaporate inside my mouth and throat in an immediate aromatic warmth, so that I gasped and choked a little, but my breath came more evenly afterwards, and I found I could control the little shaking sobs that were racking me.

'All of it,' urged Richard Byron. I obeyed him, and lay back against the deep cushions with my eyes closed, letting my body relax utterly to the creeping warmth of the drink and the smell of food and wine and flowers. My bones seemed to have melted, and I was queerly content to lie back against the yielding velvet, with the soft lights against my eyelids, and do nothing, think of nothing. I was quiet and utterly passive, and the awful beginnings of hysteria were checked.

Still from that same dimensionless distance, I heard him speaking in French. I supposed he was ordering food. And presently at my elbow I heard the chink of silver, and opened my eyes to see the big glittering trolley of *hors d'œuvre* with its hovering attendant.

Richard Byron said something to him, and without waiting for me to speak, the man served me from the tray. I remember still those exquisite fluted silver dishes, each with its load of dainty colours . . . there were anchovies and tiny gleaming silver fish in red sauce, and savoury butter in curled strips of fresh lettuce; there were caviare and tomato and olives green and black, and small golden-pink mushrooms and cresses and beans. The waiter heaped my plate, and filled another glass with white wine. I drank half a glassful without a word, and began to eat. I was conscious of Richard Byron's eyes on me, but he did not speak.

The waiters hovered beside us, the courses came, delicious and appetizing, and the empty plates vanished as if by magic. I remember red mullet, done somehow with lemons, and a succulent golden-brown fowl bursting with truffles and flanked by tiny peas, then a froth of ice and whipped cream dashed with kirsch, and the fine smooth caress of the wine through it all. Then, finally, apricots and big black grapes, and coffee. The waiter removed the little silver filtres, and vanished, leaving us alone in our alcove.

The liqueur brandy was swimming in its own fragrance in the enormous iridescent glasses, and for a moment I watched it idly, enjoying its rich smooth gleam, then I leaned back against the cushions and looked about me with the eyes of a patient who has just woken from the first long natural sleep after an anaesthetic. Where before the colours had been blurred and heightened, and the outlines undefined, proportions unstable, and sounds hollow and wavering, now the focus had shifted sharply, and drawn the bright little restaurant into sharp dramatic outline.

I looked across at Richard Byron.

He was sitting, head bent, watching the brandy swirl in the bottom of his glass, the light of the subdued wall-lamp falling upon him from behind and to the left. I found myself for the first time really looking at him without any underlay of fear and suspicion to colour my picture of him. The light lit sharply the angles of cheek-bone and jaw, and the fine line of the temple, throwing a dramatic slant of shadow from his lowered lashes – David's lashes – across the hard line of his cheek. And the first thing that struck me was the deep unhappiness of that face; it was unhappiness rather than harshness that had driven those furrows down his cheeks, and given the eyes such sombre shadowing. As he sat with his head bent, obliviously toying with his brandy-glass, the angry lines of brow and mouth were smoothed away, and instead there was a withdrawn and brooding look, an aspect harsh and forbidding enough, until it was betrayed by the unhappiness of the mouth.

His lashes lifted suddenly and he looked at me. I felt my heart jolt once, uncomfortably, then I met his gaze squarely.

'How do you feel now?'

I said: 'Much better, thank you. It was good of you to salvage the wreck – I must look like—'

He laughed, and it was suddenly like coming face to face with a complete stranger, where you had been talking to someone you thought you knew.

He said: 'You must be feeling better, if you're beginning to worry about how you look. But don't let it distress you. You'll pass, indeed you will.'

He lit a cigarette for me, and suddenly his eyes were grave over the flame and very intent. He said, quietly: 'There are only two things I want to ask you just at this moment—'

My face must have changed, because he added sharply: 'Don't look like that. Please. I've been every kind of a damned fool, and I'm sorry, but for God's sake don't look at me like that any more. They're very harmless questions, but if you'll tell me the answers, I'll leave you alone till you feel like telling me the rest.'

He paused, and all of a sudden it was as if the room were as still as the pole.

Here it comes again, I thought. He looked down at his glass, so that I could not see his eyes, but under the noncommittal voice I could feel the urgency that had frightened me before.

He said: 'How is David? Does he seem well – and happy?'

I looked at him in surprise; I had expected a very different question. I said: 'As far as I could see, he is very well indeed. But I don't imagine that he's happy. For one thing, he's lonely, and for another, he's too scared.'

'*Too scared?*' He looked at me this time. He set his glass down so sharply that the brandy splashed and sparkled, and then his hands came down to grip the table's edge, the whites of the knuckles showing. From the ash-tray, where his cigarette burned unheeded, a pencilled blue line of smoke spiralled up between us. Richard Byron stared at me through the smoke, and he repeated, very softly: 'Too scared – of what?'

I raised my eyebrows. 'Of you, of course.'

There could be no doubt about his first reaction to that uncompromising reply; it was stupefaction, sheer, speechless stupefaction. He stared at me across the table, and his eyes widened. Then, suddenly, as if he had understood or remembered something, the old bitter look was back in his face, and he seemed to withdraw once more into himself. He said, in a curiously flat voice:

'Of me? Are you sure it's of me? Did he say so?'

Then suddenly, I knew. I felt my own eyes widening as his had done, and I sat staring at him like an owl.

'Why,' I whispered, 'why, I don't believe you killed your friend. I don't believe you ever hurt David in your life. I believe you love him. Don't you. *Don't you?*'

Richard Byron gave me a queer little twisted smile

that hurt. Then he picked up his cigarette again and
spoke lightly.

'I love him more than anything else in the world,' he
said, quite as if it didn't matter.

Then suddenly, the bubble was broken, and the illu-
sion of privacy dispelled. The head waiter came hovering, his face split with a smile, his hands fluttering
before him like large pursy moths.

'Madame has enjoyed her dinner? Monsieur has fed
well? The *Chapon marseillais*, he is good, yes? He is the
specialité de la maison, you understand, Madame. . . .'

We assured him that everything had been perfect,
and, wreathed in smiles and mothlike swoops of the
hand, he bowed himself off, and another waiter, with
the faint air of apology that is worn by a man commit-
ting an act in questionable taste, sidled up with the bill.

Richard Byron glanced at it, put a quite staggering
amount of money down on the salver, and waved the
bowing waiter aside. Then he hesitated oddly, and
looked at me.

'I know it's useless saying I'm sorry for what has
happened,' he said, 'but as far as the inadequate phrase
can go, I *am* sorry. I've been a damned fool and a blind
one. I should have known that someone like you
wouldn't have been mixed up in this thing. I promise
not to pester you again – but could we go somewhere,
take a walk or something, and will you let me explain?
It's quite a long story, and somehow I'd rather you
knew it.'

His face looked white and strained in the subdued

light. I had a sudden sharp memory of David's face, wearing much that same look, and of a hesitating childish voice asking me: '*How did he look?*'

I said: 'If it concerns David, I'd like to hear it. And as for what's in the past, shall we forget it for a while? It looks as if you're not the only one who's made mistakes – and mine, perhaps, were the bigger.'

'You had the more excuse.'

He smiled his sudden warm smile, and to my own amazement, I smiled back, and rose.

'If I promise not to climb out of a back window, may I go and powder my nose?'

'You—' he bit off something he had been going to say. 'Yes, of course.'

As I went I saw him get out another cigarette, and settle back in his chair to wait for me.

We went out into the dark streets that ray from the Old Port and turned, instinctively and as if by mutual consent, towards the sea. Presently we found ourselves in a cobbled street which slanted along the sea front, with tall houses to the left of us, and a low sea-wall to the right. Away ahead, floating in the starlit air like a vision, glimmered the gold statue of Our Lady who stands high on the summit of Notre Dame de la Garde.

The houses were dark and secret, and the occasional lamps cast only a furtive light on the cobbles. Boats bobbed and curtseyed at the water's edge, rubbing each other's shoulders, the sea lipping at them with small sucking sounds. Where the shamefaced lamp-light let fall a reflection on the water, the shifting surface cast a pattern of light upwards on to the bellies of the boats, so that they seemed to be swimming, netted in a wavering luminous mesh. Further out in the bay, the green and red and golden riding-lights of the bigger ships drowned themselves in long liquid sha-dows. The ropes looked as fragile and as magical as gossamer.

We stood looking over the sea-wall. A group of sailors, noisily talking and laughing, went past, then a man and a girl, absorbed. Nobody seemed to pay any attention to us, and once again I felt the beginnings of that strangely dreamlike feeling I had experienced before, only this time it was not brought about by weariness, but by something else I could not quite understand. It was as if Richard Byron and I were alone in a bubble of glass, enclosed in its silence, into which nothing could break, and out of which we might not go. People, like the dim denizens of some under-sea-world in which our bubble was suspended, came and went, floating, soundlessly, amorphous, outside the glass, peering in perhaps, but having no power to intrude upon the silence that enmeshed us. To this day I still remember Marseilles, the noisiest city in the world, as a noiseless background to that meeting with Richard Byron, a silent film flickering on a screen in front of which we two moved and stood and talked, the only living people there.

I turned to face him.

'You said there were two questions you were going to ask me, and you've only asked one. What was the other?'

He looked at me without speaking, and in that dim light his expression was unreadable, but I got the impression that he was oddly at a loss.

I said: 'I think I know; in fact, I can hardly help knowing, can I? It should have come first, shouldn't it? – it's the more important.'

I saw the corner of his mouth lift in a smile.

'Possibly.'

I said, deliberately: 'David is at the Hôtel Tistet-Védène, Avignon.'

For a long moment he was motionless, then suddenly his body swung round to face me, and his hands shot out to grip my wrists. Again, as in Nîmes, his grip hurt me, but this time I made no attempt to get away. I could feel his heart beating in his hands.

'Charity,' he said roughly, 'why did you tell me that? Why – suddenly? I haven't told you the story yet – haven't explained. I haven't even told you I was lying when I said I'd murdered Tony. You've no reason on earth to think you can trust me – I've bullied you and hurt you and abused you and all but made you ill. Why the hell should you suddenly make me a present of this before I've even started to say my piece?'

It was as if his heart was an engine, and its pounding was driving mine as well. It started to race.

'I – I don't know,' I said lamely, and tried to pull my hands away.

He shifted his grip, and his eyes fell on my bruised wrist. For a second or two he stood with his head bent, staring at the ugly dark mark, then his mouth suddenly twisted, and he pulled me into his arms and kissed me.

After a long while he let me go, and I leaned back against the low parapet, while he turned abruptly and gazed out to sea.

'I suppose that was why,' I said shakily.

'The hell of it is,' he said, 'that I've wanted that ever since I walked into the Temple of Diana and saw you sitting there, with tears on your eyelashes. And all the time I thought you were a crooked little—'

'Bitch.'

He grinned a little. 'Quite,' he said. 'Yes, all that time, when I thought you were in with them, a cheap little crook mixed up in a particularly filthy game of murder – the sort of game that plays with a child's life and sanity as if it were a – a plastic counter you could lose, and never miss it.'

He looked away from me suddenly.

'Your refusing to tell me where to find David – was it because *David* wanted you to?'

'Yes,' I said gently.

'And I thought you were helping them to keep him away from me. You looked so guilty, so guilty and scared, and of course I'd no idea that David himself—'

He broke off sharply.

'I'm sorry, but that's how it was. He wanted to – to avoid you, so I helped. I thought I was doing the right thing.'

He gave me a little smile. 'Yes, I see that now. But you must see how all the evidence went against you, even while every instinct I've ever had rose up and screamed that the evidence was wrong . . . It was just one more thing, after all those that had happened, one

more thing which could shake one's values to smith-
ereens, and make yet another safe road as shifty as
sand. Another thing that *couldn't* be, but *was*.'

'I know,' I said. 'How does it go—?

> *Sith there is yet a credence in my heart,*
> *An esperance so obstinately strong,*
> *That does invert the attest of eyes and ears;*
> *As if those organs had deceptious functions,*
> *Created only to calumniate . . .*

Isn't that what you mean?'

He smiled again, more naturally. 'Yes, exactly,
though I can't say it puts it much more clearly. Poor
Troilus – he says it better later on, you know—

> *If beauty have a soul, this is not she . . .*
> *If there be rule in unity itself,*
> *This is not she . . .*

But I was luckier than Troilus, wasn't I? For me, the
rules did hold good – that no one who looks and moves
and speaks as you do *could* be the bitch you seemed to
be. But it was hell while it lasted, reason and instinct at
war, and both violated.' He turned his head. 'You do
understand, don't you?'

'Of course. Didn't it happen to me too? I thought
you were a beast and a murderer, I was scared of you,
and yet – this happened.'

'This happened,' he repeated, 'and reason goes out
of court – for both of us.'

'Yes.'

He said slowly, looking down at the dark opaque

shifting of the water: 'But you got the question wrong, Charity. You didn't really think I was going to throw that one at you again, did you, before I'd explained why I still had the right to an answer?'

'I got it wrong? You weren't going to ask where David was?'

'No.'

'What were you going to ask, then?'

He stood, watching the water, leaning on his elbows on the low wall. He said, heavily, for the fourth time:

'Who's Johnny?'

15

Madam, will you walk—?
(Old song)

The dark water heaved below the wall, oily looking, webbed with a flotsam of straws and pieces of cork. It was strangely fascinating, as well as soothing, to watch the lift and fall and sway of the drifting fragments in the shallow gleam of the street-lamp.

I said: 'Johnny was my husband.'

'Was?'

'Yes,' I said.

'Oh, I see. I'm sorry.'

I turned, like him, to face the sea, leaned my elbows on the wall and concentrated on the moving water.

'He and I were married in the war – he was in the R.A.F. We had two years, so I suppose we were lucky. Then he was killed over Pas de Calais.'

'Bomber?'

'No. Fighter escort.' Away out over the sea the milky haze had begun to withdraw from the moon. The horizon swam up out of darkness to meet her faint light.

'Some day,' I said, 'I'll tell you about Johnny. But not now.'

He glanced at me quickly.

'Because of this – because of what's happened?'

'Because you kissed me, do you mean?'

'Because I love you, Charity.'

'No,' I said. 'Not because of that. What happens to me now doesn't alter what happened to me before. What was between me and Johnny was a real thing that we built very carefully for ourselves, and, when we built it, it was perfect and satisfying. But because it was blasted to bits by a German shell, that doesn't mean I'm never to try and build anything else among the ruins. Johnny isn't a ghost, you know, tagging along at my elbow, reminding me to mourn.'

'When I first saw you,' he said softly, 'you were crying.'

'I know,' I said. 'And it's true I was thinking about Johnny. But the memory of my life with him isn't likely to get up and forbid me to live any more, or any differently . . . One ought to build even better the second time, and I can still build. And Johnny—' I said, turning to Richard Byron, 'why, Johnny would have egged me on.'

He straightened up, and his arms went round me, this time very gently. He was smiling, and his eyes had a little steady flame deep in the grey. He held me a little away from him and looked at me, his lips curving.

'I love you, Charity,' he said again. 'You're so sweet and you're so sane. My God, I think you could almost make the world seem a sweet, sane place again, the way it used to be . . . Am I to take it that you're telling me to go ahead and kiss you again?'

'Why, no, I—'

'Because I'm planning to,' said Richard Byron.

And did.

It seemed hours later, and the moon had laid her trail of silver out to sea, when we stood again, side by side, elbows on the wall again, and began to talk.

'. . . Enough of this side-tracking,' said Richard. 'I've got to think, and you're got to help me, so you've got a right to know the story. It's a pretty filthy one to drag you into—'

'It seems to me,' I said mildly, 'that I'm in fairly deep as it is, and entirely through my own efforts.'

He mused a little, and I could see the lines etch themselves again deeply round his mouth, those bitter little lines that made his face suddenly harsh and frightening.

He began to talk . . .

It was certainly not a pretty story, and as I listened, I could feel some of the anger that burned even now in Richard's voice, licking along my own veins.

Briefly, it was this.

Richard Byron, who was reasonably well-to-do, lived at Deepings, in Surrey, and had acquired some reputation among those who knew, as a dealer in various kinds of antiques. 'It started in a strictly amateurish sort of way,' he said. 'I bought things I liked, and occasionally sold again to people who saw them and wanted them; then bit by bit I came into it as a business, because I got interested. I didn't have to make a living that way, but I gradually learned more about it, and began to travel after stuff, and in time became really keen on certain aspects of the business – old silver and jewellery particularly. I'm supposed to know quite a lot about it now.'

The war had put a stop to it, of course, and he had joined the Air Force – 'Flying a ruddy great Lanc. over the Ruhr,' said Richard. 'That was where I got to know Tony, of course.'

'Tony?'

'Tony Baxter. The lad I'm supposed to have murdered.'

'Oh.'

'He was my navigator, and one of the nicest chaps you could ever know. The idea that he could ever have fallen for Loraine—'

'You did, yourself,' I reminded him. 'After all, you married her.'

He shot me a look from under his brows. 'Yes, I married her. David was twelve and Mary had been dead seven years, and I thought—' he broke off. 'Well, hell, you've seen her, and if you don't know why I married her you ought to.'

I had a sudden vivid memory of Loraine Byron's lovely face and blue eyes, of her long white throat and the full breasts outlined by the silk of her dress.

'I can guess,' I said.

He sent me another look. 'I met her in Paris,' he said. 'I opened my Paris office in the spring of last year, and I was over there several times during the year. In September I went over to attend a big sale of silver, and I took Tony with me, with some idea of showing him the ropes and persuading him to come in and work for me. Loraine was at the sale – I didn't see who with. Then I met her again soon afterwards at a party; she was there with a man I knew, Louis Meyer, the London representative of a big Paris dealer. He introduced me to Loraine. We met again, several times. I was at a horribly loose end, just then, and I—' he paused. 'Anyway, I married her about a month later, and took her back to Deepings at the end of October.'

His mouth twisted, and his voice took on the hard unpleasant undertone I had first heard in it.

'It didn't work,' he said shortly. 'Naturally. As soon as we were married I knew I'd been a fool. In the first place, she hadn't wanted to go to England at all: she wanted me to settle in France, in the South. But there was Deepings – and David – and I insisted. Then of course there was trouble. And – again of course – it just didn't work with David; she couldn't be bothered with him, and he had no time for her. He's a courteous little devil, and he said nothing to me, but I could see he was unhappy about it . . . We had a highly unpleasant few weeks, and then Tony came to stay for Christmas.' His voice went flat and dead. He might have been reading out of the police report. 'He was found dead in his bed at three o'clock on the morning of January 19th. He had been strangled. There was a thin cord knotted tightly round his neck. It was the cord from my window-blind, and my finger-prints were on the little acorn gadget that you pull the blind down with.'

'Of course they were,' I said. 'I expect you'd pulled the blind down at some time or other, hadn't you?'

'Yes. That's the sort of thing that saved my neck in the end. They could think what they liked, but there was an innocent reason as well as a guilty for most of the things they found. Then ten minutes after Loraine discovered the body—'

'Loraine found him!' I exclaimed.

'Yes,' he said, with the edge back on his voice. 'She went to his room – at three o'clock in the morning. She was quite open about it, all in the cause of justice. The police were impressed. She admitted she'd been there before – often: it was a lovely motive for me to kill him, handed to the police on a plate. What do you think about that?'

'I think that three o'clock on a January morning's an awfully funny hour to be waking your lover up,' I said.

He gave a hard little laugh. 'You're right at that, sweet Charity. It's a hell of a funny hour. But she did, and then when she had fainted with the shock, and someone went to the bathroom to get some water, they found David there; my little David, unconscious and as cold as ice. When I got there, I thought for a minute that he was dead too.'

The hard voice stopped, and he stared at the sea. But I knew he was not seeing the white path the moon paced across the water, but a small body huddled on a cold tiled floor.

'He couldn't remember much about it,' he said at length. 'When he was fit to talk he told them that he'd woken with the tooth-ache, and gone along to the bathroom to fill a hot-bottle. He didn't remember

the time. But as he switched on the bathroom light
somebody struck him from behind.'

'He had no idea at all? He didn't hear anything – a
skirt swishing, or high heels? Nothing to tell him
whether it was a man or a woman?'

He gave a wry smile. 'Believe me, if there'd been the
faintest scrap of evidence that could have pinned it on
Loraine, I'd have pinned it,' he said viciously. 'Because
she was in it, all right. You can't live with a woman for
half a year, even the way we lived, and not know when
she's lying in her teeth. She knew all about it. But she
didn't hit David. It was a man. David was facing the
bathroom mirror – it hangs opposite the door, and he
just saw the arm raised over him, for a fraction of an
instant, before it happened. It was a man's arm, in a
navy sleeve.'

'Not a dressing-gown?'

'No, not a dressing-gown.' He grinned a little, and
his hand moved till it covered mine. 'You're very quick
on the evidence in my defence, aren't you? Yes, that
was one small thing: I'd been wearing a grey suit that
day, as well. And I don't possess a navy one.'

'Well, why—?'

'They didn't attach much importance to David's
testimony, you see. He's only a child, he'd had a bad
shock, the glimpse he'd had was too slight and might
have been imagined, and besides, he might be expected
to be a pretty partial witness, of course. He insisted
from the very beginning that it couldn't possibly have
been me – not for any reason, except that it just
couldn't.'

'And so you were arrested?'

'After a bit, yes. Oh, the police were very thorough and really very decent over the whole thing. It was all done by kindness. But one thing and another mounted up, and everything pointed the same way – so I was arrested.'

He regarded the water sombrely.

'I'll spare you the next part. Standing your trial for murder, even when you get off, isn't a thing to go back to, even for a moment, in your mind. It's like having a filthy and contaminating disease – degrading, exhausting, leaving pock-marks on your spirit that never smooth out. Again, everybody was very decent – surprisingly decent. And, though I got to hate the prosecuting Counsel more then anyone else on earth, it was a fair trial. The fact that I'm here proves that . . . oh, I've nothing against the police, even if she did lead them right up the garden path and back again. Other mugs had taken that walk before them.'

'But, Richard, did *she* do it? The murder, I mean? And *was* there a man in a navy suit? Who was he?'

'I wish I knew,' he said heavily, 'I wish I knew. They never traced him. But I think there was a man there with her, an accomplice, whom she let in to do the job. He may have come in through the bathroom window – it was open, by the way – and have hidden behind the door when he heard David coming. It was he who knocked David out, to prevent his seeing him. Then either he or Loraine killed Tony. I myself think that he, not she, did it – or why did she have him there at all?'

'Her lover?'

'Possibly. But even if he were spending the night with her – you'll have gathered that she and I had stopped sharing a room – and even if Tony had found out, that's hardly a motive for murder. No, she let him in to do the job.'

'Burglary, perhaps? And Tony—'

'Nothing was touched. And Tony had never moved from his bed. They said he was strangled as he slept.'

'But why—'

'That's it, Charity, that's the big thing. Why?' His voice exploded suddenly. 'My God, *why*? Night after night after night I've spent wondering *why*? If I only knew that . . . he was one of the decentest souls God ever sent, Charity. An ordinary, decent boy that nobody on this earth would want to kill, you'd think. They must have meant to do it, planned to do it, quite deliberately, but what the motive was I do not know. That was the strongest thing against me, of course – the fact that there wasn't a shadow of motive for anyone else to do it. And when Loraine confessed to being Tony's mistress that gave me the strongest motive there is.'

He was silent for a moment, his brows drawn. Then he gave his head a little shake, as if to rid it of the thoughts crowding through his brain.

'Try as I will,' he said, 'I can't see why Loraine should either do it herself, or connive at its being done.'

'What if he'd turned her down?' I suggested. 'It can take women that way, can't it?'

'*Hell hath no fury?* I suppose it could . . . but then what about the other man? Why should he help in that situation?'

'You seem very sure there *was* a man.'

'Yes,' he said. 'David may be only a kid, but he's intelligent, and he doesn't get rattled easily. If he said there was a man's arm then there was a man's arm.'

'Couldn't he have been trying to divert suspicion from you?'

'He told them the story as soon as he was fit to talk, and he had no idea what had happened, or that I'd even be remotely suspected. No, he told the truth. He thought he'd surprised a burglar.'

There was a pause.

'It's a stinker, isn't it?' said Richard.

'It certainly is.'

'And that's only half the story. I don't know yet why Tony was murdered, or why, apparently, Loraine should be so very anxious to see me dead.'

'But how can you be sure −?' I interrupted, then broke off as, like a whispering echo, I remembered her voice repeating in the frightened dark: *he ought to be dead and done with, dead and done with, dead and done with* . . . What was it they did to murderers? Buried them in quicklime, so that there was nothing of them left?

I shivered in the still warm air, and his hand closed sharply over mine, warm and strong and very much alive.

His voice was sombre, and he spoke with a conviction that chilled me again.

'Because,' he said, 'I'm next on the list. She couldn't get me hanged, but she staged another murder. And the second time, I was the victim.'

16

Madam, will you talk—?
(Old song)

'It was after the trial,' he went on. 'I was allowed to go, of course, and someone handed me a note as I was leaving the court, to say that Loraine wanted to see me at Claridge's, where she had a room. I got a taxi and went to see her. She was alone, and she had some news for me. Good news. She told me, quite plainly, that she was going back to France, and that there was no need for me to institute divorce proceedings.'

'No need? What did she mean?'

'She had just discovered, she said, that her previous husband, who had been missing and presumed dead since 1943, was still alive. Our marriage, therefore, was never valid.'

'But – was this true?'

'She showed me her marriage certificate – naturally, I knew she had been married before – and then a letter from a Paris laywer. The certificate, of course, was genuine; about the letter I don't know yet.'

'What was his name – the husband's, I mean?'

'Jean Something-or-other, I think.' He reached for a

cigarette. 'To tell you the truth I hardly bothered. I'd come straight from the dock, I hadn't even had a chance to wash the prison smell off my hands, I felt as if I never wanted to see her or speak to her again – and I wanted most damnably to get home and see David. He was still at Deepings, of course, and I imagined he must be half out of his mind.'

I must have made some inarticulate sound.

He said: 'Yes, I know. Well, I slammed the papers down and snarled that I hoped to God it was true, and that I didn't care what she did as long as she kept out of my way, and she could leave it to the lawyers because I didn't particularly want to stay and talk to her. And a few other things. It wasn't pretty, I can tell you.'

'I don't blame you. I'd have wrung her neck.'

'She wasn't frightened. She knew I wasn't the neck-wringing sort.'

I said drily: 'You don't give a bad imitation of it, at times.'

He grinned a little at that, then seemed suddenly to recollect the cigarette-case in his hand. We lit cigarettes.

'Well, our loving talk finished with Loraine throwing the car keys at me, and telling me she'd left the Rolls at Redmanor station and would I *ficher le camp* – only the phrase she used was more – direct, shall I say? – than that.'

I laughed. 'I get it.'

'You shock me. Well, I did as she suggested; I got the hell out of it, and, what with one thing and another, by the time I got down to Redmanor I was half sick with worry and reaction, and in a flaming temper into the bargain. The Rolls was there, all right, and I went off at the hell of a lick, with only one thought in my head: David.'

'And there was an accident?'

'Right first guess; there was an accident. There's a place where you turn off the main road, about a mile from my house, where the road skirts a quarry. There's a sharp bend about half-way down, with the quarry on your left, and a bluff of rock to the right – the road swings right-handed round it. In general it's safe enough, because above the bluff it's open, and before you reach the bend you can see if anything's on the road below. Well, as I say, I was going the hell of a lick. I could see the chimneys of Deepings through the trees in the valley, and there was nothing on the road, so I took a run at that hill. And just half-way round that bend I met another car, on its wrong side. I was well over to the left, but there wasn't time, and he held on . . . There was just room, only just, if I went into the verge; and he kept coming. I yanked the wheel over, something snapped with a crack like a gun, and we went clean over the edge.'

'Richard!'

'Oh, they had no luck,' he said grimly. 'The off-side door wasn't caught – I'd been in such a hurry that I hadn't noticed – and it fell open as we went over. I fell out. The car dropped to the bottom of the quarry and went on fire, but some bushes broke my fall, and I only got concussed on a ledge.'

'But – are you sure – couldn't it have been a real accident?'

'I told you I'd seen there wasn't a car on the road. He must have had it parked, waiting for me. I've had plenty of time to think about it, there in hospital, and this is what I think happened. There's a phone box a mile or so along the road, and he could have been waiting there as soon as he heard the trial was over. They must have known I'd make straight for Deepings.'

'But, Richard, why bother to tell you about the marriage business, if they'd planned to kill you?'

'She had to know just when I started for Deepings, and besides, she wanted to give me the keys and make sure I'd take the car. Then, when I left her, I think she must have phoned him. He had his car parked behind the barn near the foot of the hill, and waited for me with field glasses. It was a cream-coloured Rolls coupé, and pretty unmistakable. He had only to time himself, so that he'd meet me on the bend, and he could reckon it would happen just like that, if the steering had been damaged beforehand. I tell you, it went with a crack like a gun, and the wheel just spun in my hands.'

'Wasn't he taking a big risk of being hurt himself?'

'You have to take risks to get away with murder,' returned Richard grimly. 'But, after all, the risk wasn't so very great. He may have meant to swerve at the last minute, if I didn't try to crowd into the edge, but he could be pretty well certain that I'd pull as far to the left as I could, and of course, with the steering column damaged, it was a hundred to one I'd go over.'

'Didn't the police find what had been done to the steering column?'

'No. That was Loraine's one piece of luck. The car burned right out – there was hardly a piece left recognizable, they told me.'

'I suppose her accomplice had damaged the steering while the Rolls was in the station yard?'

'I imagine so. I found the car unlocked, anyway, and my own keys inside it. But that proved nothing. No, my story was more than the police could swallow, I think; after all, motiveless murders, and an invisible, elusive murderer – it was too much. They were quite right, of course, it *was* too much. I'd started by insisting I was being framed for Tony's murder – *why?* Then I'd talked of an attempt on my own life – *why?* It wouldn't wash, Charity. We're back where we were – where is the motive for these attempts?' He gave a sharp little sigh; and threw his cigarette-stub out into the water. 'The police were very patient, all things considered, but I could see their minds were beginning to run in all sorts of curious channels, so eventually I shut up and allowed them to write it off as accident.'

'What sort of curious channels?'

'Oh . . . suicide, for instance.'

'Richard!' I cried again.

'Oh, yes. Disgraced Man's Mind Unhinged by Trial . . . you know. The papers got it, of course, and said as much as they dared. But again, there was no proof.'

'And David?'

'The last time I saw David,' he said slowly, and with great bitterness, 'was when they arrested me and took me away. I wouldn't let him visit me in prision, of course. Then, when I was in hospital after the smash, Loraine did as she'd promised. She went back to France. But she did more, as you know. She took David with her. He never even came to see me in the hospital before he went . . .'

He stopped, apparently absorbed in watching the floating butt of his cigarette discolour, split, and disintegrate into a little mess of sodden tobacco, among the débris floating below the wall. I said nothing.

'As soon as the doctors would let me, a fortnight ago, I came over. I traced them as far as Lyons, heading south . . . and the rest you know.'

'But, Richard, I don't understand. David didn't believe all that about suicide, did he? And he thought you were innocent of murder; you said so. Why did he go with Loraine?'

Richard's voice tautened. 'I don't know. I suppose, if she never told him she wasn't legally my wife, he'd assume that, as his step-mother, she had the right to look after him when I was ill. And he's only a child. He'd do as he was told.'

'But why didn't he *write?* Why did you have to "trace" them? Why didn't—?'

He turned to look at me, and the slanting lamplight slid over his face, sharpening the finely drawn angles of cheek and jaw-bone, and setting his face into a mask of great unhappiness. His eyes were full of such misery and uncertainty that I looked away.

He said, heavily: 'I don't know, Charity. I don't know. Don't you see, that's what's such a hell for me?

I've stopped giving one single damn about Loraine or her precious confederate, or her shots at killing me, or even poor Tony's death. I want to see David again, and get things straight with him. I want to find out what lies they've told him to make him go off like that without a word. Perhaps, in the end, they got him to believe it all . . . that I was a murderer, I mean . . . and he didn't dare to wait and see me—' He broke off.

His voice, when he spoke again, was very quiet.

He said, his head bent low, watching the water:

'But you know that side of it, don't you, Charity? You said he *was* afraid of me, didn't you?'

I saw the sudden gleam and shift of his knuckles as he clenched them, and a wave of compassion went over me, so real – I mean so physical – that it left me shaking. I could not speak.

He looked at me sharply. 'Well?'

'Oh, Richard,' I said miserably, 'I don't want to hurt you any more. It's all such a muddle, and I don't know what anything means, or what to believe at all.'

His face softened a little, and he touched my hand again, a feather-light touch.

'We can't work the muddle out until we get all the facts, my dear. Tell me your end of it – tell me everything he said, what both he and Loraine have been doing and saying. Don't worry about my feelings – they should be pretty tough by now. Just tell me what you know, from the first moment you met him.'

I saw, as if a brush had suddenly sketched it in across the moonlight, the slight delicate branches and paper-thin leaves of the tree Yggdrasil . . . that shook and swayed as the cat clawed up the stem, then dissolved again into moonlight. I said suddenly: 'Do you know a man called Marsden?'

He frowned, thinking.

'Marsden? No, I don't think so. What's he like? Why?'

'I remembered something.' I said abruptly. 'I think David was perfectly right about there being a man in the house that night.' I began to tell him about the conversation I had overheard up at the Rocher des Doms. 'And I remember his very words,' I finished. 'He said: *I got you out of the mess before, didn't I? I got you out of England, didn't I, and the boy too?*'

Richard had turned sharply as I spoke, and his eyes were very intent. When I had finished he was smiling, with a kind of grim satisfaction.

'So we were right. So far, so good. It's only a very little, Charity, but it's something. I wonder just where this man Marsden could tie in with Loraine's missing husband, Jean-Something-or-other, who appeared so providentially?'

'If he did appear.'

'If, as you say, he did appear.' He straightened up suddenly. 'We'll soon know if *that* part of the story's true: I've got someone investigating it in Paris. It's beginning to matter, rather, too.'

He grinned.

'Well, who knows what else you've seen and heard? We'll have it cleared up before dawn at this rate – long before dawn, my dear, because you look tired, and no wonder. Come and get a drink, and we'll find somewhere to sit while you tell me your story.'

17

Madam, will you walk and talk with me?

(Old song)

'I shall probably get it very muddled,' I said, 'because of course a lot happened before I began to notice things particularly. And I doubt if I have the gift of narrative. But I'll do my best.'

So I began to tell him what I could remember: David and the dog, Mrs. Palmer and her account of the Byron trial, the trip to Nîmes, and David's reactions to his father's presence. The drive home, and David's half-confidence and strange childish insistence that I should tell Loraine Byron nothing at all. The snatch of conversation heard in Loraine's bedroom that night. And everywhere, the presence of the man Marsden – lighting Loraine's cigarette, loitering in the dark at the foot of the Rocher des Doms, driving to Nîmes in the bus, going up to the gardens with David next morning . . .

Richard Byron listened in silence, tracing little patterns in spilt wine on the table-top, his head bent, his brows frowning.

'So you see,' I said finally, 'why I behaved in the silly way I did. I didn't even tumble to the fact that

David hated her when he insisted that his name wasn't the same as hers. I just thought I had to keep you away from him. I – I rather fell for David,' I finished lamely.

He shot me a look that brought the blood to my cheeks, then returned to his drawing on the table-top.

'Yes, David,' he said slowly. 'We always come back to David. And the old questions: why he went away like that without a word; what he believes, now, about that horrible night; why he's afraid to meet me . . . Why, d'you know, I even thought they might have done away with him, too, until I got the anonymous letter from Paris.'

'Anonymous letter?'

'I got dozens,' said Richard briefly. 'The usual filth that always starts flowing when a murder trial opens the sewer. This one was posted in Paris, and whoever wrote it apparently knew me, and knew David, and had seen him there. It included, of course, a lot of abuse about – oh, well, that doesn't matter, does it?'

'Richard, how beastly!'

'But it gave a clue, you see. My housekeeper had told me that David went off with Loraine, and Loraine had told me she was going to France. This gave me a start. So I raised heaven and earth and the R.A.C. and shipped the car across on the next boat. And at my *appartement* in Paris – I have a room over my office – there was another letter waiting.'

'But who on earth—?'

'Loraine,' he said, grimly. 'Dear Loraine. This time it was signed, and it was written, not typed, but there was something about the style that made it just a continuation of the first one.'

'Was it still about David?'

'It was. She and I, it said, must have a long talk, some time, about his future. But, as David didn't want to see me, and she herself didn't feel like facing me yet, she was taking him away from Paris, and would get in touch with me later. That wasn't all, but that was the gist of it.'

'What did you do?'

'The letter was postmarked Lyons, so of course I went down there. I hunted about for a couple of days, café-haunting, and asking questions, until I picked up what looked like a clue. Loraine's pretty conspicuous, as you know, and the barman at one of the hotels remembered seeing her, and remembered too, that she'd spoken of going south. I won't bore you with the rest of it, but I traced them fairly easily as far as Bollène, and then I went wrong. They had been seen on the road to Pont St. Esprit, and that, as you know, is across the Rhône from Bollène, and on the way to Nîmes. Well, I followed my nose, and landed in Nîmes on a chance. It was a wrong chance, as it happened, but it turned out to be near enough.'

I said: 'No wonder you wanted to kill me when you got so near to David, and I got in the way.'

He said, remorsefully: 'I thought you must be in with them. You see, I didn't believe for a moment that David himself didn't want to see me. I thought she – they – must be keeping him under some sort of duress so that he couldn't write. I thought you were part of it, and I wanted to kill you.' He smiled. 'Poor little Charity, did I scare hell out of you?'

'You did. Is that why you told me you'd done the murder?'

'Of course. I didn't know how much they'd told you of the truth, and I wanted to frighten you. And I did. I made you faint. I want whipping for that.'

'It's done with,' I said. 'I was really scared because I thought you were—' I stopped abruptly.

'You thought I was what?'

'Nothing.'

'Come on. All the facts. You promised.'

'I thought you were mad,' I said, not looking at him.

He did not speak, but I saw his hand arrested in the middle of drawing a circle on the table.

'I only knew what Mrs. Palmer had told me,' I said quickly. 'And then when you – you were so violent, and David was so frightened, I thought you must be mad. I thought you'd have to be mad to have hit David that night . . . After I'd met you in Nîmes,' I finished miserably, 'I thought you'd done it, you see.'

There was a little pause.

'Charity.'

'Oh, Richard—'

'Charity, tell me something.'

'What?' I asked. Here it comes, I thought, here it comes.

'Did David say anything that led you to believe that I was mad?'

'I – I don't know,' I floundered.

'You're lying, Charity. You ought to know by now that you can't lie to me. Did David tell you I was mad?'

'Yes,' I said.

When I looked at him at last, he was smiling.

'You silly little owl,' he said. 'Don't worry so. It makes it reasonably simple.'

'Simple?' I echoed stupidly. 'But I thought you'd—'

'I mean, its something definite,' he said. 'Something we can fight. He did say it himself?'

'Yes.'

'In so many words?'

'Yes.'

'I see. Well, that means simply this: they've persuaded him to believe that it was I who bashed him on the head and/or tried to commit suicide with the Rolls. That's all that could be construed as mad, unless they threw in the actual murder for good measure. And, since I'm morally certain that they couldn't get him to believe either that I killed Tony or attacked David himself, then it's probably the attempted suicide.'

'So?'

'Well, as I see it, we're now in a fairly strong position to fight this belief. He trusts you, doesn't he?'

'I think so. Yes, I'm sure he does, after the way I helped him at Nîmes – to get away from you.'

'Don't look so rueful. You'll have to go back and talk to him, convince him, somehow, that I'm as sane as you are, and get him to meet me somewhere and talk to me. Then we'll get this thing straight, and have done with it once and for all.'

'You mean, take him straight away?'

'Of course. D'you think I'd let him go back to her? She and her lover – husband, what you like – can go their way, and David and I will go ours . . .' His glance met mine. 'And yours.'

'It sounds easy when you put it like that,' I said. 'But, Richard, if they *are* determined somehow to kill you – well, will Deepings be any safer now than it was before?'

He put a hand to his head, in a gesture at once indescribably weary and very youthful.

'It's the same old answer, Charity,' he said. 'I don't know. My own home . . . and for some strange reason it's no longer safe for me or for my son . . . *for some strange reason*: that's the centre of the matter. This whole crazy story – it's like a tale told by an idiot, held together by some lunatic logic that we can't follow till we've delved back through his mad past and found—'

'Freud in the woodshed?'

He grinned a little at that, and finished his drink at a gulp. 'If you put it that way, yes.'

By now the café was almost empty, and the steady flow of people on the broad pavement had dwindled perceptibly. A few Negro sailors went by, arm in arm with brightly dressed girls. An Arab boy, slim and golden-brown, who might have sat to Polyclites as Hylas, slipped between the tables, begging. People flung him lumps of sugar, which he caught with quick, greedy, graceful fingers, while his monotonous degraded voice mumbled for more.

'Sometimes lately I've thought I really would go mad,' said Richard suddenly. 'The murder and the trial, then the car smash and the weeks in hospital, and the appalling headaches I still get. And David. A sudden and complete disruption of my whole life, and David's life, out of the blue. And it's the basic unreason of the business that's getting me down; certain facts are there, but they can't *be* facts; there's no sane pattern to which they fit. That's what I meant before, Charity, that's what made me behave like a devil; I find my values slipping till my brain – how does it go? – *suffers then the nature of an insurrection.* Nothing makes sense; things have turned upside down.'

'*And nothing is,*' I quoted softly, '*but what is not.*'

He said quickly, half eagerly: 'Yes, that's it. That's what *Macbeth*'s about, isn't it? Nothing keeping to the rules any more?'

I said: 'But you forget. Macbeth broke the rules first and upset the balance. There was a logic in it, after all; and Richard, there still is. There must be an explanation, a reason, for your idiot's tale, only we just haven't hunted deep enough in the woodshed.'

He did not speak, but his eyes lifted to mine for a moment, and something in them made me speak urgently.

'Richard. I *know* I'm right. Don't you remember, only an hour ago, on the quay, when you said the same thing – about me – and you said that the rules *did* hold good, no matter what the evidence to the contrary seemed to be? It's *true*, my dear. You'll find there *is* a pattern that'll fit the facts. There always is.'

'But if it's an idiot's tale – if you're dealing with the borderland of sanity—'

'You're not,' I said flatly. 'And even if you were . . . why, in Looking-Glass Land itself they kept to the rules of chess. The rules don't break themselves, Richard.'

'In fact—'

'In fact,' I repeated, 'there is no such thing as "basic unreason".'

His eyes were on me, and they were suddenly very bright. He said, softly: '*Charity never faileth.* Yes, you're right. You're right. How very right you are . . .' He laughed then, and straightened in his chair. 'Forgive me, my darling. I've been living so long on the edge of nothing that it's addled my wits. Let's have some coffee, shall we? What'll you take with it this time?'

'The same, please.'

'*Garçon. Deux cafes-cassis.* No' – the vigour was back in his voice as he spoke to me – 'nothing really matters except David, and that part of it'll soon be straightened out. Once I've seen him . . . How tired are you, Charity?'

The abrupt turn startled me. 'Tired? I don't feel tired now.'

'Sure?'

'Quite.'

He smiled his sudden, devastatingly attractive smile. 'Then, on your quite unwomanly assumption that there's a logic in everything, we'll begin again at the beginning, rake over the ashes till we discover what makes them tick, probe every avenue to the bone—'

'I get you,' I said. 'Leave no hole and corner un-turned. All right. I'm on.'

18

The mordrynge in the bedde . . .
(Chaucer)

Half an hour and two coffees later, our minds were almost as mixed as our metaphors had been. We had taken out every fact we knew, aired it, shaken it, and set it in its place, and, while certain things had become clearer, the centre of the mystery remained dark.

'The motive,' said Richard for the twentieth time. 'Tony murdered, and two attempts to murder me – and no motive.'

'Murder needs a pretty strong motive,' I said stoutly. 'There's one somewhere, if we knew where to look. What do they say are the recognized motives – gain, passion and fear? It's not murder for money, or for love, apparently, but the third motive's the strongest of the lot.'

'Fear? But who's so afraid of me that they've got to kill me?'

'Obviously someone is, because they've tried. Is that logic, Richard?'

He smiled, though the smile was a little strained. 'All right. Go on from there. You're not going to tell me that Loraine's sufficiently afraid of me to want to murder me?'

'No. I thought we'd decided she was working for somebody else.'

'Our old friend X; the man in the car. Yes?'

'X tries to kill you,' I said, 'not for gain, not for jealousy, but because of something you can do to him. You, alive, constitute a threat to him, to his liberty – or livelihood – or life.'

The glint of amusement in his eyes was genuine enough. 'In fact, we're arrived at another hoary old friend; there's something I know that I don't know I know?'

'Well, it happens,' I said stubbornly. 'Don't try to muddle me. There's something else that struck me, too, about your chase after Loraine and David.'

He shot me a quick look. 'Yes?'

'It was too easy, Richard. If they had really wanted to hide—'

He gave a little nod, as if of satisfaction. 'Exactly. That's one of the things that puzzled me. It was too easy by half. She told me she was going to France, she sent me the letters, clearly post-marked as she knew they must be . . . she left a trail, in fact, up to a point.'

'You see what it means?' I said. 'She – or X – wanted you over here. You told me she tried to get you to come here after you were married. She still wanted that. That's why she took David in the first place. You'd never have followed Loraine herself, would you? If she'd written to ask you to meet her again you'd have left it to a lawyer—'

'I certainly should,' he remarked grimly.

'So, to make sure of you, she took David to act as bait, and headed you neatly to the South of France.'

'Towards X, I suppose? You're implying, are you, that, having failed to kill me in England, X is getting ready to have another shot over here? Laying a trap?'

'Granted they brought you over here deliberately,' I said uneasily, 'and it looks as if they did, then I don't see why else they should have done it.'

'All right, we'll grant that. They lead me to the South of France, but lose me at Pont St. Esprit, either by accident or design.'

'Which do you think it was?'

He said slowly: 'I rather think it was an accident. The wrong trial that I followed to Nîmes was genuine enough; another couple had been seen setting out for Nîmes, a couple that might have been Loraine and David from the description I got. I must have gone tearing off after them before Loraine's clue, whatever it was, had a chance to reach me.' He laughed shortly. 'So there they were, marking time in Avignon, while I lost myself chasing red herrings!'

'No wonder she began to lose her nerve,' I said. 'She sounded really frightened that night at the Rocher des Doms.'

'And no wonder they were quite pleased to let you take David about,' returned Richard. 'With me loose in the vicinity, looking for him, there was quite a chance I'd see him, and pick up the trail again.'

I objected to this. 'What was to stop you talking to David, putting things straight with him, and just taking him away?'

'Mr. X,' said Richard simply.

I looked at him, startled. He nodded. 'Loraine, who had lost her nerve, was better out of the way in Avignon. But where David went, you may be sure Mr. X went too.'

I drew a long breath. 'On the Tarascon bus,' I said.

Richard nodded again, and his eyes gleamed. 'D'you know, I believe we're getting somewhere. If we're right, it must have been a bitter moment for Mr. X when you so neatly scooped David out of my reach again, sweet Charity – and incidentally led me right away from X and all his works! It seems I may owe you quite a lot.'

'But what could he possibly hope to do in Nîmes?' I protested.

He shrugged. He sounded almost indifferent. 'God knows. It's a wild half-deserted country. Anything could happen. A body could lie in that scrub for months, and the kites would—'

'Don't!'

'Well, there it is. It's a good part of the world for a quiet murder; and that, no doubt, is why I'm being decoyed here.' He smiled without mirth. 'I wonder where the trap was to be sprung orginally? Avignon? It seems unlikely.'

'Loraine said they were going south in a day or so,' I said quickly. 'Nice and Monte Carlo.'

'Did she indeed? If that was true, it could mean anything . . . there's some lovely lonely country down here, with nice dangerous cliffs—'

'And a nice dangerous city,' I put in.

He lifted an eyebrow. 'Marseilles? Well? Why not? X fails twice in law-abiding Surrey, so he—'

'Gets you on to his own ground,' said I.

'You're jumping at this thing, aren't you?' said Richard, amused. 'So Mr. X lives in Marseilles now?'

'He may call himself Marsden,' I said doggedly, 'and read T. S. Eliot – which, incidentally, I saw him doing upside down – but I'll bet he's French, and I'll bet he's Loraine's first husband Jean Something-or-other, and I'll bet he has some definite reason for wanting you down in this part of the country!'

The amusement in his eyes deepened. 'So it's all solved, is it? If only I could remember what I know that I don't know I know!'

'Well, *try*, Richard!' I said, hopelessly. 'No, don't laugh at me. I thought this was serious! Think!'

'My dear child, certainly? But what about?'

I hesitated. 'Tony's murder. Murder's the only thing serious enough to make X go to such lengths, isn't it? I mean – if you knew something that would hang him?'

But Richard shook his head. 'That horse won't run, Charity dear. There's nothing there, I'm certain of it. The police went into everything, and I – God knows I've had long enough to turn it all over in my mind, every grain, every particle, every atom of fact in my possession. You get a lot of time to think in prison, you know.'

'Yes, I suppose so. I'm sorry I reminded you.'

'Don't worry; it doesn't matter nearly so much as it did half an hour ago.' He gave me a brief smile. 'But we're forgetting one thing, you know. Tony was murdered too, and also without apparent motive. What if X wants, not me for anything connected with Tony's murder, but *both Tony and me* for something we were in together?'

'The antique trade?' I said hopelessly. 'Here we go round the prickly pear.'

He shrugged again, and reached for his cigarette-case. 'Well, there it is. That's all the connection Tony and I ever had, except the War.'

'Had you flown together for long?'

'Not really. It was fairly near the start of my third tour that I pranged. Tony had been with me since half-way through the second.'

'That, and your meeting after the War – that was absolutely all?'

'Absolutely.'

'No shady dealings in Paris?'

'Not more than usual.'

'No witnessing a grisly crime in Montmatre?'

'No.'

'But you must have done,' I insisted. 'Think again. You and Tony must at least have witnessed a murder.'

He grinned. 'No.'

'Not even a very small one?'

'Not even a—' He checked suddenly in the act of striking a match, and his voice changed. 'How very odd!'

'What?' My voice must have sounded excited, because he shook his head quickly and struck the match.

'It's nothing; nothing to do with this affair. But, oddly enough, Tony and I did once see murder done.'

He held a match to my cigarette, and smiled at my expression. 'No, really, it's nothing to do with this. It was during the War; part of the general frightfulness.'

'You don't mean the bombing?'

'Lord, no. I wasn't young enough to class that as murder; that was just a job. No, this was cold-blooded murder, rather particularly beastly.'

'Tell me about it. It might, after all, have something to do—'

'I very much doubt it. And it's not a nice story.'

'Never mind that. Tell me, just the same.'

'Very well. It was when Tony and I were being taken up to Frankfurt for interrogation after the crash – we were the only two commissioned in the air-crew – and there'd been some bomb-damage on the main line, so we were hitched on to a little goods train that went by another route, up the Lahn valley. We had to stop in a siding to let an express go past. It was a filthy grey winter's afternoon, with snow everywhere, and a sky like a dirty dish-cover clamped down over it. God, it was cold . . .'

He was staring at the cigarette between his fingers, talking more to himself than me. I think, indeed, that he had forgotten me completely, and was back in that desolate little siding beside the Lahn.

'. . . There was another train waiting, too – a lot of boarded-up trucks, with some chalk-marks scrawled across them. We didn't tumble to it until we saw a little bunch of S.S. guards standing about, and then we realized what was going on. It was a train-load of Jews going East to the slaughter-houses.'

He drew on his cigarette, and expelled the smoke almost fiercely. 'For a long time, nothing happened, and then, everything seemed to happen at once. We heard the express whistle a short way off. Then there was a yell, a shot, a whole babel of shouts, and the S.S. guards seemed to be running in all directions. All, that is, but the officer; he never even turned his head. I heard two more shots, and a man screaming. Then the screaming stopped, as if he'd bitten his tongue, and the guards were dragging him out from between the trucks of the other train. I suppose he'd made a break for it, poor little bastard. Just a little chap he was, a little thin scarecrow of a man, bleeding a bit, and scared silly. He was crying when they dragged him up to the officer, and they hit him in the face to stop him.' He shifted in his chair. 'It was all so quick – far quicker than I've been able to describe it: There were we, hardly grasping what was going on, stuck with our guard behind the carriage-windows, and outside – that, all over as quickly as a curse. There wasn't a sound but the screech of the express, and the little chap crying. And the officer hadn't even bothered to turn round.'

'What happened?' I was feeling sick, but I had to know.

'Oh, one of them spoke, and he turned and looked at the little man, and smiled. Quite a pleasant smile. Then he just moved a hand, idly enough, and said something. We couldn't hear what it was, because the express was coming up, roaring between the sheds, but the little Jew screamed again, and began to struggle.'

'Oh God,' I said.

'They threw him down across the line,' said Richard. 'He seemed to lie there for ever, like a little black broken golliwog in the snow, then that damned great express engine burst out from behind the sheds and went by like a shrieking guillotine. I – I don't know what we were doing. Our carriage was locked, of course, but I remember battering at the door and cursing like a fool and our guard trying to stop me, because he knew the officer and was afraid of him – and of course we weren't supposed to have been there at all.'

'Did the officer see you?'

'Yes. After the express was gone he heard the racket we were making, and he turned and saw us. We were hauled up in front of him then and there, and I think we'd have been shot out of hand if we hadn't been on our way to being interrogated by General von Lindt, who was a bit more important even than Herr Ober-führer Kramer.'

'That was the officer's name?'

'Yes. Max Kramer. A great big blond handsome brute with eyes like slate. He stood there, staring at Tony and me, and I think it was the worst couple of minutes I ever had in my life. He wanted to shoot us – my God, how he wanted it! His mouth went wet, and his gun-hand was shaking a little.' He shook his head sharply, as if to dodge a memory. 'I can see it at this moment – that gun pointing at us like a wicked little eye, and that hideous hand curled round the butt; there was an ugly scar running right down the forefinger, and the nail was twisted and deformed. I remember how the scar showed white, and the whole thing, hand and gun, shook with a kind of lust. . . .'

I broke across it. 'But he had to let you go.'

'Oh yes. We went. I never saw him again. Our train moved off straight away, and we ended up, conventionally enough, in Oflag XIV. But Charity—'

'What is it?' The shadow was deep in his eyes. I wanted to tell him to forget it all, to stop talking about it, but I knew that the time had not yet come when he would be able to forget. 'What is it?' I said.

'The little Jew. I recognized him.'

I stared back in a kind of horror. 'You mean, you *knew* him?'

'Oh, no, not like that. I'd met him once, that's all, in a Bond Street gallery. He was a painter – a good painter, too. His name was Emmanuel Bernstein.'

'I see. Yes, that does make it worse.'

Richard's mouth twisted as he stabbed out his cigarette viciously in the ash-tray. 'One of the best things he'd done,' he said, 'was called *Landscape under Snow*.'

19

I say, there is no darkness but ignorance; in which thou art more puzzled than the Egyptians in their fog.

(Shakespeare)

It was very late. It seemed absurd that it was only a few hours since I had stepped on to the Marseilles quay straight into Richard Byron's arms. Then he had been my enemy, my nightmare, and now . . .

'I seem to have been sitting talking to you over café tables all my life,' I said inconsequentially.

He looked up at that, and seemed all at once to come out of his dream. He smiled, 'And I've been talking too much,' he said. 'I shouldn't have told you that beastly story. It's over and done with, and, as you see, it has nothing to do with this affair.'

'It certainly doesn't seem to,' I agreed. 'And there's one thing certain, that Mr. X is not Kramer – at least Marsden isn't Kramer. He was never a big blond in his life.'

'So that's that.' Richard looked at his watch. 'Time for bed. More coffee?'

'I couldn't drink another drop.'

'I'm with you there. Now we're going to decide what's the next thing to do, and then I shall see you back to your hotel.'

His plan was very simple. I was to return next day to Avignon, tell Louise what had happened, and get David to go sightseeing with me once more. I was to deliver him into his father's hands, and then Louise and I were to remove ourselves quietly from Avignon, to a hotel Richard knew in Aix. Here we were to lie low for a day or so. Richard would take David to some friends of his, the Dexters, who were spending the summer at Hyères, further along the coast, and then would get into touch with me again.

'Now that I'm forewarned to some extent,' he said, 'I should be able to deal with Mr. X, or whoever is following David about, providing he's on the job alone. And then, when I've put things straight with David, and got him tucked safely away with Bill Dexter, I'll be able to work out what to do. With David still in the open, my hands are tied.'

'It's all nice and clear and simple when you put it like that,' I said, 'if only it works. Where shall I take David sightseeing to meet you?'

He gave me a grin of pure malice. 'What about the Cathédral at Tarascon?'

'Beast!' I said, with feeling. 'I wish I was a good liar. Don't remind me of it!'

'Well, what about Arles – the arena, above the main gate? I'll be there by ten-thirty, and I'll wait all day if necessary. Of course, if you could lose Mr. X on the way . . . but don't take any risks. If anything should go wrong, you can ring up the *Légionnaire* at Nîmes, and leave a message – for Richard Coleridge, remember. Right?'

'Right.'

We stood up, and he paid the waiter. Then we moved out into the bustling throng of the Canebière. There was still, for me, something dreamlike in the teeming, sparkling, roaring streets of Marseilles. The crowd flowed round us, jostling and chattering, the buses clanged past, the cafés were hives of laughter and music, but for me, still, the only real thing in all that glittering pageant was the feel of Richard's hand on my arm.

'This way,' he said, and we were suddenly out of the throng and walking up a dark, half-empty street. 'Where did you leave your car?'

I fished in my bag for the little paste-board slip, and read it aloud: '*Bergère Frères, 69 Rue des Pêcheurs*. But I haven't the foggiest idea where it is, I'm afraid.'

'I know it. I'll call at your hotel in the morning, say eight-thirty; we'll have breakfast somewhere, and I'll take you to get your car. Then we'll go in procession again up the road to Avignon.' He grinned. 'And don't try running away again, my girl.'

'I won't.'

'You nearly foxed me at Cavaillon, you know. Who on earth taught you to drive, by the way? You're pretty good.'

'Johnny.'

'Oh, of course. It would be.'

'It was his hobby,' I said. 'It had been his job, before

he joined the R.A.F. He'd raced cars practically ever since he'd had a licence. He was wonderfully good.'

'He certainly taught you a thing or two.'

'Did you pay my bill at Les Baux?' I asked suddenly. 'Because I ought to ring up—'

'I had to,' said he, with grim amusement. 'I'd asked for it, after all, hadn't I, after spending the night in your room? I managed to avert arrest by some story about your being ill recently, and a bit unstable—'

'Dash it—!'

'Don't worry, you're getting better rapidly, but you're still prone to sudden impulses: it was quite a good story, anyway, and she believed it, mainly because it was less trouble to believe it than otherwise, and I was paying anyway. The French are realists; so don't you bother about Les Baux.'

'I'll never dare go back again.'

'One of the things that really began to puzzle me about you,' said Richard, 'was why the devil you should go up there at all; and why you should go armed with a book of medieval French poetry in any case. I somehow couldn't see an accomplice of Loraine's sitting alone up there reading the *chansons de toile*. And there you were, admiring the dawn like any tourist . . . You're a woman of parts, aren't you, Charity? Did Johnny teach you to read Middle French as well?'

'I taught French before I was married,' I said, 'and there are translations in the book anyway.'

'Well, I thought—' Then his voice broke off, and I heard his breath drawn sharply between his teeth. His hand gripped my arm, and I felt him stiffen. He stopped.

'What on earth—?' I said startled.

There was no one to be seen. We were half-way down a narrow, badly lit street, which curled its seedy way to join two wider thoroughfares. It was a street of tallish, faintly furtive-looking houses, which had seen better days, and now masqueraded as offices, garages, warehouses, and even shops. It was at one of the latter that Richard was staring now. I followed his gaze. The shop-window we had been passing was the only lighted one in the street, but apart from that I could, at first, see nothing remarkable about it. It was long and low, and was crammed with an artful and rather attractive confusion of chairs and tables, faldstools, jugs, and ivory chessmen.

I read the legend above the window: '*Werfel et Cie, Paris et Marseilles, Objets d'art* . . . Antique dealers!' I said reproachfully. 'Richard, you shop-hound—'

And then I saw it, too.

It was lying, beautifully placed on the sweep of a velvet drape, glittering in the light of the single lamp. It was a silver bracelet, where the arms of a noble house were wrought about with lilies and griffins and the wings of birds. And I had seen it before.

Richard's arm had relaxed under mine, and he gave a little sigh. 'How odd to see it there!' he remarked. 'I gave that bracelet to Loraine before we were married. She must have sold it in Paris, and it's found its way here. It startled me to see it, I don't know why.' He turned away. 'Let it lie,' he said.

I said: 'If she sold it, then she sold it today in Marseilles.'

He swung round at that. 'What d'you mean?'

'I mean I've seen it before, too – or one very like it.'

'It's unique,' he said shortly. 'Fifteenth-century Italian. It was made for Lucrezia di Valozzi, and there isn't another like it.'

'Then Loraine was wearing it yesterday morning,' I said.

There was a pause. I was angry to find myself beginning to shake. Richard's hand, hard and excited, gripped my arm. His voice was apprehensive, but I knew the fear in it was not for himself. 'David,' he said. 'We've got to find out what's happened to David. This means Loraine's in Marseilles already.'

'The trap,' I said shakily. 'The trap . . .'

'Trap be damned,' said Richard curtly. 'They'd take a shorter chance to catch me than this. They've none of them seen me since Nîmes, I'll be bound, and Marsden wasn't on the road today. Now listen—' He had drawn me back from the lighted window, and his voice was low and urgent: 'I'm going in to see who hocked that bracelet, and when. Your hotel is in the street at the end of this one, the Rue Mirabell; turn to the right, and it's about fifty yards along. Go straight there, and telephone your friend Louise at the Tistet-Védène. Find out from her when Loraine left, if Marsden's with her, and David – anything she can tell you. You know what to ask. Then come back here. Got any change?'

'Plenty. But, Richard, I don't want—'

He loomed over me in the darkness. His face was all at once grim, remote, frightening, the face of my enemy. His voice, too; it was hard, and the edge was back on it.

'You'll do as I tell you,' he said, and pulled me towards him and kissed me hard upon the mouth.

Then I was half walking, half running up the dark street, and, as I went, I heard the shop-door open and shut behind him.

Louise's voice, across ninety-five kilometres of crackling French telephone-wire, sounded surprisingly clear, and blessedly unruffled.

'Why, Charity! I'd been wondering if you meant to come back today. How's the ghastly village with the ghosts?'

'Not too bad,' I said. 'Louise, can anyone hear you?'

'Only the concierge, and he's as deaf as a post,' said Louise very sensibly.

'Well, listen: I'm speaking from Marseilles—'

'From *where*?'

'Don't repeat it aloud, for goodness' sake; Marseilles. Listen, Louise, I haven't time to explain now, but I just want you to answer me a few questions; it's terribly important. I'm in a bit of a jam, and—'

Louise's calm voice spoke in my ear. 'Is David with you?'

So it was true. She had taken David away. The damned woman had taken David away.

'. . . Charity? Are you there?'

'Yes.'

'Are you all right? You sound a bit odd.'

'I'm all right. Are you trying to tell me that the Bristols have left the hotel?'

'Yes indeed. Such a flap,' said Louise placidly, 'as you ever saw. Mrs. Bristol screaming and throwing hysterics and swearing you'd abducted him, and Mr. Palmer and the Germans and that handsome Paul Véry out searching—'

'Louise! Do you mean that David's *run away*?'

'This morning. He left a polite note for his mamma, and moved out, complete with dog. They found out at lunch-time. So he's *not* with you?'

'Of course he's not!'

'Well, I just wondered,' said Louise reasonably. 'You've been so thick with him, and then you suddenly announced that you wanted to go to Les Boos, or whatever it is, which seemed an odd thing to do. However, I'm glad you're not a kidnapper.'

I was thinking furiously. 'Louise, I suppose it's all genuine? I mean, he really *has* run away?'

'My lord, yes! There was nothing phoney about the way Mrs. B. went for me today and demanded to know where you'd gone. She was as white as a sheet, and—'

'Did you tell her?'

'No,' returned Louise calmly. 'I didn't imagine you'd kidnap anyone without due cause, and I don't like the woman anyway. What's the matter?'

'Nothing,' I said. 'Nothing at all. Louise, you are the most wonderful woman in the world.'

'Well, it wasn't anything to laugh about. In fact, the hotel was so awful that I just went away for the rest of the day. Naturally.'

Naturally. 'Go on. Tell me what's happened. Is Mrs. Bristol still there?'

'No. Apparently she champed around all day while the various men hunted about in cars and things, and then she left just before dinner.'

'Alone?'

'As far as I know. I didn't get in till after dinner. I must say I was glad to find everyone gone.'

'Everyone?' I asked sharply. 'Has Mr. Marsden gone too?'

'Yes. He left this morning. And the Germans—'

'Before David disappeared or after?' My hand was sticky on the receiver.

'Nobody knows. He checked out at about ten, but of course no one saw David go.'

'I – see.' I leaned against the wall of the telephone booth, with my free hand pressed to my brow, trying to sort it out. David had vanished. And Marsden too. That didn't look so good. But then, I thought confusedly, Marsden couldn't have gone *with* David, or Loraine Bristol wouldn't be so upset that she had gone to the lengths of accusing me of kidnapping.

'Was there any suggestion of going to the police?' I asked.

'Well, there was, of course,' said Louise. 'Madame wanted to, but Mrs. Bristol wouldn't hear of it. She quietened down after a bit, and said she'd been hysterical with shock – which was true – and she apologized for what she'd said about you. Then, apparently, she said she thought she knew where he might have gone, and that no one was to worry further about a boy's prank, and she herself would go to find him. So she packed up, according to Mrs. Palmer, and left on the seven o'clock train for Marseilles. If I were you, I'd come straight back to Avignon, Charity, my dear.'

'I shall, very soon. Has anyone else left the hotel?'

'I wouldn't know. I wasn't in to dinner, and the Palmers were the only people in the court when I got back. I can't say I was sorry; it's been a trying day, on the whole. I say, Charity?'

'Yes?'

'Do you know anything about this business?'

'A little,' I acknowledged, 'but I didn't know David had bolted; and I don't know where he is. I wish I did. Had he any money, d'you know?'

'That's just it,' said Louise's tranquil, faraway little voice. 'He hadn't. That's why he took Mrs. B's brace-let. He pinched that *and* his passport. He explained in the note that he needed the money and he'd send her the pawn-ticket.'

'I – see,' I said again. My heart had begun to jolt, painfully. Two facts: David was in Marseilles, and Loraine was on her way. And Mr. X . . .

'Louise, I must go. One more thing – did David say anything else in the note?'

'No. I saw it. She was brandishing it all over the place. It just said he was going, he was taking the bracelet because she'd never liked it anyway, and good-bye. Charity, tell me—'

'Dear Louise,' I said rapidly, 'be the utmost angel that you always are and forgive me, but I can't explain now. Don't ask me about it; I've got to go. I'll ring up later on. Angel. Goodbye.'

The voice in the telephone rose the barest fraction of a tone. 'I wasn't going to ask you about it, whatever it is. But please just tell me where you're staying. If,' finished Louise on the faintest note of interrogation, 'that's not a secret too?'

'No. The Belle Auberge, Rue Mirabell. Got it?'

'Yes, thank you. Good-bye.'

And she rang off.

20

By the pricking of my thumbs,
Something wicked . . .
(Shakespeare)

When I came out of the telephone booth I found, in spite of the warmth of the night, that I was shivering. I hesitated, wondering if I dared spare the time to fetch my coat. I looked at my watch. The call had taken less than ten minutes. My room was on the second floor, and the lift was standing empty; it was the work of three more minutes to go to my room, pick up my coat, and reach the lobby again. I said a polite and, I hope, normal, good night to the concierge, and ran out into the Rue Mirabell, hugging the comfort of my coat close round me as I turned the corner and plunged once more into the dimness of the narrow street. Round the next bend in the road, past the shuttered Boucherie Chevaline, past the double warehouse doors and the heap of sand and stone where the pavement was being repaired, and there, across the street, was the long low window of the antique shop, with the bracelet on its velvet drape under the lamp. My steps faltered, slowed, and stopped. I stood in the shadows, staring across the road, while the night seemed suddenly colder.

The bracelet was still there. I could see it, pale against the velvet. But the lamp was out, and the shop had the still, deserted look of emptiness. Richard was nowhere to be seen.

I don't know how long I stood there, stupidly staring at the shop, gazing up the street and down the street, alternately, as if somehow I could conjure his presence out of empty air. I even started back the way I had come, as if I could have passed him unseen on my way from the hotel, but I told myself sharply not to be a fool, and went back to my post in the shadows. Firmly I thrust back the stupid, formless fear that was fumbling at me with chilly fingers. I was over-excited, I told myself; I had had an exhausting day, and, before that, a shocking night. There was no reason to suppose that anything untoward had happened at all. I must simply wait. It was only fifteen minutes since I had left him, and after all – with a lovely wave of relief the simple explanation burst over me – after all, Richard had probably gone through to the back of the shop, into the proprietor's office. I bent forward, peering, and then smiled to myself. There was, indeed, a line of light on the floor at the rear of the shop, that seemed to come from under a door.

I hesitated for a moment. Richard had told me to come back here. Should I wait where I was till he came out, or go across into the shop myself? I stood in the shadows, undecided.

Streets away, the traffic's roar sounded like the

surging of a distant sea. Twenty yards off, on business or pleasure bent, a scrawny cat slunk purposefully across the pavement. Somewhere near at hand an engine coughed, and a car moved away with a roar and a shocking gear-change. I realized that I was shivering again, whether from apprehension, or nerves, or cold, I did not know. But I was not, I decided, going to stand in the street any longer.

Sometimes, even now, I dream of that moment, of what would have happened if I had walked across the road, and of what it might have meant. And sometimes, in my dream, I do actually walk out of the shadows, over the road, into the shop . . . then, if I am lucky, I wake up screaming . . .

I was actually beginning to move forward when the blare of a car's horn, as it swung into the little street, startled me, and made me take an instinctive backward step. The oncoming car was a taxi, and it shot down the narrow road, skidding to a stop beside me. Almost before it had stopped the far door opened, and a woman got out. She thrust money into the driver's hand, and hurried across the pavement into the antique shop. The taxi jerked forward and roared away. I heard the shop door slam behind her, and the tap-tap-tap of her heels across the shop. I saw the door at the rear of the shop open, and she stood for a second, as brightly lit as if she had been on the cinema screen. It was Loraine.

I no longer had any desire to move out of the shelter of my doorway. Thankful for my dark coat, I crouched back, my mind racing, wondering how Loraine had traced David so quickly, wondering if Richard was still in the office, and, if so, what sort of a scene was taking place in there at this moment.

I was to know soon enough. The office door opened again, and swung wide. There were three people in the room. I saw Loraine quite clearly; she was standing gesturing furiously with a cigarette, talking to a man who sat in an arm-chair with his back to the door. I could see his arm in a short blue shirt-sleeve, and one navy-blue trouser-leg. It was certainly not Richard. There was another man, whom I took to be the owner of the shop; he it was who had opened the door, and now he paused for a moment to fling a remark at Loraine before he moved out of the lighted office towards me. He was big and broad, and, though his hair was grey, he did not walk like an elderly man. He closed the office door behind him, and came forward to the shop-front.

Really frightened now, I pressed myself back, closer into the shadows. But he did not come out into the street; he was only locking up. I heard the sharp *click* of the doorlock, and then he moved to the window and reached for the blind to pull it down. It came slowly and quietly, hiding his head, his chest, his body, until the whole shop-window was a blank, but for the big white hand that gripped the edge of the blind. In that uncertain light the hand, disembodied, looked like some monstrous white sea-beast, a squid or octopus, floating in the nebulous murk behind the glass. A monstrous, deformed creature of the dark . . . *deformed.*

I pressed the back of one shaking hand to my mouth, as I leaned against the wall, cold and sick. Even at that distance, and in that light, it showed quite clearly. The hand was crooked, and an ugly, puckered scar ran across the back of it, and down to the twisted finger-nail.

The blind clicked down.

It was the trap.

21

Will you walk into my parlour?
(Nursery rhyme)

I don't believe I thought at all. There was certainly no plan in my head. I just stood there, in the dark doorway, looking at the shop. It did not occur to me that I had exactly no chance at all against them, that I was a woman, alone, unarmed; that even if I had had a weapon I would not have known what to do with it. It did cross my mind, since I am a normal law-abiding person, to go to the police, but imagination quailed before the prospect of explaining, in a foreign tongue, an incredible situation to a sceptical officialdom. And there was not time. Richard and David were in there, and they must be got out.

I walked quietly across the road towards the shop.

The street was luckily still deserted, and no sound came from within the locked and shuttered shop. I had noticed, two doors from it along the street, a broken door which seemed to give on to a narrow tunnel running through the block of buildings to the back. I pushed this open. It creaked slightly, and I slipped through, groping my way down the tunnel into what seemed to be a warehouse yard. The dark shapes of buildings loomed up to right and left; there were piles of old boxes, and an orderly stack of crates; ahead of me I could make out a pair of solid double gates, and, beside them, the darker cavern of an open garage.

I waited for a moment in the mouth of the alley, until I had got my bearings, and in a very few seconds I found that I could see fairly clearly. The moon that Richard and I had watched rise was dispensing a faint light from somewhere beyond the roof-tops, and, in rivalry, the glow of the city streets threw the same chimneys into warmer silhouette. One lighted window on my left cast a line of light like a yellow bar across the blackness, but it was a smallish window, about ten feet up, and the shaft of light went high, to be lost among the deeper shadows of the open garage.

I threw one apprehensive glance at this window, which I guessed to be that of the antique-dealer's office, and then I started on a hurried tiptoe search of the yard buildings. The garage offered the only real hiding-place, and I slid into its black cave like a ghost. Save for some boxes and a few drums of oil, it was empty. But a smell of stale exhaust still hung in the air, and with a flash like the springing open of a door I remembered the car I had heard drive off only a few minutes ago. I bit my lip in an agony of indecision and frustration. Perhaps Richard was no longer on the shop premises. Perhaps he – his body . . . I thrust the thought back into the limbo whence it peered and grimaced, and tried to discipline my thoughts. *He was not dead: he could not be dead* . . . with a little sob of a prayer that was not so much a supplication as a threat to the Almighty, I turned to leave the garage, and found myself staring down at a dark stain that spread hideously on the concrete floor.

It gleamed faintly under the oblique light from the office window. Its surface was thick and slimy. I don't know how long it took me to realize that it was only oil. My flesh seemed to shrink on my bones as I bent down, put a testing finger into the viscous pool, and sniffed at it. Oil. Nothing worse. I was straightening up when, out of the corner of my eye, I saw something on the floor of the garage. It had fallen behind an oil-drum, and, if I had not stooped, I should not have seen it. It showed squarish and pale in the shadows.

Now was the time, I thought, with the tiny remnant of irony that insisted on denying the realities of my situation – now was the time to discover the mono-grammed handkerchief with the message scrawled in blood – or oil, amended the other part of my mind, rather hurriedly. I picked up the pale object, which was, at any rate, certainly not a handkerchief, because it was hard, oblong, and about a quarter of an inch thick. It felt as if it could be a book.

It was a book. It was a smudged and ruffled copy of T. S. Eliot's *Four Quartets*.

In something less than twelve seconds I was across that yard, and crouching in the shelter of some crates under the lighted window, with Marsden's book thrust deep into the pocket of my coat. Suspicion, then, was certainty. Marsden had been in that garage; Marsden, in fact, might have been driving the car that I had heard.

But in this last supposition, it soon appeared, I was wrong, for, quite clearly from some four feet above my head, came the voice I had heard that night on the Rocher des Doms.

'. . . Why you had to behave as if all hell was let loose, Loraine. Couldn't you—?'

I had not missed much. They were still discussing Loraine's outburst at the hotel. Her voice cut in, petulant and brittle: 'It *was* all hell. That hotel . . . you don't know what it was like—'

'Don't I? I was staying there myself.'

'Yes, but you had something to *do*. Following that damned kid around. I hadn't. I tell you—'

'You still needn't have lost your nerve to quite that extent, my dear.' He spoke cuttingly, and she flared back:

'It's all very well for you, blast you. What d'you think I've been through, this last few months? You were sitting pretty while I – I've had nothing; no fun, nothing to do except cope with that – that bad-tempered iceberg, damn him. Then *l'affaire Toni*, and the police, and now this last business . . . all that waiting: d'you wonder it's got me down? I tell you, *I couldn't help it*. I've done my best, and for God's sake, Jean, leave me alone.'

Jean. Jean Something-or-other, the husband. John Marsden.

A new voice cut across the interchange, a deep voice, speaking a guttural French that I found hard to follow.

'Stop it, both of you. Loraine, pull yourself together; and you, Jean, leave her alone. She's behaved like a fool, but there's no harm done; what's happened today has cancelled out any mistakes either of you may have made.'

Jean spoke soberly: 'My God! we've been lucky! When I think of it – the kid walking in here as large as life, and his father after him!'

The antique dealer was curt: 'All right, we've been lucky. Then it seems my luck has got to make up for your carelessness.'

'Damn it, Max—'

Max. Max Kramer; John Marsden. The pieces fitting smoothly into place. The rats in the woodshed.

There was a crash as a fist hit the table. Kramer snarled: '*Lieber Gott*, will you listen to me? This isn't the time to wrangle over what's past. We've got those two to dispose of, and it isn't until I see them officially reported as accidental deaths that this thing's over. *When* that happens, and not before, you'll get your money.'

'And the papers,' put in Loraine sullenly.

'And the papers; and we'll cry quits, and you two can go to perdition in your own way, and leave me to go mine. Is that understood?'

'All right. What do we do?' This from Jean.

Loraine said, still sullen: 'I don't even know what's happened yet. Are they dead?'

'No,' said Kramer, and I felt a muscle jump and tighten in my throat. 'The boy's asleep; he should stay that way for quite a time; I gave him enough to keep him quiet till it's over.' He laughed. 'I've always had a kind heart. His father's had something to keep him quiet, too; perhaps it wasn't administered quite so gently, but then Jean and I were hardly prepared. . . . He'll be out for a bit – quite long enough, unless we waste any more time.'

His voice dropped, and I strained closer. 'Now listen. I've been thinking hard since this happened, and I've seen how we can use things the way they've played themselves. It works out pretty well with what we planned before. The boy and his father will be found dead at the foot of the cliffs – at our arranged spot. They'll be together in the wreck of Byron's car.'

'Have you got it?'

'His keys were in his pocket, along with the garage chit. It's in one of Bériot's lock-ups.'

'And the story,' said Jean, with triumph lighting his voice, 'will be that the boy bolted to meet his father; the two of them set off – for Italy, perhaps; and *pff* – an accident in the darkness!'

'Exactly,' said Kramer, with satisfaction. 'The child really played into our hands by running away. He even stole his passport to take with him. There'll be no reason why anyone should think about – murder. No one will look in that boy's body for drugs.'

'And any signs of violence on the man will be accounted for—'

'Exactly,' said Kramer again.

Then the purr of satisfaction faded, and his voice went hard and precise: 'André's taken the two of them, tied up in the van. He's been gone about fifte minutes. We should be there almost as soon as he is. He's a bit of a fool, as you know, and he's afraid of trouble; I told him we'd have to wait for you, Loraine, but that one of us would go after him as soon as possible, Jean—'

'What?'

'My car's in the garage on the other side of the street. Here are the keys.' I heard the jingle as he threw them. 'You get straight after André. See that he parks well out of sight.'

'Right. And you?'

'I've got to get Byron's car; it won't take me long. If either of them wakes up and makes trouble—'

'I'll know what to do.'

'*So*,' said the German.

Loraine said: 'What about me? Can't I come? I want to watch.'

Jean sounded amused. 'Chief mourner? What on earth did the poor sod do to you, *ma belle*?'

'You'll go with me,' said Kramer flatly. 'I want Jean's mind on his job. Get going, Jean.'

'Okay. Throw me my coat.'

I heard the chair-springs creak as he got up. I heard the small jingle of the car keys as he dropped them into his pocket. He was going. He took three steps, and the door opened. They were on their way to kill Richard and little David, and there was nothing I could do. Nothing. Somewhere out in the night, along that cruel coast, Richard and his son would hurtle to their deaths, and I would not even know where they lay, until I saw the headlines in the morning papers.

I suppose I was praying. I only know that my cheeks and lips were wet, and my hands were gripping the edge of a crate until the bones seemed to crack. *Dear God, don't let them die* . . . not Richard, not little David; there must be something I can do . . . perhaps, even now, the police . . . there must be something I can do. There must be. If only I knew where they'd been taken, I'd find something, somehow . . . if only I knew where they were. *Dear God, won't you tell me where they are?*

'Max,' said Jean's voice above me, half laughing, half casual, 'I'm damned if I can remember whether it's the first fork right after Aiguebelle, or the second.'

'*Lieber Gott!* The second!' said Kramer. 'The first only goes to a cottage on the cliff. The track you want drops steeply away from the road just beyond those big parasol pines on the left. This is a hell of a time to ask a question like that!'

'Isn't it?' said Jean insolently, and went out, whistling, into the shop.

I heard Kramer say: 'Loraine. Quickly now. Get on the telephone to that hotel of yours—' and then I was across the yard and fumbling for the catch of the double gates that opened on to the back alley. With Jean at the street door I dared not go that way. I must chance finding my way through the alley, back to the Rue Mirabell, and thence to locate my car. The road to Italy, the coast road, past Aiguebelle . . . I found myself whispering frantically as my hands clawed at the heavy catch of the gate: '*Bergère Frères, 69 Rue des Pêcheurs . . . 69 Rue des Pêcheurs* . . . my car, please, quickly . . . the second on the right after Aiguebelle; on the left the parasol pines.' And then, again, like a refrain: '*Bergère Frères. . . .*'

The bolt was rusty, and my fingers slipped and strained. There was sweat on my hands. I thought I heard the outer door of the shop open and shut in the distance. I thought I heard a soft whistle in the street. I couldn't move the bolt. I strained and tugged to move it, and it would not come, and something inside me strained too, and stretched to snapping-point. I couldn't get out. They were going to murder Richard, and I couldn't get out.

In another moment I'd have broken: I'd have been caught by Kramer screaming in his warehouse yard and beating the gates with my hands, but, just as the panic inside me swelled to bursting-point, a little door in the gate swung open like magic in front of me, and I was free. It was one of those little man-doors they cut into bigger ones, to save having to haul the latter open every time somebody wants to get out; and it swung wide in front of me, creaking ever such a little.

I bent down and stepped through it into the narrow back alley-way.

As I straightened up, something hit me. It caught me full on the chest, and I staggered back against the gates, pinned there by my assailant's weight, and with his breath on my cheek.

22

Needs must when the Devil drives
(Proverb)

Before I had time to do more than draw breath for the scream I dared not utter, my attacker gave a little snuffling whine and began licking my face.

'*Rommel!*' Relief made me weak. My legs shook, and I wanted, insanely, to laugh. I pushed the delighted dog down with a warning whisper and a hand over his muzzle, while my other hand groped for his collar. The inevitable piece of string was there, about two feet of it, the end snapped and frayed. David must have tied the dog up when he went into the shop, and the poor beast had eventually broken the string and come wandering in search of him. As I ran down the back alley in the direction of the Rue Mirabell I was busy with the new and minor problem; what on earth could I do with the dog?

I could abandon the poor beast, of course, if he would let me, but something in me shrank from such an action. I could leave him in my hotel, but the thought of the fuss, the explanations, the waste of time, was more than I dared face. He was running happily beside me, panting with the pleasure of having at last found a friend, and it occurred to me, too, that I was in no position to reject help of any sort. I might yet be glad, even, of Rommel's friendship.

I was proved right about thirty seconds later, as we plunged across the Rue Mirabell into another dark little alley, and a drunken Negro rose straight out of the shadows to lurch across my path. I tried ineffectually to dodge him and slip by, but, even as he gripped my sleeve, Rommel gave a snarl, and leaped for him, hitting him in the groin. The man doubled up and staggered back with a curse, reeling against the wall. I fled by, and Rommel with me, the pleasure on his silly face greatly enhanced by the satisfactory little episode. For me, remembering suddenly the reputation of the city through whose dubious streets I was adventuring alone, the sound of the dog's lolloping feet and excited panting were now enormously comforting. I gripped the frayed string more tightly, and we ran out of the alley into a street that I vaguely remembered.

This was a main street, well lighted, the road, in fact, down which I had come from Avignon into Marseilles. I had turned off it some way further west, in my attempts to dodge Richard, so the garage of Bergère Frères must lie somewhere in the maze of streets between this one and the docks. It couldn't be far, I thought hopefully, as Rommel and I crossed the street and hesitated on the further pavement; I remembered that I had not walked a great distance before re-crossing this street and finding the hotel in the Rue Mirabell.

I looked round me. It was not a street of cafés, and

there were surprisingly few people about. The news-
paper kiosk at my elbow was shut, so was the *boulan-
gerie* in front of me, but thirty yards away was an open
garage, the lights of its petrol-pumps glowing like
beacons. Someone there would certainly know the
way to the garage in the Rue des Pêcheurs. I tugged
Rommel in that direction.

One garage-hand was busy at the pumps, attending
to a car, but as I hurried forward another emerged from
the garage door, carrying a bucket. He put this down,
and, at my breathless query, pushed the beret back on
his head and scratched his hair.

'Rue des Pêcheurs, mam'selle? Why yes, but—' he
eyed me dubiously. 'It's no sort of place for you to be
going, this time of night.'

'But I must!' My insistence was such that his stare
became curious. 'It's most urgent. Which is the way?'

He rubbed his ear, still staring. 'I'll point the way out
to you, sure enough. But I tell you—'

'I must!' I cried again. He meant kindly, no doubt,
but my heart was hammering in my throat, and the
engine of every car that passed was like the whining
hum of a minute-gong. I took a step towards him.
'Please, m'sieur!'

His stare was all over me now, taking in my smudged
hands, my dusty sandals, the plaster-marks on my
coat, the desperation in my face. There was a glint
in his eyes now that was more than curiosity. 'I'll tell
you what I'll do.' He passed his tongue over his upper
lip, and smiled quite pleasantly. I wondered if he were
thinking of telephoning the police. 'I'm off in ten

minutes,' he said. 'If you like to wait I'll take you there myself.'

I grabbed at the edges of my patience and politeness. 'M'sieur, you are kindness itself. But I repeat, this is urgent; I cannot wait. I have to leave Marseilles immediately, and I must have my car. So—'

'Car?'

'Yes. At Bergère's garage. It's in the Rue—'

'I know that. But it's shut.' He spoke curtly; he was losing interest. He half turned away and picked up his bucket.

'*Shut?*' The world stood still, then began to spin. 'Are you sure?'

He shrugged slightly. '*Mais certainment.* It's a repair garage: it shuts at eight.'

'Perhaps someone – it's so very important . . . where do they live?' I found myself beginning to stammer; I was groping for words, my French slipping from me as my brain panicked again: 'I could go to the house—'

He spoke a little more gently: 'I don't know where they live. You could perhaps ask at the houses near the garage.'

A tram bucketed down the street behind me, the noise of its speed mocking me. A car turned in beside the petrol pumps, and the swish of its tyres on the gravel made the hairs prickle along the nape of my neck. I dropped Rommel's string on the ground, set my foot on it, and began to grope in my handbag with shaking hands.

'No, that's no use. I've no time. I must go now. I must hire a car. Please get one out immediately and fill it up. How much—'

'There is no car.' Interest, curiosity, perhaps even compassion, these were still in his eyes, but deepening there, too, was suspicion. Heaven knows I didn't blame him: if he could read my face as I read his, he must be able to see something sufficiently out of the ordinary. My whole bearing must speak my fear. I dragged at a handful of notes and held them out. 'A car, m'sieur, for God's sake—'

He eyed the notes, but made no move to take them. 'It is the truth. We have no car for hire. I am sorry.' His shrug of regret was genuine, and final. He turned away.

I just stood there, numbly, clutching the notes, and in me, the hope that had never been a hope at all, drooped and died. It was no use. Richard was dead. I could go to the Rue des Pêcheurs, I could knock from door to door, breathless, hurrying, desperately fumbling for words. I could find M. Bergère; I could explain to him: I could persuade him to open his garage. I could get my car out, and drive along the coast road to Aiguebelle and the parasol pines, I and this silly fluffy dog of David's. And when I got there there would be nothing to see except the moonlight on some car-tracks in the dust, and nothing to hear except the grating roar of the sea on the shingle at the foot of the cliff. I was too late . . .

Rommel turned his head and wagged his ridiculous tail. Someone spoke behind me.

'Mrs. Selborne!'

I turned, as in a dream. A tall man in a dark suit was standing by the petrol-pumps, looking at me. He spoke again, in English, and took a step towards me.

'It *is* Mrs. Selborne, isn't it?'

I knew him now: it was the handsome Frenchman from the Tistet-Védène. I smiled mechanically. 'Monsieur – Véry?'

He smiled back and gave a charming little bow. 'I never expected to see you here, madame; this is indeed a pleasure.' Then as I, at a loss, stammered something, his eyes fell on Rommel. They widened, and he turned on me a look half amazed, half quizzical, and wholly amused.

'So it *was* you?' he said. I did not reply, but he appeared to notice nothing odd in my demeanour. He laughed. 'Tell me, where have you hidden him – the little boy you stole?'

'I – I—'

He made a gesture. His dark eyes were alight with amusement. 'Figure to yourself, madame, what it was like at the *hôtel*, this morning! The cries, the tears—'

'Tears?' I repeated the word dully. I was not taking this in. All my attention was on the trivial task of folding the notes very neatly, and putting them back into my bag.

'We–ell, perhaps not tears.' He grimaced slightly. 'There is no love lost there, *hein*? But *you*' – his eyes were dancing – '*you* the criminal! Tell me, why did you do it? He was unhappy, the little one? Did he tell you, perhaps—?'

'No, no. I didn't—'

'You haven't been caught yet, anyway?' He chuckled. '*Bon*. You caused a lot of trouble, you know, but it was *fort amusant*, just the same. I thought I was going to have to miss the end of it; I had to leave today for Nice, and I was *désolé* that I should never know what happened. And now, by the purest chance, I pull in here' – he gestured to the pumps – 'and here you are, with the evidence of the crime, red-fingered . . . or is it red-handed?'

But I was not listening. My eyes had followed his gesture, and for the moment my whole world was filled with what they saw.

The mechanic was just screwing the cap back into the petrol-tank of Paul Véry's car. And what a car! Long, low, and open, with *power* written along every gleaming line of her, the Mercedes-Benz lay along the garage-front like a liner at a fishing-jetty. From where I stood she looked about thirty feet long.

'Monsieur Véry—' It stirred in me, that crazy little hope that wouldn't die. My heart began to thud.

At something in my face his expression changed. The amusement dropped like a peeled-off mask. His eyes scanned me. 'I am sorry. I shouldn't have jested about it. You are in trouble.'

'Yes. Great trouble.' I came close to him and put out a hand that was not steady. 'You're going to Nice, you say . . . could you, *would* you, take me with you part of the way?'

'But of course. The boy—?'

'It's to do with the boy,' I said shakily. 'I know where he's gone. Please understand – it's terribly important to hurry; let me explain as we go. I – it's so urgent—'

His hand closed over mine, for a brief, reassuring

moment. 'Don't worry, *ma belle*; we shall hurry. That car – it is difficult, with her, to do anything else.'

Two minutes later, with Rommel safely tied in the back seat, the Mercedes flicked through the traffic in the Canebière, and turned her nose to the east.

23

Tyger, Tyger—
(Blake)

Almost at once, it seemed, the glare and rattle of the Marseilles streets thinned around us, and we were threading the tree-lined suburbs, whose ever-sparser street-lamps and high shuttered houses flickered past in a gathering darkness. If there was a speed-limit here, Paul Véry ignored it. He drove fast, cutting dangerously through the remaining knots of traffic in a manner that made me at one moment feel glad of the speed we were making, and at another wonder if he reckoned the risks he took. If we should be stopped by the police . . . for the Mercedes made no secret of her speed, it did not need the klaxon blaring at the crossing to advertise her coming: on a rising snarl she swept through the last of the thinning streets, and roared down the tunnel of her own undimmed lights, racing like a homing tiger for the forests of the night.

The gleaming tram-lines of Marseilles vanished from under our wheels: the lights of the last house flickered through its cypresses and were gone; and we were in the open country. A wind had risen. The wind of our own speed beat against us, whining along the great bonnet and clawing at the wind-screen, but I could tell from the drift of the high clouds against the starlight that the upper air, too, was alive. The moon had vanished, swallowed by those same clouds, and we raced through a darkness lit only by faint stars, save where the car's great lights flooded our road for what seemed half a racing mile ahead. And down that roaring wedge of light she went, gathering speed, peeling the flying night off over her shoulder as a comet peels the cloud. Along that rushing road the pines, the palisaded poplars, the cloudy olives, blurred themselves for an instant at the edge of vision, and were gone. The night itself was a blur, a roar of movement, nothing but a dark wind; the streaming stars were no more than a foam in our wake.

The road whipped wickedly under us like a snake. The world swung in a sickening lurch as the tyres screamed at a bend. Then we were straight again, tearing hell-bent down our long tunnel of light.

Paul Véry glanced at me with a little smile. 'Is this fast enough for you?'

'No,' I said.

In the glow of the dashboard I saw him look momentarily disconcerted, and I realized that, in taking so literally my demand for speed, he had expected me to be scared. Even at that moment I could feel a wry twinge of amusement at the idea that anyone who had lived with Johnny could ever be afraid of speed again: this bat-out-of-hell flight through the roaring darkness had been Johnny's normal way of driving home. But then, Johnny had been – Johnny: I admitted to myself, on a second thought, that I had had several qualms tonight already as we had bullied our way out of Marseilles. I had been in this kind of car too often not to know just what she could do with half-a-second off the chain.

'Nevertheless,' said Paul Véry, decelerating, 'it is as fast as is safe.' He, too, then, had felt that moment at the bend when the tiger had nearly got away from him.

'I'm sorry,' I said. 'I was worrying. I'm watching all the time for their tail-light, and I spoke without thinking. I'm most terribly grateful to you for taking me at all.'

'It's a pleasure.' He accompanied the formal words with a smile so delightful that, in spite of my heart-aching fear and apprehension, I smiled back. I found myself watching him as he leaned back in his seat, and settled the car down to a steady sixty-five, his eyes narrowed on the extreme arrow-tip of light ahead. In its reflected glow his face was a handsome mask of con-centration.

The road tore towards us. Once my heart jumped and fluttered in my throat as a red light appeared in the blackness ahead, but it was only a small car, stationary, with a couple in it, a man and a girl. I sank back in my seat, and the blood seemed to seep back from my tingling finger-tips and slowly start to feed my heart again.

Paul Véry had glanced sideways at me, and now he spoke.

'That is not the tail-light you are looking for, I take it?'

'No.' I smiled a little uncertainly at him. 'I suppose you must be wondering what it's all about?'

His gaze was back on the road. 'But naturally. You talk of urgency, and you are anxious and afraid. Who would not wonder, madame? Believe me, I am eager to help . . . but there is not the least need to tell me your affairs if you would rather not.'

'You're very good. I – I told you it was something to do with the boy David.'

'*Eh bien?*'

'I *didn't* take him away, you know. But I do know where he is now. That's where I'm going.'

His hands moved a little, as if with surprise, on the steering-wheel, and the car gave a wicked swerve. He cursed it under his breath.

'Sorry,' I said. 'I didn't mean to startle you. But the rest of my story's a good deal more startling than that. I told no more than the truth when I said I was in trouble. I am: desperate trouble.' My voice wavered as the spectre of that desperation once more gibbered at me out of the dark. 'Life-and-death trouble,' I said, on a little sob.

'And you need help – badly.' It was almost a question, spoken very softly, without looking at me. There was a curious lilt to his voice, and I turned my head to look at him, the sob caught in my throat. Help . . . of course I needed help. Up to this moment, stupid with weariness and dazed by my terror for Richard, I had thought of Paul Véry only as a miraculous means of my reaching the little road beyond Aiguebelle. Further than that I had not gone. But now . . . the miracle was complete: I and Rommel were alone no longer, we had an ally, and our immediate objective was apparent. André was ahead of us, with Richard and David, and he was alone on the job. It was by no means probable that Jean, also, was before us: he would have had little, if any, start of us, and, at the rate we were going, we would almost certainly by now have caught any car going at a more normal speed.

André was alone, and there were two of us – and Rommel.

My heart lifted, and I turned gratefully to my companion. He was smiling; he looked extremely handsome, and also, I realized, entirely formidable.

'And where are "they" taking this little boy, *hein?* And who are "they"?' The strange note was back in his voice, and all at once I knew it for what it was. It was enjoyment. He sounded amused, excited, and not at all apprehensive. He had, of course, no idea yet of the real danger of the situation: it was the unusualness of it, the lady-in-distress touch, the mad speed through the dark – all this must be appealing to some sense of adventure in him. But I knew, too, as I looked at him as it were with new eyes, that no threat of danger to come would damp that enjoyment.

I found myself heartened by his demeanour, the lift of excitement, almost gaiety, in his voice and look. It was catching, and it was certainly, to anyone in my desperate plight, heartening, to be suddenly given an ally at once so eager and so redoubtable.

And redoubtable was by no means too strong a word. There was about him an impression of force, of energy leashed in only precariously . . . the whole personality of the man was, at such close quarters, almost overwhelming. I had, I realized, failed to estimate Monsieur Paul Véry. It was not only the headlong speed of the car that snatched at my breath as I began the explanation that was his due.

'It's a long story, and a nasty one,' I said quickly, 'and I mayn't have time to tell it all to you before things happen. But the main thing is that David, whose real name is David Byron, is going to be murdered tonight, along with his father, if we can't do something to prevent it.'

He shot me a startled look. 'But—'

'I know!' I cried. 'It sounds fantastic! But listen: I'll try to tell you a little about it . . .'

I began, stumbling a little in my haste, to tell him what I knew about Kramer and Richard and Loraine. He listened in silence, but when at length I came to Marsden's part in the affair, he interrupted me with an exclamation that sounded amused.

'Monsieur Marsden? *That* one? The rest, yes; I will believe it because you tell me so, and because I think you really are in bad trouble. But *this* I cannot think, that the good Monsieur Marsden is a murderer. Besides, he is English.'

'He *says* he's English,' I said sharply. 'But I tell you he *is* her husband, and he's in Kramer's pay. You've *got* to believe me. The good Monsieur Marsden, as you call him, is on his way at this moment to murder both Richard and David Byron, unless we can do something to stop him!'

I could see his face in the dim light. He was smiling a little still, but his brows were drawn with bewilderment.

'*Mais, ma belle*—'

So I was to be spared none of the nightmare. The ordeal by unbelief was to be part of it . . . and in my own bewildered terror I must try and sort out the affair's lunatic logic, so that this man might believe and help me. I clutched my shaking hands together, and fought to marshal my knowledge. I remember that the only clear thought in my head was a wish that Paul Véry would stop calling me '*ma belle*'.

'Listen, monsieur,' I said carefully, 'I am telling you no more than the truth, as I know it. There is no time to go back to the beginning. I can only tell you what is happening now, tonight, and beg that you will believe me. I'm not quite sure of this man Kramer's reasons for employing Loraine and Marsden to do murder for him, but I *think* it's because of something that happened during the War, Richard and a friend of his witnessed a – an atrocity, I suppose one would call it – in which Kramer was concerned.'

'That does not matter.' He spoke all of a sudden with sharp impatience. 'I have said that I will believe you. All this talk of the War . . . there is no time. Tell me now what you think this man plans to do – what *you* plan to do, now, tonight.'

The relief was so sharp, so intense, that the darkness blurred round me, and I shut my eyes and pressed the palms of my hands against them. I felt the car slow down, and took my hands away, to find that we were threading a decorous enough way between walls and houses. A festoon of street lamps swung up into the darkness, a lighted tram rattled out of a side-street, and suddenly we were plunged into a brilliance of neon-lights and cafés and the impatient blare of traffic.

'Toulon,' said Paul Véry. 'Go on. Tell me your plan.'

'Very well,' I said. 'Here it is, without trimmings. Somewhere along this road is a village called Aigue-belle. A little way beyond it, on the left, there is a group of parasol pines, and opposite them a lane branches right-handed off the road, along the cliff top. There, unless we overtake it on the road, a van will be waiting, in the charge of a man called André. In that van are Richard and David Byron, unconscious and, I believe, tied up. André has orders to wait there for the others, then they're going to stage an accident. Kramer's bringing Rich – Byron's own car, and Loraine's with him. But Marsden left before them. And at the rate we've been travelling, he's hardly had a chance to overtake us, but he won't be so very far behind.' I drew in my breath. 'He'll hurry a bit, of course,' I added, 'as André's alone on the job, and a bit of a fool into the bargain.'

I stopped. There was a pause, filled with the rushing wind. The town was behind us, and once again we were plunging down our lighted tunnel into the lonely night. I did not look at Paul Véry: I had pleaded my cause abominably, I knew, but weariness, bewilder-ment, and agony of mind were my excuse. I bit my lip, and waited.

His reaction, when it came, was unexpected. I heard him give a long-drawn whistle of stupefaction, then he swore softly, and laughed. But even as I opened my mouth to speak he moved one hand off the wheel to drop it lightly over mine.

'Forgive me, I did not mean to laugh . . . but you seem to be so deep in the confidence of this murderer. How do you know all this?'

I slid my hand from under his, and began to fumble in my bag for a cigarette. At least he was not alarmed, I reflected. I said: 'Does that matter now? You said we'd got to think of what to do.'

'Yes indeed.' He removed his hand at that, and reached in a pocket to produce a flat silver case. He handed it to me without looking at me. He seemed all at once to withdraw into his own thoughts; it was as if he had forgotten me, forgotten all but the immediate problem of action. When he spoke, his voice was abstracted, and he used his own language for the first time.

'Why did you not . . . light me one too, will you, *ma belle*? . . . why did you not go to the police?'

I answered in the same tongue: 'I hadn't time.' I took a cigarette from the case, and bent low behind the wind-screen, shielding my face from the draught as I flicked my lighter.

'And the dog . . . how did you come by the dog?'

The lighter went out, and I had to flick it two or three times to relight it. I huddled lower in the car, making a little draught-proof cave, and tried again. I did not reply, but he hardly appeared to notice; he was talking almost to himself, still in that preoccupied, almost absent voice.

'And the man Marsden; why should you be so certain that the man Marsden is the husband of Loraine?'

The lighter flared, and burned steadily. I lit the cigarette, and handed it up to him out of my cave. I fumbled in the open case on my knee for another. 'Does it matter?' I said again. 'Have you by any chance got a gun?'

'As it happens, I have,' said Paul Véry, and I could tell by his voice that he was smiling again. 'But tell me, how do you come to be in Marseilles anyway? And what is your connection with this Byron?'

I held the lighter to my cigarette, and drew at the flame. Then I froze, crouched there under the dashboard of the car, while the flame of the lighter, illuminating my tiny cave of blackness, flickered over the open lid of Paul Véry's cigarette-case.

There was an inscription there, beautifully tooled in the silver. It was only his name, and a date.

It read:

> *Jean-Paul.*
> *A jamais,*
>   *L.*   17.8.42

The lighter went out. Above me in the darkness, his voice said, ever so slightly mocking: 'Don't worry about it any more, *ma belle*. It'll be all right, I'll see to that. And you trust me, don't you?'

That phrase, softly spoken in French in the darkness

. . . the voice of the Rocher des Doms; the voice I had heard less than an hour ago in Kramer's office . . . And, like another echo behind it, too late, whispered the ghost-voice of Louise: '*Paul Very . . . something to do with antiques . . .*'

'You do trust me, don't you?' repeated Jean, smiling into the darkness above me.

24

Who rides the tiger cannot dismount
(Chinese proverb)

It was cold. The Mediterranean night-wind, pine-scented, sea-scented, sang past my cheek in a warm dark tide, but I was shivering as I hugged myself deep into my coat and fought down the rising hysteria of hopelessness.

Fool that I was! I had heard Loraine's husband – I still thought of him as Paul Véry – go for his car. In the time it had taken me to escape from Kramer's yard and run as far as the garage he could just have got his car out and driven across to fill her up. In spite of his connection with the Tistet-Védène, in spite (I told myself savagely) of his now obvious eligibility for the rôle of Loraine's husband, I had not tumbled to it. I had run to him in thankfulness, like a fool, putting our last pitiful little chance straight into his hands. Murderer's hands.

The lights of Hyères swam up in front of us; they swooped by, and were engulfed in our dark wake. I huddled deeper into my seat, and stole a glance at him. Now that I knew . . . oh, yes, now that I knew, it was plain to see, the glint of amusement below the insolent lids, the arrogant tilt of the chin, the whole formidable confidence of the man. And I was aware again, sharply, of the impression of excitement that I had received before: somehow, it was there, banked and blazing, under the smoothly handsome exterior: the faint gleam of sweat over his cheek-bones betrayed it, the nostrils that flared to a quicker breathing above a rigid upper lip, the hands, too tight upon the wheel. Murderer's hands.

The dim road hurtled towards us. A village, a huddle of houses, flickered by like ghosts. Ahead two eyes gleamed: they stared, then darted like fire-flies as the rabbit turned to run. Paul Véry gave a little laugh, and deliberately thrust down his foot. I heard the rabbit squeal as we hit it: behind me Rommel whined, sharply. Paul Véry laughed once more.

'Frightened?' The question came again; he must have heard me make some sound. This time I could honestly give him the satisfaction he wanted.

'Yes. Do we have to go as fast as this?'

He smiled at the tremor in my voice, but, to my surprise, slackened the car's headlong speed.

'And did you have to do that?' I said.

'Do what?'

'Kill that wretched rabbit.'

He laughed again, a charming, gay little laugh. He looked extraordinarily handsome. 'You don't like killing?'

'Of course not.' I hoped there was nothing in my

voice but an austere disapproval, nothing of the cold creeping terror that was shaking me.

The car slowed still further. The speedometer, under its masked light, showed a decorous fifty as Paul Véry took a hand off the wheel and dropped it over mine. The contact, warm, vital, and wholly mocking, sent a new shock through me: it was as if the man were giving off tangible waves of excitement.

'Do you?' I asked, knowing the answer.

'If something gets in the way, *ma belle*, it's asking to be killed, isn't it?' Warm and strong, his hand tightened over mine. The car's speed dropped further, and he turned his head to smile down at me. 'Not afraid any more?'

I said 'No,' coolly enough, but I drew on my cigarette as if for succour, and my lips were unsteady. For I knew now what I was in for. I would have to be killed along with Richard and David; that much was obvious. Like the rabbit, I had got in the way. I knew, too, that Paul Véry was a real killer, who enjoyed the act of killing, and that this mad ride through the dark towards his dreadful objective had touched in him some ghastly stop of pure excitement. And my presence was the final titillation. Darkness, speed, danger, murder . . . and a girl. Nothing was to be missing from Mr. Véry's white night.

The Mercedes sang down to thirty, twenty-five, twenty . . . We were crawling at ten miles an hour down a sloping black tunnel of trees, and Paul Véry had thrown away his cigarette; his arm had slid round my shoulders and his handsome face was bent close to mine. I leaned back against the arm but it was like a bar of steel. At my involuntary movement of resistance it tightened brutally, and I saw something begin to blaze in the eyes above me.

I suppose real terror is mercifully paralysing. I shut my eyes as he pulled me to him, only vaguely wondering if he would kill me here, or send me over the cliff with Richard. I even found myself wishing that he would watch the road when he was driving.

His rapid breathing was hot on my cheek. His voice said, with something ruffling its deep velvet caress: '*Ma belle* . . .' I felt his mouth searching for mine, and jerked my head away. He said again, on a note of surprised reproach: '*Ma belle* . . .'

And even as I wondered half hysterically why a victim should be expected to want to kiss her murderer, the cobwebs of terror blew aside for one moment, and I remembered that he still had no idea that I knew him for what he was. His pained reproach held no hint of mockery: passion had left no room for that. He was simply so damned handsome that no woman had ever refused him a kiss before.

My knowledge was my only weapon: it was a pitiful enough tool, a despicable tool if you like, but it was all I had. I didn't hesitate a second. I opened my eyes, and smiled Delilah-wise into his. 'It's only . . . do *please* watch the road,' I whispered.

I heard his little soft laugh of triumph as he turned his head away to glance at the road. I relaxed against his shoulder, and the arm tightened round me as the Mercedes drew to a sliding halt at the side of the road.

I threw away my cigarette with my free hand.

'Oh damn!'

The car slid to a stop.

'What's the matter, *chérie?*'

'My bag,' I said crossly. 'It went overboard when I threw my cigarette out.' I sat up and made as if to pull away from him.

He pulled the handbrake on with a sharp movement, and turned to prevent me, taking me in both arms and drawing me back towards him. 'Does it matter?' It was the brown velvet voice, irresistibly caressing, flatteringly urgent. He had forgotten to switch the engine off.

I hung back, pouting like a chorus starlet: 'Silly! Of course it matters! Get it for me, there's a dear.'

'Later,' he said, his voice roughening. His mouth came down on mine, and I sighed tremulously, and slid my arms round his neck. I began to wonder how soon we might expect Kramer in the Bentley . . .

It seemed an age, a ghastly crawling age, before he relaxed his embrace a little and spoke again: 'Trembling, *ma belle?*'

I managed a breathless little laugh, which became half genuine as I saw the satisfied vanity in his face. It never occurred to him to doubt my surrender. I hastened to make him even surer of me.

'Paul.'

'*Chérie?*'

'You like me?'

'A silly question, *ma belle!*'

You're telling me, I thought. I said: 'Even looking the way I do now?'

He laughed complacently. 'Any way, madame. Tell me – what is Richard Byron to you?'

He must have felt me jump in his arms, but he put it down to startled recollection. 'Oh!' I cried. 'How *dreadful* of me! I'd actually forgotten!' I tried to push him away. 'Monsieur Véry, hadn't we better go on? I can't imagine what I was thinking about!'

'Can't you?' He was laughing again, and I had to control a sharp impulse to strike him across his beautiful complacent mouth. 'Answer me, *ma belle*. This Richard Byron—'

'I don't know Richard Byron,' I said quickly. 'It's the little boy I care about, little David – let's go on, Monsieur Véry!'

'You called me Paul a minute ago.'

'Paul, then. If we're not in time—'

'There is plenty of time.' He pulled me close again, and I went as if in spite of myself. I knew he had no intention of going on yet. I was afraid of pushing my hand and making him suspicious. I relaxed against him for another long, agonizing minute, while I strained my ears for the sound of Kramer's car, and the darkness pressed in around us. The silence seemed thick and heavy under the trees. Only by the faintest quivering of her body did the Mercedes betray that her engine still ran. Paul Véry either did not care, or he was too preoccupied to notice. I wondered just how long it would be before things got beyond me, and guessed that it would not be very long now. Would I be strangled, like Tony, or—

I gave another long sigh, and drew away. 'We must

go,' I said huskily. 'The little boy, Paul, *chéri* – we mustn't forget him. I'd never forgive myself if anything happened to him because we'd—' I stopped and put up a hand to his cheek. 'Let's go on, Paul.'

He was as taut as a wire, and breathing fast. There was a queer look in his eyes, a kind of cold blaze that was uncanny, a blank look that I knew, suddenly, was the look of the killer. His hands moved, blindly. Things would be beyond me any moment now.

I pushed his hands away gently. 'Please!' I said. 'Get me my bag and then we'll go.'

He didn't move, but sat there still with his eyes on me.

I smiled at him. 'All right, handsome,' I said. 'We don't go. But get it for me anyway. I feel a fright and I want my mirror.'

I leaned forward quickly and kissed him, as earnest of good intentions, then reached across him and opened the door. He hesitated, then with a little shrug he got out of the car. *Humour the victim; she'll come quietly* . . .

I had dropped the bag before the car stopped, and I judged it to be about twenty yards back.

He walked back up the road, peering at the dark verge.

I counted his steps, and put my hand on the hand-brake, releasing the ratchet. I held it there, waiting.

Five, six, seven . . . he paused and I thought he glanced back.

'Can't you find it?' I called. 'Shall I come?'

'It's all right.' He moved on slowly.

Eight, nine. . . .

I reached a foot over to the left and threw out the clutch. We were on a slope; I eased the gear-lever into second.

Ten, eleven. . . .

'Here it is,' he said, and stooped to pick it up.

In a flash I was in the driver's seat. I shoved the brake off, opened the throttle with a roar, and let in the clutch. Behind me, I heard a shout and a curse. The Mercedes jerked forward sharply – too sharply. For a moment I feared I would stall her, and threw out the clutch again. Then she caught hold as a race-horse takes the bit, and we were away.

But my moment of fumbling with the unfamiliar controls had cost me dear enough.

As I swung her out to the crown of the road and changed up, I heard his hoarse breathing and the thud of feet, and felt the lurch as he flung himself on to the running-board of the car.

'*Rommel!*' I screamed above the rising snarl of the engine. '*Get him, Rommel!*'

I heard the dog give an excited bark, but there was no movement of attack. After all, the dog had seen me kissing the man only a few seconds before. Then I remembered that Paul Véry had a gun, and called, for the dog's sake, even more urgently: '*Down, Rommel!*' and heard Paul Véry's ugly little breathless laugh.

The Mercedes gathered speed with a roar. The man was cursing behind me as he clung to the rear door. We plunged out of the tunnel of trees, and went up a hill with the sickening swoop of a swing. Ahead of us, once more, our great flood-lights made a funnel into the dark, and we hurtled down their narrowing glare.

In control now, my hands on the wheel, I felt suddenly, beautifully, icily cold. The needle began to creep over to the right of the dial. We slashed through a tiny village. The name Euzès swam up for a second into the light, and vanished, while I knitted my brows and tried to remember the map.

The Mercedes roared on, and out of the corner of my eye I saw Paul Véry, clinging like a remora, give a heave of his muscles and lift a leg to climb inboard. I waited till the leg was just about to slide over the door, then I gave the wheel a jerk that sent the car across the road in a sickening, screeching swerve.

I heard him scream, saw him lurch outwards, but somehow he managed to retain his grip. He clung there, huddled together, yelling God knew what blasphemies at me.

I gave him a moment or so, and then I did it again. The tyres tore at the road, and I listened indifferently enough. If I had a burst, it would be just too bad, but unless I could get rid of Paul Véry and his gun, then I might just as well die this way as any other. I drove my foot down and dragged at the wheel again. The rear wheels skidded savagely, and the car bucked like a mad stallion. The lights careened dizzily across the night, and the darkness swung in a great arc round us. For a moment I thought I had done it too violently, and had lost control. Paul Véry was yelling again, and I heard the frightened dog give a sharp howl as he was flung down. The car, rocking madly, lunged forward again at the same wicked pace. The beam swung ahead, swung and steadied like a searchlight. Two fir-trees flickered by like ghosts, and then the lights met – nothing.

The road ahead had switched sharp left. I saw the verge of it leap towards our wheels, and beyond it a yard of dusty ground where thin grass waved spectral antennae against an immensity of darkness. Stars and wind, and a strange shifting luminous abyss of darkness. The edge of the sea.

This time I skidded the Mercedes in earnest. The wheel kicked like a live thing, and the dust mushroomed up behind us in an atomic cloud. We only missed hitting a rock with our off-front wheel because both off-side wheels were a foot from the ground.

Then we were round. There was blood on my bottom lip, but I was feeling good.

Then I realized that the left-handed swerve had helped Paul Véry to heave himself inboard at last. Cursing, half sobbing, he flung himself into the car, and, almost before I knew what had happened, he had scrambled into the front seat and was crouched beside me, thrusting a shaking hand into the pocket of his coat.

25

In this heedless fury
He may show violence to cross himself.
I'll follow the event . . .

(Tourneur)

'Come on, you——,' he said, in an ugly voice. 'Pull her up, or you'll get it! I warned you I carried a gun!'

I didn't even glance at him. The second turning past Aiguebelle, I was thinking . . . by the big parasol pines . . .

'In the belly,' said Paul Véry, and added a filthy word.

I laughed. I was as cool as lake-water, and, for the moment, no more ruffled. The feel of that lovely car under my hands, in all her power and splendour, was to me like the feel of a sword in the hand of a man who has been fighting unarmed. The Mercedes was my weapon now, and by God! I would use her. I knew just how frightened Paul Véry was: I had watched it all, the gradual stretching of his nerves . . . the savage excitement of his murderous assignment, the acute pleasure of baiting me, the speed, the anticipation of the final thrill . . . and then, this. The man's nerves were rasped naked. I had realized, watching him driving, that he was more than half afraid of his own speed. The delicious excitement of frightening himself, of terrifying me, had been half the thrill. No first-rate driver – I could hear Johnny telling me yet again – no first-rate driver is ever excited at speed. Driving, he would add, is just a job, and you can't afford to let your brain revv up along with your engine. Then he would give that little smile of his, and the hedges would accelerate past us into a long grey blur. *When you let excitement in*, Johnny would add, in a lecture-room sort of voice, *fear will follow*.

And fear was in the car with us now. I could hear it raw in his voice. I could smell the sweat of it.

And I had in my hands the weapon to break him with. If I could smash his nerve completely before we reached the parasol pines . . . if I could get that gun away from him . . .

So I laughed, and drove my lovely shining sword slashing through the night.

'Put the thing away,' I said contemptuously. 'If you shoot me, what d'you suppose would happen to the car – and you?'

I heard his breath hiss, and thought for a moment that he was far enough gone to shoot without thinking. But he didn't. He merely cursed again, and moved up to me until I could feel something hard pressing against my body through my coat. It was shaking a little.

'I mean it,' he said hoarsely. 'I'll do you, you – ! Pull in, I tell you, or I'll blow a hole in your guts and take the chance of stopping the car myself!'

We were on a long straight stretch of road. I drove my right foot hard down, and the Mercedes tore up the straight with a rising scream. The needle swung hard to the right and held there.

'Some chance,' I said derisively, 'but go ahead. It's Kramer's car, after all; and he's a fool to lend it you when he must know you're a lousy driver.'

The gun wavered. I heard him let out a quivering breath. 'If you tickle me with that thing at this speed,' I added, 'I can't answer for the consequences.'

The gun withdrew. Ahead, the road curved, and I let my foot up a bit. Above the roar of the overdrive I heard him begin to curse again . . . 'If I'd guessed you knew, you –, if I'd guessed—' he said between his teeth, and told me what he would have liked to do to me. He was speaking in French, and gutter-French at that, so I missed a good deal of it, but I had to stop it somehow, before it took my mind off the road.

I cut across the stream of filth. 'But it was obvious that I knew, monsieur.'

That shook him. 'How?'

My voice dripped contempt like an icicle. 'Do you really imagine that I'd have let you maul me about like that because I *liked* it? My dear Monsieur Véry, as a lover you'd hardly even pass the first test—'

Then he lurched at me. In lashing his precious vanity, I had gone too far. I thought he was going to shoot me and damn the consequences, but instead he lunged savagely at the wheel. I thought he had it, and that we would all go over the cliff; but he missed his grab, and fell against me, clawing at my legs.

I jerked the wheel, stamped on the brake, and sent the rear of the car round again in a left-handed skid. He was flung away from me against the side of the car.

'Keep your hands off me, please,' I told him, rather breathlessly, and straightened the Mercedes up.

He did not answer. He stayed slumped against the righthand door of the car, breathing noisily through his throat. Poor Rommel, behind us, was whining with fear. I began to wonder just how much more assault and battery the tyres would stand.

And at that moment we roared by a fork in the road.

The first fork to the right. Not far to go. For the first time I glanced briefly at Paul Véry, and experienced a sense of shock at what I saw.

He, at least, had had as much assault and battery as his nerves could take. Gone was the immaculate Frenchman of the Tistet-Védène, gone the velvet-voiced Don Juan of the Mediterranean night; in their place huddled a man with twitching hands and a face shining with sweat. Nothing, not even fear, could strip Paul Véry of his extraordinary good looks, but, some-how, they had cheapened in front of my eyes: the man who sat there, staring in fascinated horror at the hurtling road, might have been brought up in any Paris gutter.

Formidable no longer. The power and competence that had seemed the very essence of the man had vanished: defeat – defeat by a woman – had knocked the props from under him. But he was still dangerous. The menace had not disappeared, it had only changed in quality. I was facing, instead of a powerful and relentless executioner, a mean and unpredictable thug.

What was more, I thought, a stupid thug. Only a stupid man, knowing how much I knew, would have talked to me as he had, taken the risks that he had taken, all for a moment's self-gratification. The significance of his final exchange with Kramer suddenly struck me: only a conceited fool would have forgotten, or pretended to forget, such information at such a moment. Paul Véry was a tool, and, up to a point, a good tool. But shake him out of his master's grip, and he was lost.

These speculations, flashing through my mind in the brief moment before I turned back to watch the road, effectively silenced any further attempts on my part to bait Paul Véry. In deliberately trying to crack his nerve, I had been running a far graver risk than I had known. He was, actually, quite stupid enough, in a moment of blind rage, to have shot me as I drove. The last incident had proved it, when, maddened by my mockery, he had flung himself at the wheel. If, at that moment, he had had his gun in his hand . . .

My heart gave a jerk in my breast, then seemed to tip over, sickeningly, and spill chilled blood down all my veins, so that even my fingers tingled.

If he had had his gun.

Clearly, in imagination, I heard his voice again, as I had heard it in Kramer's office. '*Throw me my coat.*' Would he have spoken so carelessly if there had been a gun in the pocket? I remembered him standing, dark and handsome in his well-fitting suit, by the petrol pumps in Marseilles. No bulging pocket had spoiled the fit of that coat . . .

I flashed a look at him as I lifted my foot a little. His eyes were fixed on the road.

I drew my left hand softly off the wheel, and, with a breath that was a prayer, felt down beside me. There was a pocket on the car door. I slipped my hand into it.

Cold, deadly, and infinitely comforting, the gun slid into my grasp.

And at that moment, like great grey clouds billowing in the furthermost tip of our beam of light, I saw the parasol pines.

26

We will die, all three
(Shakespeare)

Like a flash, I cut out the headlights, but Paul Véry had seen them. I saw him stiffen, and shoot his neck out like a bird of prey.

There was only one thing to do. I must drive straight on past the turning, ditch my companion some way beyond, and then return to deal with André alone. It seems odd that it never occurred to me to shoot Paul Véry – though perhaps not; I had never handled a gun in my life.

'Listen to me,' I said rapidly. We were nearly there. The pines stood back from the road, making a great grove like a tent. 'I've got—'

But I was too late. Even as I spoke the first of the great trees loomed over the car, shutting out the stars, and our dimmed lights had picked out the shape of a van, parked on the beaten dust a little way ahead, and, beside the van, the figure of a man. André, who was a bit of a fool, had not parked out of sight.

Paul Véry let out a yell: '*André! Ici Jean! Au secours!*'

I switched the headlamps full on, and trod on the

accelerator. The beam of light shot out, catching the man who ran forward under the cover of the pines.

It was Marsden. He had a gun in his hand.

'*A moi! André!*' yelled Paul Véry. He was standing, leaning forward, half out of the car.

Marsden had reached the edge of the road. Was in the road. I put a fist down on the klaxon, and my foot hard down on the boards, and, with a little sob of pure terror, I drove that ton or so of murderous, screaming metal straight at him.

I saw him jump; at least, I think I did, but the next few seconds were just a terrifying blur. I remember Marsden's face, white in the roaring light; his mouth was a gaping hole; he was yelling. There was a scarlet stab of flame: another. Then the car hit something, and the whole world heeled over in a rocketing, exploding skid. The Mercedes seemed to rear straight up in the air, and her headlights raked a dizzy arc of sky. Then they went out, and darkness stamped down on us as a man stamps on a beetle. Clinging to that crazily kicking wheel, blinded, half-stunned, wholly automatic, I fought the car. For a moment I thought I had her, then she swept into a bucketing turn. The night split, wheeled, hung suspended for a million years, then shattered into splinters of flame. Then silence, broken only by the tiny tinkle of falling glass.

There was a shout, a thud of feet running. The door of the Mercedes was wrenched open, and hands seized me out of the darkness.

There was a roaring in my ears. The night, the stars, were spiralling down an enormous, narrowing funnel.

Somewhere, far down the gyroscope, I heard a rough exclamation, then another shout – voices, urgent, sharp with something that might have been fear. Hands moved over me, patting, searching. Someone had hold of my head, and was forcing liquid between my teeth.

I choked, gasped, stirred, and the gyrating universe whirred slowly to a standstill, re-focusing itself around me. The stars steadied themselves, and hung, only faintly tremulous, in a still pall of sky. There were two men beside the car. One was holding me; the other bent over me in the darkness, peering down. His face blurred palely in front of me; it was Marsden. I was conscious, first of all, of a tremendous wave of pure relief; I hadn't killed him after all. Then I began to struggle feebly against the arms that held me.

'I've got a gun,' I said firmly.

Amazingly, somebody laughed, and the arms tightened.

'Lie still, you little fire-eater. Haven't you done enough for one night?'

I turned my head and blinked stupidly.

'*Richard!* But – but you're tied up in the van. I was going to rescue you.'

He laughed again, a little shakenly. 'Yes, I know, my darling. But there's no need to run over the police in the process.'

'*Police?*'

Marsden was grinning down at me. 'Strictly unofficial, madam. But Scotland Yard in person!'

'I – I'm awfully sorry,' I said feebly. 'I thought you

were André. One of *them*, anyway. And you shot at me, didn't you?'

'We both did,' said Marsden ruefully. 'I knew it was Kramer's car, and I thought he'd seen me and was getting away.'

'But he was yelling for help.'

'My French isn't all that good,' said Marsden simply, 'and I couldn't really hear him anyway. There wasn't a great deal of time to think, you know.'

Richard spoke. 'Can you move all right, Charity? You'd better get out of the car. It's in a rather uncertain position, to say the least.'

I sat up out of his arms and felt my limbs gingerly.

'I think I'm all right.' With their assistance I climbed out of the Mercedes. Now that my eyes were accustomed to the darkness I could see quite clearly in the starlight. The car had skidded clean off the main road, and had ended up some yards down the track on the right, facing the way I had come. She was standing, decorously enough, on the seaward verge of the track, and for a moment I could not see what Richard meant. Then I saw. The night swayed perilously, and I was glad of the support of Richard's arm. The edge of the little road was the edge of the cliffs. A yard beyond the near-wheels of the car, the ground dropped sheer to the sea, three hundred feet below.

'I – I had some luck, didn't I?' I said shakily. 'What did we hit?'

'Nothing. Marsden got one of your front tyres. You turned round twice and skated backwards down here.

The car's not even dented – except for a headlamp. I did that.'

I pushed my hair back from my forehead, and took a deep breath of the sweet night air. Things had steadied round me, and I felt a good deal more normal. Richard and Marsden were gently urging me across the road and under cover of the trees.

'It sounds like some very pretty shooting,' I said, then memory flooded back. 'David!' I cried. 'Where's David?'

'He's all right; he's still asleep. He's safe in a ditch a hundred yards or so away; we moved him from the danger zone.'

'And – and Paul Véry?'

'Alive,' said Marsden grimly. 'He's unconscious, and of course I don't know how badly he may be hurt. I haven't looked yet. He didn't look too good. Byron got him out of the car; he's lying behind it. I'll go back and have a look at him in a minute.'

'Right,' said Richard, 'but we'd better let Charity put us in the picture quickly, in case things start to move again. What were you doing in Kramer's car with that man? And where's Kramer? Marsden said Kramer was going to follow the van out.'

'Kramer's coming,' I said. 'He and Loraine are following in your car. It was to be sent over the cliff with you and David in it, Richard.'

'My car, eh?' His voice was hard. 'We might have thought of that, Marsden. And I suppose that thug I laid out just now is Loraine's real husband?'

'Yes.'

'The man who murdered Tony and hit David. . . .'

His expression was ugly, but it changed as we reached the shelter of the trees and he spoke to me again: 'Are you sure you're all right?' He made me sit down behind an enormous double-trunked tree, with the van between me and the road.

'Yes, perfectly. Don't worry about me. Go and – oh!' My hand flew to my mouth. 'Rommel!' I said, aghast.

'What?' Richard's voice was blank.

'Rommel, the dog. He was in the back of the car. I'll never forgive myself if he's hurt.'

'There wasn't any dog in the back of the car.'

'But there must have been—'

'I assure you there wasn't.'

I was on my feet, steadying myself by the trunk of one of the trees.

'He must have been thrown out. He'll be lying around somewhere. Perhaps he's hurt—'

His hand steadied me. 'We'll look presently. Now sit down again. Have some more brandy.'

'No, thank you.'

'Come on; do as you're told.'

I obeyed him. 'You seem to spend a lot of time forcing spirits down my throat, Richard.'

He corked the flask and put it down beside me. 'You seem a lot more worried about this dog than you do about friend Paul.'

'It's David's dog. Besides, Paul Véry ran over a rabbit,' I added, as if that explained everything.

'What—' began Richard, then checked himself and spoke rapidly: 'Now listen. Only Kramer and Loraine are coming in my car?'

'As far as I know.'

'How far behind you?'

'I don't know. He had to go to your garage first to get the car.'

'I see . . . well, that wasn't very far. You came fast, I take it?'

'Pretty fast, yes. We did stop once on the road; that wasted about five minutes, I'd say.'

'Did you indeed? What for?'

'A spot of love-making,' I said levelly.

'I – see.' He was silent for a moment. 'Of course. That was when you changed places, I suppose?'

'Yes. But Richard, tell me what's happened? This man Marsden—'

'Later. Listen; as things have turned out, we've every chance of winning. They'll stop when they see the van and the Mercedes, and we're two men armed, with surprise on our side. It'll be all right in a very short time, you'll see.'

'What are you going to do?'

He gave a little laugh. 'I've no idea. No doubt inspiration will come in the moment of crisis.'

'Where's Mr. Marsden?'

'Gone to take a look at our friend Paul . . . *listen, is that a car?*'

We froze, straining our ears through the myriad noises of the night's silence. I became conscious of the whispering of the sea; not the breathing, bell-tolling, ebbing-and-flowing sorrow of the northern tides I knew, but the long, murmurous *hush-hush* of the land-bound waters. And above us sang the pines.

'No,' I said presently in a low voice. 'I can't hear a car.'

He stayed for a while with his head cocked to listen, then he relaxed, and I saw the faint gleam of a gun as he turned it over in his hand.

'There was a gun in the car,' I said quickly. 'I had it on my knee when we skidded. If we can find it that makes three of us—'

'No.' His voice was flat. 'Indeed it doesn't. You'll stay behind the lines, lady – in the trenches, in fact.' I saw his arm lift, and point inland. 'About forty yards back of these trees there's a rocky bank, with a dry gully beyond it. David's there. You'll wait with him, please.'

I opened my mouth to protest, but at that moment Marsden interrupted us, looming suddenly out of the darkness.

'He's still unconscious,' he said in a rapid undertone, 'but nothing seems to be broken. We'll bring him over here, to be on the safe side, and tie him up in the van. We don't want to take the risk that they'll see him lying there, and be warned before they stop that there's something wrong. Is there any rope left?'

'I doubt it.' Richard was on his feet, and the two of them were moving about the van. 'I think we used all there was.'

I felt an absurd desire to laugh. 'On André?'

'Mmm?' Marsden's voice was muffled. He seemed to be investigating a tool-box. 'André? Who's he?'

'The driver of the van.'

'Oh. Yes. He's tied up in there. He's all right.'

Richard spoke softly from inside the van: 'Nothing here. Charity, is there a belt on your coat?'

'No.'

'Oh hell.' He landed beside me, soft-footed on the pine-needles. 'This is beginning to have all the elements of farce, isn't it? Too many villains, and nothing to tie them up with. And for the life of me I daren't give you my trouser-belt.'

'I doubt if he'll give much trouble,' said Marsden, 'but I'd rather be sure. There may be a rope in the boot of the car. Coming, Byron? We'll go and get him.'

'O.K.,' said Richard. 'Charity, if you hear a car, get back to that gully and stay with David till we come for you.'

'Yes, Richard,' I said meekly.

But Marsden was made of sterner stuff. 'I found a gun in the Mercedes. Perhaps she—'

'No,' said Richard once more, finally. 'Both you and I have had a pot at her tonight, and Kramer might be luckier.'

'Beautifully put,' I said, and Marsden laughed.

'Let's go.'

They had barely taken two paces when I was on my feet, backed against my tree, all my brittle self-confidence in fragments.

'There it is!' I said hoarsely. 'Listen!'

Through the ghostly song of the pines, through the secret breathing of the sea, we heard it, faint but unmistakable; the throb of an engine.

'Blast!' said Marsden softly.

'And coming at a wicked pace,' said Richard, and listened a moment longer. My heart was beating to suffocation. 'That's my car all right, damn him . . . Charity, please.'

'I'm going.' My voice, like my body, was shaking. I had to push myself away from the solid comfort of the pine-tree's bole. I was vaguely aware of the two men, moving like shadows in the cover of the van. I ran away from the road, through the trees. The Bentley's engine cut through the silence in a rising drone, urgent, *crescendo*. I was free of the pines, and dodging through head-high scrub. In front loomed a dark mass that might be the rocky bank. The Bentley was coming fast, her engine snarling on a wasp-note of anger . . . I reached the foot of the rocky bank, and stopped. I could not go on. I suppose it was delayed shock, or something, but I know that I was stuck there, shaking and sweating and cold as ice, staring back through the leaves and the pine-trunks, towards the road.

I saw the glare of the Bentley's lights, cutting along the darkness of the cliff-top. The sound of her engine swelled suddenly as she rounded the curve half a mile away. The parasol pines soared again like great thunderhead clouds in the moving light.

The headlamps went out, and the Bentley swooped towards us in the little glow of her side-lights, confident, menacing – the tiger coming in to kill. He had seen the parasol pines; I heard his brakes grip momentarily as he swept into the last stretch of road. Any minute now he would see the van, and stop. The Bentley's snarl deepened. She was on us, moving fast. She was swinging right-handed into the track.

Then the night was ripped, unbelievably, by the roar of another engine. The Mercedes.

I don't remember moving at all, but I must have run towards the road like a mad thing. I only knew that Paul Véry had come round; had somehow got into the Mercedes, and was giving his warning.

I saw the Bentley veer into the track on the cliff-top, I heard the shriek of her brakes. I saw the Mercedes, roaring like a bomber, leap forward, then lurch on to her burst front tyre, and plunge broadside on across the road.

The Bentley never had a chance.

There was a yell, a dreadful scream, and then the cars met in a sickening crash of rending metal and shrieking tyres. Some hideous freak of chance knocked the Bentley's switch as she struck, so that, for one everlasting moment, as the two cars locked in a rearing tower of metal, her headlights shot skywards like great jets of flame. The cars hung there, black against the black sky, locked on the very brink of that awful cliff, then the beam swung over in a great flashing arc, and the locked cars dropped like a plummet down the shaft of lift, straight into the sea.

And after that last appalling impact, silence, broken hideously by echo after echo of the sound, as the disturbed sea washed and broke, washed and broke, against the cliff below. For an age, it seemed, the agitated waves beat their terrible reiteration on the rock, till, spent at last, they sank and smoothed themselves to their old whispering.

The last clouds shifted, parted, broke under the wind, and the moonlight fell, infinitely pure, infinitely gentle, to whiten the moving water.

27

O most delicate fiend!
Who is't can read a woman?
(Shakespeare)

David was still asleep. I had gone to find him, leaving
the two men looking for a way down the cliff. They had
driven the van across the road on to the track, switched
on its lights, and turned it to face the sea. There was
not a chance in a million, Marsden said, that any of the
three in the cars was still alive, but we could hardly
leave the place without attempting to find out.

With a shudder, I left them to it, and made my way
back through the trees to look for David. As I emerged
at the top of the rocky bank, I found that I could see my
way plainly in the moonlight. Below me, in sharply
shadowed monochrome, lay the gully; under a jut of
rock and leafage, a darker shadow stirred. I scrambled
down hurriedly, to be met by a shapeless shade that
whined a little and wriggled with a somewhat subdued
delight.

'Rommel!' I went down on my knees in the dust, and
hugged him. 'Oh Rommel! Did I nearly kill you, poor
boy?'

Rommel lavished me with generous but damp forgiveness, and then ran, with a yelp of excitement, into the shelter of the rock. I followed.

David lay curled up, wrapped in a coat. He looked very young and touching, and the sweep of his dark lashes over his cheek was so like Richard's that I felt a sudden rush of some emotion stronger than any I had ever felt before. I knelt down again, beside him, and felt his hands; they were cold. I put a hand to his cheek, and was horrified to feel it wet to the touch, as if with sweat, but immediately Rommel, feverishly licking the other cheek, provided the clue. I pushed him off.

'It was very clever of you to find him,' I told him, 'but wait a minute, will you?'

I gathered David up close to me, and began to rub the cold hands. Rommel, pressing close with quivering body, watched eagerly.

And presently the dark lashes stirred, and lifted. He stared at me blankly, and his hands moved a little under mine.

'Hullo, David,' I said.

The wide gaze flickered. 'Mrs. – Selborne?'

'Yes. How d'you feel?'

'Pretty foul.' He moved his head gingerly, and blinked up at the moonlit bank with the great pines billowing beyond. 'Where am I?'

'Some way east of Marseilles. But don't worry. Everything's all right now.'

His eyes were on me again, with a look in them I couldn't quite fathom. I felt him move away from me a little. 'I remember now . . . Marseilles. How did you get here?'

I understood then. I reached out a hand and took hold of his. 'David, I tell you it's all right. I'm *not* one of them; you can trust me. I followed you out here – Rommel and I did, that is—'

'Rommel?'

He turned at that, and his eye fell for the first time on the dog, who, belly to earth, shivering with delight in every hair, was waiting to be noticed.

'He found you all by himself,' I said. 'Tracked you down.'

'Oh, *Rommel!*' said the boy, and burst into tears, with his head buried deep in the dog's fur, and his arms round its neck. I let him cry out his fright and loneliness and distrust, while Rommel administered comfort, but presently the sobs changed to hiccups, and a voice said uncompromisingly from Rommel's neck: 'I feel beastly sick.'

'I'm not surprised,' I said. 'It'll do you good. Don't mind me. . . .'

Some short time later, after a nasty little interlude, he came back and sat down beside me. I put my coat round him, and held him close. I was wondering how on earth to begin telling him about Richard.

'You'd better have a drop of this.'

'What is it?'

It was Richard's flask. 'Brandy.'

'Oh!' He was palpably pleased. '*Real* brandy? . . . ugh, it's horrible!'

'I know, but it's fine when it gets a bit further down. Have some more.'

'No, thanks. I feel all right, only hungry.'

'Great heavens!'

'What are we doing here anyway?' he demanded. 'What happened? I want to *know*. Are we—?'

'One thing at a time. We're waiting here for – for transport back to Marseilles.'

He spoke quickly, apprehensively: 'Marseilles? That shop? I don't want—'

'Not to the shop,' I said reassuringly. 'That's all over. The owner of that place has been dealt with. Will you tell me what happened there, or don't you want to talk about it?'

'I hardly remember. I took the bracelet in, and he looked at it, and then asked me where I got it. He looked so queerly at me that I thought he guessed I'd pinched it, and so I made up a few lies. He seemed all right then, and asked me into the office. He went to a drawer; I thought he was getting the money. But he turned round with a towel or something in his hand. I – I don't really remember what happened then.'

'Chloroform, I think.' The smell was still there very faintly, sweet and horrible. Kramer must have recognized him at once, I thought. Probably Loraine had rung up as soon as he was missing, and told her employer about the bracelet. My arm tightened round him. 'What on earth made you choose *that* shop, of all the shops in France?'

'Well, I had no money,' said David, 'and that beastly bracelet was all I could find. I thought Marseilles was the only place hereabouts where I could sell a thing like that and no questions asked, so I hitch-hiked here. It took *ages*. I took the bracelet into two or three places, but they wouldn't buy it. In the end one chap told me to go to that shop. He said the man was a dealer in silver and he'd probably take it.' He gave a little shudder, and burrowed his head against my shoulder.

'What were you planning to do after you'd got the money?'

'Eat.' The answer was prompt and emphatic.

I looked down at him. 'You poor wretch! D'you mean to tell me you've had nothing all day?'

'I had lunch with some lorry-drivers, but nothing since then.'

'Oh dear! And I had some chocolate in my bag, but I lost it. The only consolation is that you'd have been a lot sicker if you'd been chloroformed on top of a good meal. I dare say it won't be very long before you'll get something.' I lifted my head to listen, but there was no sound except the sighing of the pines. 'And after you'd eaten, David, what were you going to do then?'

'I was going back to Nîmes to look for Daddy.'

I was startled, and showed it. 'To look for *your father*?'

He gave me a slightly shamefaced look. 'Yes. It was really because you went away from the hotel that I decided to go.'

'I don't get it.'

'That day in Nîmes – you remember? – when we ran away from my father, and I told you I was afraid of him . . . Well, it wasn't true.'

I began to sort out my ideas all over again. 'You never really thought he was mad? You weren't ever really afraid of him at all?'

David said, with scorn: 'Of course not. Afraid of *him*? I'd never be afraid of him as long as I lived!'

I said, helplessly: 'Then for heaven's sake explain! I can't get this straight. You *said* you didn't want to meet him; you *said* it was a matter of life and death, and you said he was mad. And you did look afraid; you looked scared stiff. Now, what's it all about?'

'I was afraid,' he said sombrely, 'terribly afraid, but *for* him, not *of* him. I'll try and tell you . . . Shall I just begin at the beginning?'

'Please.'

He began to talk, in a clear little voice completely empty of emotion. It was a queer experience to hear the same beastly story of the night of murder and treachery, so soon retold in the voice of a child. It differed from Richard's in nothing but point of view.

'. . . And when I heard he'd been acquitted, I knew he would come down to Deepings straight away. But he didn't. I waited and waited, and then the police telephoned Mrs. Hutchings – that's the housekeeper – that Daddy'd had an accident, and was badly hurt. He'd been taken to hospital, they said. Of course I wanted to go and see him, but they said he was still unconscious, and I must wait. Then, quite late, *she* came.'

The pitch of his voice never changed, but suddenly, shockingly, I was aware of the cold hatred underneath it. Then, as he went on, I began to realize that David's story was more terrible, even, than Richard's.

'She came to my room. I wasn't asleep, of course. She told me she'd been to the hospital. She broke it ever so gently, you know, but – she told me Daddy had died. What did you say?'

'Nothing. Go on. *She told you your father was dead?*'

'She did. She also told me it was no use going to the hospital; she said I'd not be able to see him, because he'd been too badly burned. Of course,' said David, his mouth half buried somewhere near Rommel's right ear, 'I wasn't exactly *thinking* straight, you know. I didn't really want to go away with her, but I couldn't stick Deepings just then, and anyway, what could I do? Daddy was dead, and she was my step-mother, and I more or less thought I had to do as she said. There's not much you can do if you're only a boy, and besides, I'd not had much practice in thinking things out for myself, *then*. I have now.'

'I know that,' I said bitterly.

David went on: 'She'd taken a flat up near the Bois, and we lived there. She was quite decent to me, as I thought, and I was so dashed unhappy anyway that I didn't care what happened. I suppose I just moped around the place. I found Rommel one day in the Bois, with a can tied to his tail. After that it was better.'

I said, a little grimly: 'What happened next?'

'About three weeks ago, she told me Daddy was still alive.'

'How on earth did she explain away her lie about his death?'

'She told me she'd done it for my sake.' The grey eyes lifted to mine for a moment: they were quite expressionless. 'She said that, according to the reports she'd had from the doctors and the police, Daddy had tried to commit suicide.'

'David!'

'Yes. She implied, of course, that he *had* done that awful murder, and that it had been preying on his mind. Oh,' said David, with a large gesture, 'she spared me all she could. She said that he'd been going queerer and queerer for some time, and that he must have killed Uncle Tony – *and* knocked me down – in a sort of blackout. She prescribed it to – is that the word?'

'Ascribed.'

'Oh. She ascribed it to his terrible experiences during the War. Why did you laugh?'

'There's a certain irony in that,' I said, 'but it doesn't matter.'

'Well,' said David, 'that was her story. He was batty, and he was dangerous, so she'd removed me from the trouble zone.'

'Did you believe it?'

'No. I knew he wasn't mad; I knew he hadn't killed Uncle Tony; and of course I knew he hadn't hit me. I also knew for certain that he hadn't meant to crash his car and commit suicide, because he'd rung me up from London as soon as he got out of Court, and told me he was coming straight down.'

'Did you tell her that?'

'No.' He looked at me. 'I can't quite explain it, Mrs. Selborne, but I began to get more and more strongly the feeling that I ought to keep things to myself. There was something so – well, sort of queer and *wrong* about the whole set-up. Some of the things she said, the way she looked at me sometimes – the very fact that she'd taken me away with her when I was certain she disliked me anyway – oh! lots of things seemed odd. And now all this talk about father: I was certain that she didn't think he was mad, either. And of course nothing could excuse the lie she'd told about his death.' He paused.

'Why didn't you write to your father? Surely that—'

'It was the first thing I thought of, of course. But there was a catch in it, Mrs. Selborne. There were two chaps in the flat below – she said they were her cousins – and they were with us all the time. I never got a minute to myself. I couldn't have got a letter to him without them knowing, and reading it. What's more, she seemed to *want* me to write to him, and that was quite enough, at the time, to make me think twice about it.'

'She wanted you to ask him to come and see you?'

'Exactly.' His tone was a quaint echo of Richard's. 'She said she couldn't possibly let me go back to England till we saw how he was, and she suggested I write and ask him to come to France. She'd have read the letter; there was no question of my being able to tell him what the set-up was, and ask him what had really happened at his end. She went on and on about my writing to invite him, and in such a funny way that I got suspicious again, and just refused. I pretended that I'd believed her story about his being mad, and that I was frightened to see him.' He gave a dry little chuckle. 'Gosh! she was furious, being hoist in her own juice like that. Is that right? It sounds a bit odd.'

'I rather think you mean stewing with her own petard. But let it pass. I get it. She wrote to him herself in the end, you know.'

He shot me another look. 'Yes, I did know. I telephoned him one night.'

'You did? But—'

'He wasn't there. I – I was pretty disappointed. I managed to sneak down one night and phone from the cousins' flat while they were with *her*. Mrs Hutchings answered. She said Daddy'd had a letter marked *Paris* that morning, and he'd left straight away. I said how was he, and she told me he was all right, but just worried to death, and only just out of hospital anyway. . . . The cousins caught me on the way up from the phone. I spun them a lie, but they didn't believe me, and after that I was never left alone. Next morning we all went to Lyons, and then, stage by stage, down here. It puzzled me no end, till I began to think they wanted Daddy down here, instead of in Paris. And I could only think that it was still something to do with that murder, and that they'd harm him.'

'A trap,' I said, 'with you as bait.'

'Exactly,' he said again. 'So I wasn't going to get into touch with Daddy just to lure him in; I wanted to be quite sure, first, that it was safe. The queer thing was that the cousins left us at Montélimar, and when we were in Avignon, she let me go round alone . . .'

'She didn't,' I said, thinking of Paul Véry. 'Someone else had taken over. You were accompanied all the time.'

'*Was* I? Then I was right to run away in Nîmes?'

'Very probably.'

He spoke slowly, in an unconscious echo of his father's own bewilderment: 'It was pretty awful, not knowing what to do – not knowing whether people were enemies, or just ordinary people. It was as if' – he gave a little shiver – 'as if everything was upside down.' He shivered again.

'It's over now,' I said firmly. 'If you're cold, come under my coat again.'

'I'm not, really. I want to know what's happened, and how you know all this. I say, do we *have* to stay here, Mrs. Selborne? This "transport" you mentioned—'

'Is here now,' I said, and got to my feet. I could hear footsteps scrambling up the further side of the bank. David jumped up, looking a little scared, and Rommel bristled.

'Who—?'

Richard swung himself down the slope, and stood there in the moonlight, looking at his son. He hesitated a little, then put out a hand.

There was a rush of feet past me, and David hurtled into the moonlight like an arrow going into the gold. I saw his father's arms close round him, and the dark heads close together.

I went quickly past them, and Marsden's hand reached down to help me up the bank.

I looked a query at him.

He shook his head. 'Not a sign,' he said quietly.

We walked through the trees, towards the road where the van stood waiting, her nose towards Marseilles.

28

Two loves have I . . .
(Shakespeare)

I woke to bright sunlight and a most delectable smell of coffee. Swimming up through the billows of a deep and dreamless sleep, I found myself blinking drowsily at the white walls and red-tiled floor of a room that was vaguely familiar. The sun blazed in bright bars through a closed shutter: the other had swung open, letting in a flood of gold. From outside the cries and clangs of the city rose musically, as if muted by the light.

The door had opened softly, letting in the lovely coffee smell that had roused me. I turned my head, then sat up, fully awake.

'Louise!'

Immaculate as ever, she was standing just inside the door, looking speculatively at me across a loaded tray.

'So you are awake? Or did I disturb you? I thought it was high time—'

'Oh, Louise, how nice to see you! How did it happen? And what *is* the time?'

She set the tray on my knees, and went to open the shutter. 'High noon, my child.'

'Good Lord, is it really?' I poured coffee. 'When did you get here?'

'About an hour and a half ago. I got the first train.' She added, reasonably: 'You said you were in a jam, and I knew you hadn't any clothes with you.'

'My *dear*,' I said gratefully, 'don't tell me you've brought my clothes! I knew you were the most wonderful woman in the world.'

She laughed. 'No one can face a crisis unless they're suitably clad. How do you feel?'

'Fine – I think.' I stretched a few muscles gingerly, and was relieved. 'A bit stiff, and a bruise here or there, but otherwise' – I smiled at her – 'on top of the world.'

'Mmmm . . .' Louise eyed me as she pulled an unsteady-looking wicker chair to the bedside. 'Ye-es. Your ghastly village seems to have been a pretty exciting place after all. What happened to you?'

I chuckled through a bite of *croissant*, aware of a miraculous spring-time lift of the heart, a champagne-tingling of the blood: the nightmare had gone; this fresh sun of morning rose on a different world where the last gossamer rag of fear and uncertainty must shrink and vanish in the superfluity of light. I said: 'I was – translated.'

'Yes. You look it. I suppose you met the Wolf of Orange?'

'In person,' I said happily.

'I thought so.' Her tone was bland. 'He rang up about half an hour ago. If you're feeling fit, we are to meet him for lunch at the Hôtel de la Garde. On the terrace, at one-fifteen. And now,' said Louise, settling herself in the wicker chair and regarding me placidly, 'I am dying by inches of curiosity, and I want to be told every single thing that has happened, including why this Richard Byron who is David Bristol's father and who I thought was a murderer anyway should be ringing you up in Marseilles and asking you to lunch, and why he should feel it necessary to inform me that neither he nor Mr. Marsden was in jail as yet and that Rommel had bitten André in the seat of the pants and that I was to let you sleep late and then take you some coffee and see you took a taxi to lunch as if' – finished Louise on a faintly accusing note – 'he had known you all your life instead of – how long?'

I said, in simple surprise: 'Three days . . . off and on.'

'And rather more off than on, at that,' said Louise. 'A dictatorial gentleman, I'd have said, at a guess.'

'He is a bit.' I stirred my coffee absorbedly.

'And you like it,' she accused me.

'I'm – well, I got used to it, you know. Johnny—'

'I know. No wonder you keep getting married and I don't,' said Louise, without rancour.

I coloured, and laughed a little. 'He hasn't asked me, as it happens.'

She merely raised a beautifully groomed eyebrow and handed me a cigarette.

'Well, come along, my girl. Tell me all about it.'

'It's a long story—'

'We've got an hour before we meet the Wolf. Go on: begin at the beginning, go on to the end, and then stop.'

'– and an utterly fantastic one.'

'I am all ears,' said Louise contentedly, and leaned back in her chair.

So I told her, lying back on the pillows in my little hotel room at the Belle Auberge, with the peaceful sunlight slanting across the coverlet, and the smoke from our cigarettes winding in placid spirals between us. I told her everything just as it had happened, and, like Paul Véry, she listened silently, only staring at me with a kind of shocked disbelief.

'We–ell,' she said at length, on a long note of amazement. 'What an extraordinary tale! Not, of course, that I believe a word of it, only—'

'You'd better ask the others,' I told her. 'Mr. Marsden said—'

Louise sat up. 'Yes! Now *that* I don't follow at all. What the dickens is John Marsden doing in this *galère* at all?'

It was my turn to raise an eyebrow. 'John?'

'After you left for Les Boos,' she said calmly, 'we got acquainted.'

'Well I'll be dashed,' I said. 'If I'd known that I'd have stopped suspecting him at once.'

'On the principle that all my men friends turn out to be Boy Scouts or curates on holiday,' agreed Louise. 'It certainly shook me to hear he's a great detective. Marsden of the C.I.D. Well, well. And he's very nice, even if he does read poetry. Go on. Did he tell you how he got to this awful place on the cliff?'

'Yes. He made it sound awfully simple. Apparently he was helping at first, this spring, in the investigation of Tony Baxter's murder. Richard, it turns out, had actually met him a couple of times, but didn't remember the name when I described Marsden to him. Well, Marsden was taken off to work on another big case, but he was interested in the Baxter murder, and the man in charge of it, Inspector Brooke, wasn't at all satisfied with the way the case finished. He came at length to believe, himself, that Richard hadn't done it; the murderer, therefore, must be still at large, possibly active, and the motive undiscovered. Richard's so-called car-accident shook him a good bit. Richard was safe in hospital, but Brooke began to wonder about Loraine, and to worry quite a lot about David.'

'Good for him.'

'Yes indeed. Well, Marsden was due for leave, and offered to do a spot of unofficial guardianship. He has friends at the Sûreté, and they said right, go ahead, so he came over to France to locate David.'

'Well, well,' said Louise. 'Then that's why he disappeared from the Tistet-Védène when David did.'

'Quite. I'd noticed him hanging round where David was, and imputed sinister motives to him. Well, to cut it short, he managed, with a good deal of difficulty, to get on to David's tail south to Marseilles. Apparently it took the poor child nearly all day to get here, as he felt obliged to hide at sight of every car, and the lorries were slow, and few and far between. But he got here, with Marsden faint but pursuing, and eventually landed in Kramer's beastly little shop.'

I glanced at my watch. 'I must get up soon . . . Well, poor David was chloroformed – pretty heavily, too –

while Marsden skulked about outside not knowing what had happened. I imagine that Kramer got busy on the telephone, then, to Avignon, and told Loraine to get onto the next train. Paul Véry must have left long before—'

'He did,' said Louise. 'He took his car out soon after lunch, ostensibly to look for David. The American couple did the same, and so did those two Germans. But Paul Véry didn't come back for dinner.'

'I've no doubt he did look for David,' I said, 'and probably passed him hiding in a ditch. He must either have telephoned Kramer later, and heard of David's capture, or have driven straight down here for orders; at any rate, Marsden says, he got here a good hour or so before Loraine. I saw him myself in the office when she landed in a taxi. Marsden was still hanging about waiting for David to leave the shop, when Paul Véry arrived, and turned into the garage opposite, just as if he'd lived there all his life. Marsden recognized him, and began to wonder just what was going on, so, when Paul Véry walked into the shop, and straight through into the office, Marsden, like me, found his way through to the back, and listened under the window. It must have been just about then,' I said meditatively, 'that Richard and I were sitting talking about four streets away . . .'

'There seems to have been quite a procession into Kramer's parlour,' remarked Louise.

'Yes indeed.' I shuddered. 'Well, Marsden heard quite a bit under his window. He could tell that there were at least three men – Kramer and Jean-Paul and

André – in the office, so, even when he learned what had happened to David, he couldn't do very much about it. His French was just good enough for him to realize they were planning to move David's body, so he didn't dare risk losing track of him by going to the police. He simply stuck around and hoped for a chance to grab David.'

'Poor John,' said Louise.

'He said it was hell,' I told her. 'He waited and waited, and they talked and talked, and then the door opened, and Richard walked in.'

'That must have been quite a moment.'

'Mustn't it? Richard, of course, remembers nothing but the sight of David lying on a sofa. He started for him, and the three of them set on him straight away. Marsden, under the window, didn't see a thing, but he heard Richard say "David!" in English, and then the hullabaloo. Then Kramer said something about "putting them both in the van", so Marsden slipped across to the garage. He says he imagined they'd all three go with the van, and since his one thought was not to be left behind, he got inside it and hid under some sacks. But they dumped Richard and David in, locked the door on them, and Kramer told André to get out to that place on the coast, park under cover, and wait for him. Then he and Paul Véry went back to wait for Loraine. Marsden was furious. If he hadn't been locked in, he could have dealt with André then and there, and driven Richard and David straight off to the police-station. But he was stuck, so he lay low, untied Richard, and set about bringing him round.'

Louise sighed with satisfaction. 'So when poor André stopped the van and went to get the bodies—'

'Exactly. They knocked him cold, tied him up, and took his gun. They even took his coat to wrap David in. On the whole,' I said, 'I'm a little sorry for André. Kramer said he was a bit of a fool.'

Louise laughed. 'And now Rommel's bit him. Poor André.'

I pushed back the coverlet and got out of bed. 'Poor Rommel, you mean. He's had a lot to bear. David left him outside the shop, and the poor dog must have waited for centuries. He found his way round to the back streets in the end, and that's where I picked him up. Did you say something about bringing me some clothes?'

'They're in my room. I'll get them; I didn't want to wake you before.' She smiled at me as she rose. 'What a good thing I brought your very nicest dress!'

'*Not* the Mexican print?' I said gratefully. 'Dear Louise, you shall be my bridesmaid *again*.'

'Not on your life,' said Louise. 'It's unlucky, and anyway, I'm too old. I'll wait and be godmother.'

'You're a little premature,' I said.

'So I should hope,' said Louise, making for the door. She turned, and her sleek brows mocked me again. 'So are you, aren't you?'

'I?'

'Yes. He hasn't even asked you.'

The door shut gently behind her.

*   *   *

As I lifted my dress from the case Louise had brought, I saw the silver photograph-frame underneath. Johnny's eyes smiled up at me.

I picked up the photograph, and was looking down at the pictured face, when the fading bruise on my wrist caught, as it were, at the edge of my vision.

I smiled back at Johnny. Then I held my wrist very lightly against my cheek. Any hesitations I had had, all the doubts that my intellect had been placing in front of my heart, seemed, with the rest of the nightmare adventure, to resolve themselves and fade away. Past and future dovetailed into this moment, and together made the pattern of my life. I would never again miss Johnny, with that deep dull aching, as if part of me had been wrenched away, and the scar left wincing with the cold; but, paradoxically enough, now that I was whole again, Johnny was nearer to me than he had ever been since the last time that we had been together, the night before he went away. I was whole again, and Johnny was there for ever, part of me always. Because I had found Richard, I would never lose Johnny. Whatever I knew of life and loving had been Johnny's gift, and without it Richard and I would be the poorer. We were both his debtors, now and for ever.

I lifted Johnny's photograph and kissed it. It was the last time I should ever do so. Then I laid it gently back in the case, and picked up my dress again.

A short time later I opened my door, called Louise, and went out into the sunshine to meet Richard.

29

O frabjous day!
(Carroll)

The terrace of the Hôtel de la Garde almost overhangs the edge of the sea. It is wide, and flagged with white stone, with beautifully formal little orange-trees in pots to give it shade, and a breeze straight off the Mediterranean to cool it. The bright little boats bob, scarlet and green and white, just below your table, and the *bouillabaisse* is wonderful.

We were a gay enough party. Richard and Marsden had spent the greater part of the night and morning with the police, and both looked tired, but about the former I noticed something I had not see in him before; he was relaxed. The last of the strain had been lifted, and though his eyes were weary, they were clear, and his mouth had lost its hardness. As for David, he was in tearing spirits, and kept us all laughing until coffee and cigarettes came round.

Marsden got out his pipe and settled back in his chair with a long sigh of satisfaction. He, too, looked as if some strain were lifted, but with him it was rather a slackening of concentration, a putting, so to speak, of his intelligence into carpet slippers for a while. He had come off duty.

His blue eyes studied me over the match-flame as he held it to his pipe. At last this was going nicely.

'If I may say so, Mrs. Selborne,' he said, 'you've come out of this affair looking remarkably fit. How do you feel today?'

'Fine, thank you,' I said. 'Nothing to show but a few bruises.' I caught Richard's rueful grin, and smiled back. 'How restful it is, isn't it, now that everybody knows whose side they're on?'

'It certainly is,' agreed Marsden. He cocked an eye at Louise. 'I take it you've put Louise in the picture?'

'She told me the whole story,' said Louise, 'except for the most important thing – the reason for it all. That was just guesswork. Have you found out anything further about *why* Kramer employed those two to do the murders?'

'Our guesswork was right,' said Richard. 'The police searched Kramer's premises this morning, and there's evidence galore. The whole thing is clear enough now.'

'Tell us, please,' I said.

'I'll try.' He flicked the ash from his cigarette into the sea, then stared thoughtfully at the tip of it for a moment, before he spoke.

'We were right,' he said, looking at me. 'It all began on that beastly January day in 1944, when Tony Baxter and I, on our way to a prison camp, were witnesses to Kramer's murder of Emmanuel Bernstein – and, incidentally, to his connection with the mass-murder of the Jews.' He glanced at Louise. 'Did Charity tell you about that?'

'Yes. What a beastly affair! I don't wonder you lost your temper and blew up.'

Richard's eyes met mine. 'I do, sometimes,' he admitted. 'It's a fault I have. But this time Tony did as well. I'm glad of that, because if I'd been solely responsible for attracting Kramer's notice I'd feel a very heavy burden of guilt for Tony's death. As it is' – his face darkened for an instant, but he resumed in a normal tone: 'Well, you know what happened; we were eventually permitted to go, but Kramer had occasion to remember us, and his memory was excellent.'

He paused. 'That wouldn't have mattered at all, of course, if it hadn't been for the next connection between us: both Kramer and I were in the same line of business, the trade in antiques, and both, as it happens, particularly interested in old silver. When the War finished, and the Nuremburg witch-hunt started, Kramer somehow or other managed to disappear. He got out of Germany, and appeared in France as an Austrian refugee, one Karel Werfel. He had managed to salt away a pleasant little fortune in money and loot, and before long he was doing very nicely, with his headquarters in Paris, and branches in Lyons and Marseilles. I should mention here, perhaps, something that we found out this morning. Loraine was his' – his gaze fell on David, wide-eyed and absorbed – 'Loraine was with Kramer for a time immediately after the War.' Richard's voice was sombre, tinged with a kind of pity. 'She had a bad record; she was suspected of collaboration, and of having a hand in the murder of two French officers. Kramer helped her to avoid the consequences, but kept the proof himself and used it to gain a hold over her.'

He stubbed out his cigarette. 'By the time Tony and I appeared again on his horizon, Max Kramer had a lot to lose. He had this perfectly genuine and lucrative business, but he also had other business, even more lucrative, and highly criminal, for which the antique trade was a cloak. His real headquarters for that was here, in Marseilles. I'm not quite sure just what rackets he was concerned in, but at the moment the Marseilles police are having a fine old time rounding up some of the people whose names were in Kramer's safe. There hardly seems to be any pie he didn't have a finger in – smuggling, dope-running, and so forth, but the most important thing that came to light when his premises were searched is definite evidence that he's been mixed up in some of these underground movements to upset the present German government and bring back the National Socialists.'

'You mean those gangs of Neo-Hitlerites? Were-wolves, or whatever they called themselves?' asked Louise.

'Something like that.' It was Marsden who answered her. 'His genuine business, with its wide trade con-tracts, and the necessity for a good deal of foreign travel, made an excellent mask for the centre of a widish organization. The police think now that Kramer – or Werfel – was at the back of a good deal of organized thuggery, sabotage, and what-have-you in

Germany and Northern France shortly after the end of the War. Go on, Byron.'

'Well, into this comfortable and prosperous picture,' resumed Richard, 'came, suddenly, Tony and myself. There was a big sale in Paris, for the disposal of the Lemaire collection of silver, and naturally I was there. Kramer, apparently, was there too, and must have seen us, though neither of us noticed him. But he made enquiries, and discovered that I was in the same line of country as himself, and had, in fact, opened an office in Paris. We were bound to meet. And if Tony or I recognized him, well' – his gesture was eloquent –'even if he escaped a war crimes tribunal, there would be enquiries, and he couldn't afford the least investigation. It would be the end of Karel Werfel . . .'

'It was a pretty frightful coincidence, wasn't it,' said Louise, 'that David should have gone to *Kramer's* shop to sell the bracelet?'

'Frightful,' agreed Richard, 'but not so much of a coincidence, if you think it over. The thread that runs through the whole story, after all, is the antique-business: if Kramer and I hadn't happened to be in the same line of country, we would probably never have met after the War – and certainly the danger of our meeting more than once would have been slight. But we were both interested in the same thing, and would in all likelihood be thrown together again and again: and *that* Kramer dared not risk. Yes, the whole *raison d'etre* of the affair, you might say, was "old silver", and the bracelet would almost inevitably act as a link. I bought it for Loraine; Loraine brought it – and David and me – down into Kramer's country: once David tried to sell such a thing hereabouts it was almost certain to come to Kramer's notice pretty soon. And that's what happened; David was advised to take it to him to get an opinion on its value. No, the coincidence lies in the fact that I saw the thing in the shop-window when I did; but that was just Kramer's luck. I was supposed to be got into his den sooner or later, it just happened to be sooner.'

'Paul Véry,' I said, as he stopped. 'Where did he come in?'

'He had a criminal record as long as your arm,' said Marsden cheerfully, 'and half a dozen aliases. Kramer had enough tucked away in his safe to send Paul Véry to Devil's Island for several lifers.'

'He must have promised to hand the papers over to Loraine and Paul after Richard was safely out of the way,' I said. 'I heard him tell them they'd be free of him once the job was over.'

'Was she really Paul Véry's wife?' asked Louise.

'Indubitably. They were married in 1942, then he was posted missing the following year. She picked up with Kramer in the autumn of 1945. When Paul Véry turned up again he appears to have accepted the situation (to some extent, I imagine, under pressure), and stayed on to work for Kramer. He seems to have taken a pretty – what shall I say? – liberal view of his wife's activities. When Kramer saw Byron and Baxter at the Lemaire sale, and decided they would have to be eliminated, he picked Paul Véry for the job.'

'Greatly helped,' said Richard bitterly, 'by the fool

Byron, who, seeing Loraine at the sale, began to show signs of interest that made it easy for the precious trio to commit the first murder.'

'If you hadn't "married" her and taken her to Deepings,' said Marsden, 'they'd have managed some other way.'

'I dare say,' said Richard, 'but you can't say I didn't help. At least it's a comfort of a sort to know she was never legally my wife . . . It was Paul Véry, of course, who killed Tony and knocked David out. It was Paul Véry who tried to ram my car. And when the attempt at double murder failed, they took David to France. I doubt if they had a plan worked out at all, but David was an obvious trump card.'

'I don't quite see why, you know,' said David.

'Don't you?' said his father. 'Loraine knew very well that I'd never willingly see her again. Kramer wanted me over here, but if she'd tried to get me to see her I'd either have ignored her or put my lawyers on to it. But you' – he flicked David's cheek with a casual finger – 'I can't afford to let you go. You're a rebate on my income-tax.'

'Talking of income-tax,' I said, 'your insurance company—'

'Oh God, yes,' said Richard. 'Two cars in four months! I know. I'm going to have a gay time explaining when I get back. . . . Anyway, that's the story. You know the rest. They planned to get me down here, where there were better facilities for disposing of me, and, heaven knows, their plan might have worked, if they hadn't left two important things out of their reckoning.'

'What two things?' demanded David.

Richard said soberly, looking at Marsden: 'The integrity and human-kindness of the English police, for one. I shan't forget it, Marsden, and neither will David. I'll write to Brooke tonight. We're deeply in your debt.'

Marsden looked acutely uncomfortable, and muttered something, then turned and began to tap out his pipe on the balustrade between the table and the sea.

'And the second thing?' asked David.

Richard smiled at me suddenly, so that my heart turned a silly somersault in my breast.

'The spanner in the works,' he said, and laughed.

'The what, Daddy?'

'Chance, my dear David, in the shape of Charity.'

David looked from him to me, and back again. 'Charity?'

I said: 'It's my name, David,' and blushed like a fool.

'Oh, I see.' His bright gaze rested on me for a speculative moment, then returned to his father, but all he said was: 'I thought you meant that stuff in the Bible about *Charity suffereth long and is kind.*'

'That, too,' said Richard, and laughed again.

'Your father exaggerates,' I told David. 'The only thing I did of real practical value was to find Rommel, and then I nearly killed him.'

'Your idea of practical value,' said Richard drily, 'is a distorted one, to say the least. That ill-favoured mongrel—'

David shot up in his chair. '*Mongrel?* He's not! Anyone can *see* he's well-bred! Can't they?' He appealed to Marsden, who grinned.

'Let us say that a good deal has gone into his breeding,' he said tactfully. 'I'm sure he's highly intelligent.'

'Of course he is!' David was emphatic. 'Look how he found me! Why, he's practically *police-trained*!'

Richard said dampingly: 'I suppose that means you've trained him to sleep on your bed?'

'The police,' began Marsden, 'don't as a rule—'

But David hadn't heard him. He was eyeing his father with some caution. 'As a matter of fact, I have.'

'And a very good habit too,' I said promptly. 'He can keep the – the mice away.'

Across David's look of gratification, Richard's eyes met mine.

'I – see,' he said. 'Collusion. Conspiracy against me in my own home. I seem to be letting myself in for—'

'*Daddy!*' David's eyes were round. He looked at me. 'Mrs. Selborne! Are you going to marry Daddy?'

'Yes,' I said.

David got to his feet. 'I'm terribly glad,' he said simply, and kissed me.

Above the general babel of question and congratulation the smooth voice of the *maître d'hôtel* insinuated at Richard's ear: 'Champagne for m'sieur?' They didn't miss much at the Hôtel de la Garde. Then the magnificent bottle arrived, all gold-foil and sparkling ice and bowing attendant acolytes, and Marsden, on his feet, was making a very creditable speech, unaware of – or unconcerned by – the broad smiles and palpable interest of the people at the other tables. Behind him the blue sea danced, diamond-spangled, and in his uplifted glass a million bubbles winked and glittered.

'. . . The only correct ending,' he was saying, 'to adventure. *So they lived happily ever after.* I give you the toast: Richard and Charity!'

He sat down among quite a small storm of clapping and general laughter.

'When's it to be?' he asked me.

Richard took a folded paper from his breast-pocket. 'In ten days' time,' he said. 'That's the very soonest you can do it in France. I made enquiries this morning when I got the licence.'

I heard Louise murmur: 'Dictatorial . . .' just beside me, and then David demanded:

'But when did all this *happen*?'

Richard was laughing at me across his glass of champagne, with devils in his eyes. I said: 'Actually, it hasn't happened. I mean, he hasn't asked me to marry him at all.'

'Hasn't *asked* you—'

Richard said: 'Will you marry me?'

'Yes,' I said.

David grabbed his glass again. 'Well, then,' he said, in briskly practical tones, 'that's settled, isn't it? All in front of witnesses, too. He'll not find that easy to wriggle out of, Mrs. Selborne. I'll see he gets held to it. And now may I have some more champagne?'

'It seems to me,' I said austerely, 'that you've had quite enough.'

He grinned at me. 'It was a very nice proposal,' he

admitted. 'No words wasted, no beating about the bush . . .' He reached for the champagne-bottle.

'No!' said Richard firmly, as I moved the bottle beyond David's reach.

'Collusion!' said David bitterly. 'Conspiracy! I can see—'

'I've had a lot of practice,' I told him, 'and I'm a very managing woman.'

Richard was grinning. 'Did Johnny always do as he was told?'

'Always,' I said composedly.

Louise laughed. 'Some day,' she told him, 'I'll tell you the truth about that.' She got to her feet, and smiled at the others, who had risen too.

'Well, thank you for my lunch and the champagne. Don't let me keep you from the police and the other joys in store. Will they want David? No? Then perhaps he could spend the afternoon with me?'

'Thanks very much,' said Richard. 'If the dog'll be in the way—'

'On the contrary,' said Louise, 'I wouldn't dream of leaving the dog behind. What do you suggest I do with the pair of them?'

Richard's hand slipped under my arm as we all turned to make our way out of the restaurant.

'Most people,' he said gravely, 'begin their sight-seeing in Marseilles with a trip to the Château d'If.'

30

Epilogue

Upon the Islands Fortunate we fall,
Not faint Canaries but Ambrosiall.

(Donne)

It was late the following afternoon, and the sun slanted a deepening gold through the boughs that arched the avenue where Richard and I were walking. The columns of the planes were warm in their delicate arabesques of silver and isabel and soft russet-red. Over our heads the leaves, deepening already towards the sere time, danced a little to the straying wind, and then hung still.

'At least,' said Richard, 'we have nine days to get to know each other in before it's too late. Are you sure you don't mind being rushed into it like this?'

'Quite sure.'

'The least I can do is to leave it to you to choose a place for a honeymoon.'

I said: 'The Isles of Gold.'

'Where's that? Ultima Thule?'

'Not quite. It's another name for Porquerolles. You sail from Hyères.'

'Wonderful. We'll have a fortnight there – and

perhaps Corsica, too. The Dexters say David can stay as long as he likes and we can pick him up—'

'Oh, Richard, look!' I cried.

We were passing a shop window, and, backed against a neutral screen of porridge-grey, a single picture on a little easel was standing.

Richard turned and glimpsed it. He stopped.

'Oh,' was all he said, but it was said on a long note of discovery.

The picture was small, but against the flat background of the screen the colours in it glowed like jewels, so placed that they vibrated one against the other, until you could have sworn the boy in the picture smiled. He was standing against a shadowed ground of leaves and rock, very straight, with his dark head high, and a gallant look to him.

'It's David!' I said.

'It *is* David,' said Richard. 'See the sling in his hand? He's just setting off to face Goliath and the Philistines.'

'It's the first time I saw him,' I said, and gazed down at the pictured face, so young, and with that look I remembered so well of the grave acceptance of a burden too heavy for his shoulders. David, alone among his enemies, had faced them with just this same gaiety and temper that was written in the bearing of the young champion of Israel.

'May I have it for a wedding-present?' I asked.

'You certainly may. What a glorious bit of painting! And the man who painted that meant it with every stroke of the brush. Young Israel, up against the enemy . . . I wonder—'

He broke off suddenly as he leaned forward to peer at the narrow strip of brass along the base of the frame.

At the look in his face I cried out: 'Richard, what is it?'

'Look for yourself,' he said.

I peered through the plate glass. In tiny letters on the brass I made out the legend:

LE JEUNE DAVID

and below this the name of the artist:

EMMANUEL BERNSTEIN

And so it ended, where it had begun, with the little Jewish painter whose death had been so late, but so amply avenged. And, ten days later, with *The Boy David* carefully boxed in the back of the Riley, my husband and I set our faces to the South, and the Isles of Gold.

Now read on for a taste of Mary Stewart's next tale
of adventure and suspense.

◆

WILDFIRE AT MIDNIGHT

I

The Misty Island

In the first place, I suppose, it was my parents' fault for
giving me a silly name like Gianetta. It is a pretty enough
name in itself, but it conjures up pictures of delectable
and slightly overblown ladies in Titian's less respectable
canvases, and, though I admit I have the sort of colouring
that might have interested that Venetian master, I
happen to be the rather inhibited product of an English
country rectory. And if there is anything further removed
than that from the *bagnio* Venuses of Titian's middle
period, I don't know what it is.

To do my parents justice, I must confess straight
away that the *bagnio* touch was there in the family –
nicely in the past, of course, but known nevertheless to
be there. And my mother is just sufficiently vague,
artistic, and sentimental to see nothing against calling a
red-haired daughter after the Vixen Venus, the lovely
red-headed Gianetta Fox, who was once the rage of
London, and a Beauty in the days when beauties had a
capital B, and were moreover apt to regard beauty and
capital as one and the same thing. She was a nobody,
the lovely Gianetta; her mother, I believe, was half
Italian, and if she knew who her father was, she never
admitted to him. She simply appeared, Venus rising

from the scum of Victorian Whitechapel, and hit London for six in the spring of 1858. She was just seventeen. By the time she was twenty she had been painted by every painter who mattered (Landseer was the only abstainer), in every conceivable allegorical pose, and had also, it was said, been the mistress of every one of them in turn – I should be inclined here, too, to give Landseer the benefit of the doubt. And in 1861 she reaped the due reward of her peculiar virtues and married a baronet. He managed to keep her long enough to beget two children of her before she left him – for a very 'modern' painter of the French school who specialized in nudes. She left her son and daughter behind in Sir Charles's scandalized care; the former was to be my maternal grandfather.

So my nice, vague, artistic mother, who spends her time in our Cotswold rectory making dear little pots and bowls and baking them in a kiln at the bottom of the garden, called me after my disreputable (and famous) great-grandmother, without a thought about the possible consequences to me when I hit London in my turn, in 1945.

I was nineteen, had left school a short eight months before, and now, fresh from a West End training course for mannequins, was ingenuously setting out on a glamorous career with a fashion-house, modelling clothes. I had a share in a bed-sitting-room, a small banking-account (gift from Father), two hand-thrown pots and an ash-tray (gift from Mother), and an engagement diary (gift from my brother Lucius). I was on top of the world.

I was still on top of the world when the Morelli Gallery acquired the Zollner canvas called *My Lady Greensleeves*, and Marco Morelli – *the* Marco Morelli – decided to make a splash with it. You remember the fuss, perhaps? Morelli's idea was, I think, to stage a sort of come-back of art after the austerities and deprivations of the war. He could hardly have chosen a more appropriate picture to do it with. *My Lady Greensleeves* has all the rioting *bravura* of Zollner's 1860 period: the gorgeous lady who languishes, life-size, in the centre of the canvas is the focus of a complicated shimmer of jewels and feathers and embroidered silk – I doubt if any material has ever been more miraculously painted than the coruscating damask of the big green sleeves. As an antidote to austerity it was certainly telling. And even Zollner's peacock riot of colour could not defeat his model's triumphant vitality, or drain the fire from that flaming hair. It was Gianetta Fox's last full-dress appearance in canvas, and she had all the air of making the most of it.

So had Morelli, and his cousin Hugo Montefior, the dress-designer, who happened to be my employer. And there really was nothing against the idea that Montefior should re-create the dress with the lovely green sleeves, and that I should wear it at the showing, and that there should be a Sensation in the right circles, thereby doing the cousins a lot of good. And, possibly, me too, though this honestly didn't occur to me when Hugo put his idea in front of me. I was merely flattered, excited, and terribly nervous.

So I wore the Greensleeves gown at the show, and

Morelli got his Sensation, and I was so scared of the fashionable crowd that when I spoke at all, it was in a tight, flat little voice that must have sounded the last word in bored brittle sophistication. I must have looked and sounded, in fact, like a pale copy of that arrogant worldling behind me in Zollner's canvas, for that is what Nicholas Drury undoubtedly took me for, when at length he elbowed his way through the crowds and introduced himself. I had heard of him, of course, and this in no way increased my self-confidence: he had at that time – he was twenty-nine – three terrifyingly good novels to his credit, as well as a reputation for a scarifying tongue. I, for one, was so thoroughly scarified that I froze into complete stupidity, and under his sardonic look stammered some meaningless schoolgirl rubbish that, God help us both, he took for coquetry. We were married three months later.

I have no wish to dwell on the three years that followed. I was wildly, madly, dumbly in love with him, of course, a silly little star-dazzled adolescent, plunged into a life completely strange and rather terrifying. And Nicholas, it became very quickly apparent, wasn't on his own ground either. What he had meant to marry was a modern Gianetta Fox, a composed young sophisticate who could hold her own in the fast-moving society to which he was accustomed; what he'd actually got was only Gianetta Brooke, not long out of school, whose poise was a technique very recently acquired in Montefior's salons and the Mayfair mannequin factory.

Not that this initial miscasting was the cause of our little tragedy; love is a great builder of bridges, and it did seem at first as though what was between us could have spanned any gap. And Nicholas tried as hard as I: looking back now I can see that; if I did achieve sophistication, and a little wisdom, Nicholas struggled to rediscover tenderness. But it was too late; already, when we met, it was too late. The times were out of joint for us, the gap too wide – not the ten-years' gap between our ages, rather, the thousand-year-long stretch of a world war that to me was only an adolescent memory hardly denting the surface of my life, but to Nicholas was a still-recurring nightmare agony leaving scars on the mind which were then only precariously skinning over. How was I, untouched nineteen, to apprehend the sort of stresses that drove Nicholas? And how was he to guess that, deep down under my precarious self-confidence, lurked the destroying germs of insecurity and fear?

Whatever the causes, the break came soon enough. In two years the marriage was as good as over. When Nicholas travelled, as he often did, in search of material for his books, he more and more frequently found reasons for not taking me with him, and when at length I found he was not travelling alone, I felt no surprise, but I was hurt and humiliated, and so – I have red hair, after all – blazingly outspoken.

If I had wanted to keep Nicholas, I should have done better to have held my tongue. I was no match for him on a battlefield where love had become a weakness and pride the only defence against a cynicism both brutal and unanswerable. He won very easily, and he cannot have known how cruelly . . .

We were divorced in 1949. For the sake of my mother, who is so High Church as to be verging (according to Father), on Popish Practices, I kept Nicholas' name, and I still wore my wedding-ring. I even, after a time, went back to London and to Hugo Montefior, who was angelically kind to me, worked me to death, and never once mentioned Nicholas. Nor did anyone else, except Mother, who occasionally asked after him in her letters, and even, on two occasions, wondered if we were thinking of starting a family . . . After a year or so I even managed to find this amusing, except when I was run-down and tired, and then the gentle timelessness of Mother and Tench Abbas Rectory became more than I could bear.

So in mid-May 1953, when London had been packed to suffocation for weeks with the Coronation crowds already massing for the great day, and Hugo Montefior one morning took a long look at my face, took another, and promptly told me to go away for a fortnight, I rang up Tench Abbas, and got Mother.

'A holiday?' said Mother. 'The beginning of June? How lovely, darling. Are you coming down here, or will Nicholas find it too dull?'

'Mother, I—'

'Of course we haven't got television,' said Mother proudly, 'but we can listen to the *whole thing* on the wireless . . .'

I spared a glance for Montefior's salon windows, which have a grandstand view of Regent Street. 'That would be lovely,' I said. 'But Mother dearest, would you mind if I went somewhere else for a bit first?

Somewhere away from everything . . . you know, just hills and water and birds, and things. I'd thought of the Lake District.'

'Not far enough,' said Mother promptly. 'Skye.'

Knowing Mother, I thought for one wild moment that she was recommending Heaven as suitably remote. But then she added: 'Your father was talking about it at the Dunhills' garden-party the other day. It rained *all* the time, you know, and so we had to be indoors – you know it *always* rains for the Dunhills' garden-party, darling? – well, it did so *remind* Maisie Dunhill. They were there a fortnight once, and it rained *every day.*'

'Oh,' I said, as light dawned. 'Skye.'

'And,' said Mother, clinching it, 'there's *no television.*'

'It sounds the very place,' I said, without irony. 'Did Mrs. D. give you an address?'

'There are the pips,' said Mother distractedly. 'We *can't* have had three minutes, and they *know* how it puts me off. What was – oh, yes, the Dunhills . . . do you know, darling, they've bought a new car, a *huge* thing, called a Jackal or a Jaeger or something, and—'

'Jaguar, Mother. But you were going to give me the address of the hotel where the Dunhills stayed.'

'Oh yes, that was it. But you know Colonel Dunhill *never* drives at more than thirty-five miles an hour, and your father says – what, dear?'

I heard Father's voice speaking indistinguishably somewhere beyond her. Then she said: 'Your father has it, dear, written down. I don't quite know how . . . well, here it is. The Camas Fhionnaridh Hotel—'

'The *what* hotel, Mother?'

'Camas – I'll spell it.' She did. 'I really don't think – I don't remember – but this *must* be the one. What did you say, dear?' This to Father again, as she turned away from the receiver, leaving me listening in some apprehension for the pips, which always reduce Mother from her normal pleasant abstraction to a state of gibbering incoherence. 'Your father says it's Gaelic and pronounced Camasunary,' said Mother, 'and it's at the back of *beyond*, so you go there, darling, and have a lovely time with the birds and the – the water, or whatever you said you wanted.'

I sat clutching the receiver, perched there above the roar of Regent Street. Before my mind's eye rose, cool and remote, a vision of rain-washed mountains.

'D'you know,' I said slowly, 'I think I will.'

'Then that's settled,' said Mother comfortably. 'It sounds the very thing, darling. So *handy* having that address. It's as if it were *meant*.'

I am glad to think that Mother will never appreciate the full irony of that remark.

So it came about that, in the late afternoon of Saturday, May 30th, 1953, I found myself setting out on the last stage of my journey to Camas Fhionnaridh in the Isle of Skye. Mother, I found, had been right enough about the back of beyond: the last stage had to be undertaken by boat, there being only a rough cart-road overland from Strathaird to Camas Fhionnaridh, which the solitary local bus would not tackle. This same bus had brought me as far as Elgol, on the east side of Loch Scavaig, and had more or less dumped me and my cases on the shore. And presently a boatman, rather more ceremoniously, dumped me into his boat, and set out with me, my cases, and one other passenger, across the shining sea-loch towards the distant bay of Camasunary.

Nothing could have been more peaceful. The sea-loch itself was one huge bay, an inlet of the Atlantic, cradled in the crescent of the mountains. The fishing-village of Elgol, backed by its own heather-hills, was within one tip of the crescent; from the other soared sheer from the sea a jagged wall of mountains, purple against the sunset sky. The Cuillin, the giants of the Isle of Mist.

And, locked in the great arms of the mountains, the water lay quiet as a burnished shield, reflecting in deeper blue and deeper gold the pageantry of hill and sky. One thin gleaming line, bright as a rapier, quivered between the world of reality and the water-world below. Our boat edged its way, with drowsily purring engine, along the near shore of the loch. Water lipped softly under the bows and whispered along her sides. The tide was at half-ebb, its gentle washes dwindling, one after one, among the sea-tangle at its edge. The sea-weeds, black and rose-red and olive-green, rocked as the salt swell took them, and the smell of the sea drifted up, sharp and exciting. The shore slid past; scree and heather, overhung with summer clouds of birch, flowed by us, and our wake arrowed the silk-smooth water into ripples of copper and indigo.

And now ahead of us, in the centre of the mountain-crescent, I could see the dip of a bay, where a green valley cut through the hills to the sea's edge. Higher up this valley, as I knew, was a loch, where the hills crowded in and cradled the water into a deep and narrow basin. Out of this the river flowed; I could see the gleam of it, and just discernible at that distance, a white building set among a mist of birch-trees where the glittering shallows fanned out to meet the sea. The boat throbbed steadily closer. Now I could see the smoke from the hotel chimneys, a faint pencilling against the darker blue of the hills. Then the glitter of water vanished as the sun slipped lower, and the enormous shadow of the Cuillin strode across the little valley. One arrogant wing of rock, thrusting itself across the sun, flung a diagonal of shadow over half the bay.

'Garsven,' said the other passenger, at my elbow. I jumped. Such had been my absorption in the scene, so great the sense of solitude imposed by these awful hills, that I had forgotten I was not alone.

'I beg your pardon?'

He smiled. I saw now that he was a pleasant-looking man of perhaps thirty, with hair of an unusual dark gold colour, and very blue eyes. He was tall and lightly built, but he looked strong and wiry, and his face was tanned as if he spent most of his time in the open. He was wearing an ancient ulster over what had, once, been very good tweeds. 'This must be your first visit,' he said.

'It is. It's a little – overpowering, wouldn't you say?'

He laughed. 'Decidedly. I know the district like the back of my hand, but they still take my breath away, every time.'

'They?'

'The Cuillin.' He gave the word what I imagined must be its local pronunciation. His gaze had moved beyond me, and I turned to follow it. 'Garsven,' he said again. 'That's the one at the end that sweeps straight up out of the sea at that impossible angle.' His hand came over my shoulder, pointing. 'And that's Sgurr nan Eag; then the big one blotting out the sun – that's the Pointed Peak, Sgurr Biorach.'

'You mean Sgurr Alasdair,' put in the boatman unexpectedly from behind us. He was a sturdy Skye man with a dark square face and the soft voice of the Islands. He steered the boat nonchalantly, and now and then spat to leeward. 'Sgurr Alasdair,' he said again.

The fair man grinned, and said something in Gaelic which brought an answering grin to the boatman's face. Then he said to me: 'Murdo's right, of course. It's Alasdair on the maps – it was re-christened after some mountaineer or other; but I like the old names best. Sgurr Biorach it is, and that next to it is Sgurr Dearg, the Red Peak.' His pointing finger swung towards the last towering pinnacle, black against the sunset. 'Sgurr nan Gillean.' He dropped his hand and gave me the sort of smile that holds the hint of an apology – the Britisher's regret for having displayed an emotion. He said lightly: 'And you couldn't have had your first sight of them under better conditions. Sunset and evening star – all the works, in fact, in glorious Technicolor.'

'You must be a mountaineer,' I said.

'A climber? Yes, of a sort.'

'He's a good man on the hill, is Mr. Grant,' said Murdo.

Grant took out cigarettes, offered them to me and Murdo, then spun a spent match into the water. He said to me: 'Have you come for long?'

'A week or ten days. It depends on the weather. If it stays like this, it'll be heaven.'

'It won't,' he said confidently. 'What d'you say, Murdo?'

The boatman cast a dubious eye at the south-west, where the Atlantic merged its long and glimmering reaches into a deep blue sky. He jerked a thumb in that direction, and spoke briefly and to the point. 'Rain,' he said.

'Oh dear.' I was dismayed. This golden prospect seemed, now that I was here, to be infinitely more desirable than the rain-washed hills of my dreams.

'Never mind,' said Mr. Grant cheerfully, 'it'll improve the fishing.' I must have looked blank, because he added: 'You do fish, of course?'

'Oh no.' To my own surprise I sounded apologetic. 'But I – I could learn.'

His interest quickened. 'You climb, then?'

'No.' I felt suddenly very urban and tripperish. 'Actually I came for a – a rest, and quiet. That's all.'

His eye fell on my cases. 'London?' He grinned. 'Well, you've certainly come to the right place if you

want to get out of the crowds. You'll have no neigh-
bours except the Black Cuillin, and the nearest of them
is—' He stopped abruptly.

'Nearest?' I glanced at the hotel, much closer now,
islanded in its green valley, dwarfed and overborne by
one great solitary mountain to the east. 'That mountain? Is that one of them too? You didn't speak of it
before. What's it called?'

He hesitated perceptibly. 'That's Blaven.'

The boatman took his cigarette from his mouth, and
spat into the water. 'Blah-ven,' he repeated, in his soft
Highland voice. 'Mmph – mm . . .'

'The Blue Mountain . . .' said Grant in a voice that
was almost abstracted. Then he pitched his cigarette
into the water, and said abruptly: 'Was London so very
crowded?'

'Oh yes. It's been steadily filling up with people and
excitement for months. Now it's like a great pot slowly
simmering to boiling-point.'

Murdo turned the boat's nose neatly towards the
river mouth. 'London, is it?' His voice held a naïve note
of wonder. 'Did ye not want to stay and see the
Coronation, mistress?'

'In a way, I did. But I – I've been a bit overworked,
so I thought a holiday was a better idea after all.'

'What made you come here?' asked Grant. His eye
were still on the Blue Mountain.

'To Skye? Oh, I don't know – everybody wants to
visit Skye at some time or other, don't they? And I
wanted quiet and a complete change. I shall go for long
walks in the hills.'

'Alone?' There was something in Murdo's expression that made me stare at him.

'Why, yes,' I said in surprise.

I saw his eyes meet Grant's for a moment, then slide away to watch the approaching jetty. I laughed. 'I shan't get lost,' I said. 'The walks won't be long enough for that – don't forget I'm a city-bird. I don't suppose I'll get further than the loch, or the lower slopes of – Blaven, was it? Nothing much can happen to me there!' I turned to Mr. Grant. 'Does Murdo think I'll go astray in the mist, or run off with a water-kelpie?' Then I stopped. His eyes meeting mine, held some indefinable expression, the merest shadow, no more, but I hesitated, aware of some obscure uneasiness.

The blue eyes dropped. 'I imagine Murdo means—'

But Murdo cut the engine, and the sudden silence interrupted as effectively as an explosion. 'London . . .' said Murdo meditatively into the bowels of his engine. 'That's a long way now! A long way, indeed, to come . . .' The guileless wonder was back in his voice, but I got the embarrassing impression that he was talking entirely at random. And, moreover, that his air of Highland simplicity was a trifle overdone; he had, I judged, a reasonably sophisticated eye. 'A very fine city, so they say. Westminster Abbey, Piccadilly Circus, the Zoo. I have seen pictures—'

'Murdo,' I said suspiciously, as we bumped gently alongside a jetty, and made fast. 'When did *you* last see London?'

He met my eye with a limpid gaze as he handed me out of the boat. 'Eight years ago, mistress,' he said in his soft voice, 'on my way back frae Burma and points East . . .'

The man called Grant had picked up my cases and had started walking up the path to the hotel. As I followed him I was conscious of Murdo staring after us for a long moment, before he turned back to his boat. That simple Skyeman act had been – what? Some kind of smoke-screen? But what had there been to hide? Why had he been so anxious to change the conversation?

The path skirted the hotel to the front door, which faced the valley. As I followed my guide round the corner of the building my eye was once again, irresistibly, drawn to the great lonely bulk of the mountain in the east, stooping over the valley like a hawk.

Blaven? The Blue Mountain?

I turned my back on it and went into the hotel.

'A comfortable chair and a Mary Stewart: total heaven. I'd rather read her than most other authors'

HARRIET EVANS

'She set the bench mark for pace, suspense and romance with a great dollop of escapism as the icing'

ELIZABETH BUCHAN

DISCOVER ALL
OUR BEAUTIFUL
MARY STEWART
REISSUES FOR
2011